"Get out of here," Bolan shouted

"Let me do it—"

"Gary, get the hell out of here now!"

Manning was suddenly gone, obeying the order, as Bolan tore around the far side of the building. He found the dangling piece of fluorescent-yellow rope, grabbed it high in the air and pulled it down with all his strength.

The big house seemed to shudder, then the top half was obliterated by a blast that filled the night with unreal white brilliance. It blinded Bolan, even with his eyes shut, until he felt the rush of fire and the hammer of debris slam into him with the force of a speeding train.

Then all the brightness turned to black.

DON PENDLETON's
MACK BOLAN.
Conflagration

A GOLD EAGLE BOOK FROM
WORLDWIDE.

TORONTO • NEW YORK • LONDON
AMSTERDAM • PARIS • SYDNEY • HAMBURG
STOCKHOLM • ATHENS • TOKYO • MILAN
MADRID • WARSAW • BUDAPEST • AUCKLAND

First edition May 2000

ISBN 0-373-61472-1

Special thanks and acknowledgment to
Tim Somheil for his contribution to this work.

CONFLAGRATION

Of all the creatures that were made he (man)
is the most detestable. Of the entire brood he
is the only one—the solitary one—that possesses
malice.... He is the only creature that inflicts pain
for sport, knowing it to *be* pain....

> —Mark Twain
> Autobiography, 1924

I've faced some of the worst criminals the world
has to offer in my War Everlasting, but I can never
get used to seeing the pain and suffering one man
is willing to inflict on another all for the sake of
the almighty dollar. They say that money is the
root of all evil, and my job is to sever those roots
whenever and wherever I can.

> —Mack Bolan

CHAPTER ONE

Arlington, Virginia

The centuries-old houses of old town Arlington sat baking in the summer sun like an old man dozing on a front porch, too old and wise to do anything more than enjoy the long, slow afternoon. When a pair of slate-gray vans ripped down Beacon Street at highway speeds, a neighborhood tabby panicked and ran for cover in a basement window well. No one else even noticed.

The vans emerged from the residential section of the street into the old downtown area and barreled up a steep cobblestone drive toward a three-building office mall built in reddish brick. It was tidy and new, but was designed to blend with the city, where some buildings dated back to the time of the Revolutionary War. There was no one in the courtyard; it was too late for lunch. There were no retail establishments in the building, so no shoppers milled about.

The courtyard hadn't been designed for traffic. The two vans raced between a pair of stone benches, shoving one of them into a small brick and wrought-iron fountain, then came to a stop at a vestibule at one of the office mall buildings.

The rear doors of the vans burst open, and six men emerged, all in black pants and T-shirts and all masked in black stocking caps with extra-large eyeholes for unobstructed visibility. Each man sported an identical Bizon-2 machine pistol, which was held at port arms as if in a salute.

One man from each unit marched across the courtyard to the entrance doors to the two other buildings, quickly taking up a position in a corner of the doorway, the unfolded butts of the machine pistol wedged in their stomachs. From these positions the two men had an uninterrupted view of the courtyard, all doorways and both sidewalk entrances to the courtyard.

The other two pairs of gunmen hurried to the front of the van, yanked on the entrance doors and disappeared inside.

The van drivers immediately began to reposition themselves. First one, then the other backed across the courtyard and swung in a tight half-circle, then backed to the doorway again, ready to receive the gunmen when they exited.

Everything was prepared for a quick escape.

The gunmen turned left inside the air-conditioned hallway. The building was too small for a doorman or a security guard during the daytime. The doors to the ground floor offices—attorneys and CPAs—were all covered by blinds. The intruders turned into a doorway under an illuminated sign that read Stairs. They marched to the top floor and stepped through the door.

The gunmen grouped at the rear of a vast open area. The top floor was one large office, divided by cubicle walls, plant stands and photocopying equipment. The soft murmur of office activity continued despite their presence. There was too much space, too few people.

It seemed almost too easy for a small unit of assassins to roam a U.S. city without being spotted.

THE MEN HAD BEEN SEEN and identified, a long hour before, by the stalker who had been waiting for them to appear outside their Washington, D.C. hotel. The man had trailed them across the city and into Arlington. He was skillful behind the wheel of the car, and the gunmen never knew they were being followed, even on the quiet residential streets. They never saw him scramble out of his car, a block behind them, even as they were stepping out of their vans.

Mack Bolan, a.k.a. the Executioner, moved up the sidewalk until he could just see around the corner of one of the buildings and evaluated the scenario in the brick-paved courtyard as the vans took up their fast-getaway position. He quickly reconnoitered the office mall, which was composed of three three-story office buildings set around the small courtyard, whose fourth side faced Beacon Street.

Backtracking, he found a service entrance to the south building and made his way through the hallways to the guarded entrance.

The darkened glass of the front entrance to the south building showed the stalker that the vans hadn't moved in the thirty seconds they were out of his sight. He could see the guard at the west building entrance, while the man at his entrance was deep in the corner of the entrance vestibule and hardly visible.

Bolan wasted less than a second coming up with

a strategy for handling the gunmen: disable them however possible and ask questions of the survivors later on. If there were any.

He knew next to nothing about these men, and their target and motivation were major unknown factors—and irrelevant until the situation was under control.

Until the innocent men and women inside that building were safe.

He dragged a stout, deadly looking piece of weaponry from under his brown leather jacket. The Heckler & Koch G3-TG3 automatic rifle nudged its way through the dark glass doors of the entrance so quietly that the man standing in the corner of the vestibule just a few feet away didn't notice it, his attention fixed on the street.

The H&K G3-TG3 fired six 7.62 mm rounds that spun across the quiet courtyard and slammed into the guard at the other entrance, punching him against the redbrick wall. He stayed there, suspended for a moment, then slid to the ground.

The Executioner pushed through the glass door, swinging the autorifle toward the second guard, and triggered another burst of fire. The rounds cored him through the gut from a proximity of just a couple of paces, dropping him hard.

One of the vans was already burning rubber and Bolan quickly, efficiently snatched a grenade from the combat webbing under his jacket and thumbed it into the breech of the HK79 grenade launcher, then whipped it into target acquisition. As he squeezed the trigger, he spotted the driver of the second van targeting him with a Bizon-2 machine pistol. Bolan swung the G3-TG3/HK79 combo at this new threat and triggered the 40 mm grenade. At that instant the Bizon-2 commenced firing. The Executioner retreated inside the building through the open door and covered his face with his arm, half expecting to feel the machine-gun fire drilling into his flesh before the grenade exploded.

It didn't happen. The gunner was targeting wide and trying to home in on the soldier when the hollow-charge fragmentation grenade cracked into the van window and detonated. He was dead before the sound of the blast reached his ears, his flesh and bones ripped apart.

Bolan sprinted around the smoking ruin of the vehicle, charging into the street. The fleeing van was already accelerating down Beacon Street, making good its escape.

That left four heavily armed men inside the building, with no means of escape. If luck was with him, they hadn't heard the sounds of the melee.

Bolan headed inside.

STEPHANIE MCCORD REACHED into the core of her being for a measure of self-control she had never known she possessed and somehow managed to stifle the gasp as she turned into the cubicle. She didn't think they had seen her, and there was no startled exclamation from the rear that told her differently.

Her mind was spinning out of control. Four men in black masks with horrible looking guns clutched to their chests had invaded the office. She had no clue who they were or what they were doing here, but she knew people were about to start dying.

She acted fast, snatching at the phone and dialing 911. When the operator answered she hissed into the receiver, "There are people with guns. Lots of them. Send help."

The operator started to ask a question, but McCord set the phone receiver on the desk. The operator automatically had the address of the caller, and there was no other information she could possibly provide that would be of any help. She stood on her toes to try to see over the top of the cubicle wall. McCord was a small woman, and her eyes were just about level with the top of the five-foot cubicle walls. She spotted the movement of the gunners as they moved apart in pairs. They were going to set up a perimeter in the office, trapping the people inside.

She darted out of the cubicle. The way was clear, if she was guessing correctly, and McCord raced along the hallway to the office at the end of the open room. The only personnel with offices of their own were the president and vice president. She slipped through a door, then she closed it softly behind her.

Lipetsk Enterprises' Vice President of Technology, Serge Gordetsky, looked up curiously but continued to speak into the telephone. McCord stepped across the room and depressed the disconnect on the phone.

"Stevie?"

"Shut up, Serge. There are men with guns out there."

"What?"

Gordetsky was getting to his feet when the sound of rapid gunfire and the eruption of screams and shouts reached them. Gordetsky sprang for the door, but McCord grabbed his wrist and held on.

"Stevie, I must go help!"

"No! I called the police—let them take care of it."

There was another blast of gunfire and Gordetsky stepped to the blinds that covered the office window, parting them to see the activity in the office. He exclaimed something softly in Russian, then stepped back from the window, glaring at the door with a mixture of fury and fear.

The door crashed open and a gunman stood looking at them, his eyes unreadable behind his mask.

"Who are you? What do you want?" Gordetsky demanded.

"Are you Serge Gordetsky?" the gunner asked. His accent was strange, and McCord couldn't place it. Suddenly she was filled with the terrible realization—they were after Gordetsky!

"I've called the police," she said. "They're on their way."

"Are you Serge Gordetsky?"

"No," McCord explained. "Mr. Gordetsky isn't in the office today."

The gunman turned and looked over his shoulder, although the boxy gun he had aimed into the office never wavered. He nodded to one of his companions, and another gunman stepped to his side. They spoke in a whisper, too low to hear but loud enough to tell it wasn't English. The second gunman, a slightly taller twin to the man who held them hostage, produced a photograph and they examined it for all of three seconds. Then they looked at Gordetsky.

"That's him," the taller man said emotionlessly. "Kill him."

The gunman shrugged and took a step into the office.

"No!" McCord screamed. She took a single step toward the gunner, as if to block the shots she knew were coming. She was too late, too slow. The machine pistol throbbed in the gunman's grip, and Serge Gordetsky threw his hands into the air, rolling his eyes to the ceiling, and sprawled onto his back. Stephanie McCord collapsed in a crouch with her arms gripped around her head. Sobbing, she somehow sensed the gunman walking across the room. He was coming for her, she thought. He was going to place the evil little weapon against her nape and pump a few shots into her. She found she really didn't care.

But then she realized the gunman was standing over the body of Serge Gordetsky. There was a flash of white light.

The man had just taken a photograph of her murdered lover.

McCord snapped. Fury and adrenaline rushed through her body, and she launched herself at the gunner like a striking tiger, snarling with rage. Her hands slashed at his face like claws ripping into the soft flesh of an easy kill, tearing through his nylon ski mask and gouging his flesh. The gunner shouted in pain and twisted hard, his big bulk flinging her small, slim body onto the cluttered desk. Somewhere in the back of her consciousness McCord felt a crack of pain that traveled up and down her back and ribs, but she ignored it. Instead she twisted off the desk, fell to the carpet on all fours and leapt into the air again, roaring from deep in her stomach. She saw the man raising his gun, and she knew with a surge of bitter excitement that she would be on him before he could fire. Her hands landed on the weapon as her one hundred pounds slammed into the man, pushing him backward.

As he lost his balance, he dragged the gun with him. McCord refused to let go and felt herself pulled on top of him. They ended up in a tangle on the floor, with the gunner moaning in pain. Something was wrong with him. Then McCord realized he had landed on the inert body of the man she loved, and his back had bowed backward over it. McCord pushed away from him, trying to take advantage of his momentary dazedness to wrest the weapon from his hands, but he held tight and rolled to the side, leveraging the gun out of her fingers. Suddenly, he was in a sitting position, aiming the gun at her. Her luck had run out.

Blood was coming out of his mouth and his left eye, and he glared at her with the hatred a boy had for the bee that just stung him.

"Stupid bitch," he muttered as he rose to his feet.

Stephanie McCord knew she was about to die, and she wouldn't give her murderer the satisfaction of any kind of a response.

Then she heard shooting from outside the office.

CHAPTER TWO

Where had the gunmen gone after entering the building? Mack Bolan's answer came from above when gunfire filtered down from the third floor. He raced up the stairs. The doors at the top of the stairs had only narrow, steel-mesh reinforced windows, which showed him nothing.

He cautiously opened a door and found himself in the middle of what was clearly a hostage situation. Twenty people were visible, their hands in the air. The large, low-ceilinged office stretched twenty yards from one end to the other, and it was almost totally open space, partitioned with flimsy cubicle walls.

"Hey there!"

One of the gunners had taken up a watch position, standing on a desk or chair so that his head was touching the ceiling and he could see over the cubicles. He spotted Bolan and raised his gun.

Between the Executioner and the watch gunner was the crowded knot of frightened hostages. Bolan knew he couldn't let the man fire into them to reach him. He sprinted away and slammed flat onto the floor behind a desk, then crawled over the carpet, catching glimpses of the gunner as he moved from cover to cover behind office furniture. Halting behind a file cabinet, he crouched for a three count. As he was about to move again, he heard the watcher-gunner trigger his weapon and felt the thumping of the rounds slamming into the file cabinet. Bolan half expected to feel the bullets cutting into his flesh, but they never reached him. The flimsy aluminum cabinet wouldn't stop the rounds, but the packed-in file folders and paperwork did the trick. He listened for the pause in the firing he knew had to come.

The gunfire stopped. The Executioner rose swiftly to his feet, slamming the magazine of the G3-TG3/HK79 on the top of the file cabinet and triggering a long, high burst. The first rounds went wild into the ceiling, to deliberately avoid hitting an unplanned target as he got his bearings, but he adjusted his aim into the high-placed lookout so quickly the gunner didn't have time to fire his weapon again. The first 7.62 mm round pierced his forehead. His eyes rolled upward, as if he were trying to spot the round hole in his flesh and bone. The rounds that slammed into his throat and chest were overkill. The gunner withered out of sight.

Bolan scanned the office, but the only people he saw were the frightened, huddled office workers. He used a chair to step on top of the nearby desk, then onto the file cabinet that had shielded him. He was taller than the lookout had been, and he had to crouch slightly with his head pressed into the flimsy ceiling panels.

Two women had started to scream when the guard was shot, and they were being comforted by the other office workers. Their sobbing stopped when they saw the figure standing above them. He was a few inches over six feet with a slim, muscular build, but on his towering perch he was like some brutal monster of a human being. His blue eyes flashed, taking in everything and processing the information with marked alertness. There was nothing that he missed.

The office workers seemed to hold their breath as one. They didn't know who he was. They knew he had killed one of the men who was terrorizing them, but they couldn't bring themselves to believe that this dark man was their savior.

He raised his weapon and triggered a blast of fire that was all the more frightening for its brief accuracy. The second gunner screamed as the hand and part of a leg that had been exposed behind the divider were ripped by the rounds. The gunner was insensible with the pain and he thrashed into the open, throwing away his gun. The dark, blue-eyed man towering over the scene was waiting for that to happen. His target was now fully exposed. The dark man triggered a controlled brief burst and the second gunner dropped, abruptly silent.

STEPHANIE MCCORD OPENED her eyes, surprised that she hadn't been killed. The gunfire from outside the enclosed office of her dead lover told her something had gone wrong for the assassins in the ski masks.

"Oh, God," she said as the meaning became clear. Somebody in the office had to be trying to put up a fight. The gunfire she was hearing could only be more of her people getting cut down by the assassins.

"Shit!" exclaimed one of the two gunmen. "Who's that?"

"How should I know?" the other answered.

They pulled away from the window, hiding behind

the door with their weapons pointed at the ceiling, staring into space. Even behind the masks McCord sensed a change in their expressions.

Were they suddenly concerned? Perplexed? Maybe even afraid?

Was it possible that help had arrived so soon?

"In here! They're in here," she shouted.

The assassins at the door focused their guns on her, but she jumped to her feet and raced across the room, diving as if into water and landing behind the protection of the desk. There was a quick retort of near-proximity gunfire, and she listened to the rounds crack into the desk and hit the wall above her head.

"Stop it! Now they know we're in here!" one of the assassins admonished the other.

"I'll kill that bitch if it's the last thing I do!"

McCord felt the murderous words crawl down her spine.

"Later! Can you see how many are out there?"

McCord heard the slight scrape of the blinds on the window being parted. She wondered suddenly if Serge Gordetsky had stored a handgun in his desk. She flipped on her back and eased open the nearest desk drawer, feeling inside. There was nothing in the drawer but files and an empty ceramic mug. She grabbed the mug. It might make a good missile.

She almost laughed when she thought of defending herself against automatic weapons with a coffee cup.

AL ZELLER WATCHED the dark monster of a man step down from his high perch as lightly as if he were a ninja walking down a castle wall in medieval Japan. The figure crossed to him in a few long, low strides, and crouched.

"There's only two others," the dark man said to him without preamble. "Got a fix on them?"

Zeller didn't have a chance to wonder where the dark soldier got the information he had. He answered at once. "They're in that office, both of them."

"Hostages?"

Zeller swallowed. "Yeah. Two people. One is Serge Gordetsky. He's our technology VP. The other is Stevie McCord. She's—"

"Good enough." The man was watching the office, with its closed door and blinded windows, as he changed out the box-type magazine on his large automatic rifle. Zeller could almost see the wheels spinning inside the man's head, evaluating and strategizing.

Bolan stood quickly, stepped from behind the cubicle wall and opened fire on the office, sweeping the rounds across the top of one office window for precisely ten rounds. The window disintegrated noisily, and the blinds jumped and danced. The second burst of ten rounds cut through the second window on the other side of the door, stitching it at ceiling height and bringing it down in a waterfall of crashing glass. The rifle came up empty, and Bolan dropped it at Zeller's feet unceremoniously, dragging out a big handgun before the glass had stopped crashing. He strode to the office door and opened it with a powerful kick, slamming it into the bodies of the two gunners ducking behind it. They cried out and shot in different directions.

One of them never got his balance and fell heavily on the glass-covered floor, spun quickly and tried to line his machine pistol on the intruder. He never got the chance. Bolan leveled the .44 Magnum Desert

Eagle at his chest and triggered once. That was all it took. The machine pistol thumped on the carpet, and the body deflated and sagged.

The second man got to his feet, but the door had cracked him hard in the rib cage and he felt himself slew to the side. The desk stopped his progress, and he leveled his weapon swiftly, ignoring the pain. It seemed incredible, but the intruder had already lined up the big handgun on his chest.

And he wasn't shooting.

Bolan saw movement behind the gunner and willed himself not to fire, although his finger had almost squeezed the trigger to the firing point. The powerful .44 Magnum round would almost surely not miss the masked gunman, but at this range it could very well pass completely through him and into the woman, whom the warrior had to assume was an innocent.

"Get down!" he ordered fiercely.

The woman's eyes went wild.

The gunner's confusion came and went in the blink of an eye, and he spun on the woman just in time to see something deep blue and gold flashing at his head. It was a damned coffee cup. The thing cracked into his left eye, pulping the eyeball and sending him flying across the room.

His legs worked frantically to keep him balanced, but then his foot slipped on shards of glass and he fell backward, his spine slamming into the wall before he collapsed to the floor.

Bolan made his move toward the gunman, but the guy was still highly functional, unfazed by the pain or the blinded eye. He triggered a burst of rounds at the woman as Bolan triggered one deadly blast from the Desert Eagle. The round chopped into the Bizon-2 and sent it flying, leaving the gunner's right hand mangled. The gunner grunted, but the adrenaline was still coursing through his body, and he pulled out another weapon with his left hand. The slim .25-caliber pistol was aimed at the woman. Somehow the gunman knew he was dead. And all he cared about in his last moment of life was cutting down the woman who had cracked him in the head with the coffee cup.

Bolan didn't have time to reach the man and knock the pistol away. His only choice was to fire the Desert Eagle again, and he blasted the man's arm away at the shoulder with the powerful round. The elbow shattered and the forearm flopped uselessly, hanging by tattered flesh and stretched tendons.

The gunner raised his arms, staring at the ruin that had been done to them, and his eyes were wide in deepening shock. Then he leaned forward, glaring insanely at the woman.

"Bitch!" he said, as if she were to blame for his failure and mutilation.

Then he pitched onto his side, the blood pouring out of him.

THE WOMAN STARED at the corpse for a long moment, then sobbed suddenly, bending slightly as the grief poured out of her. She bent over the body that had been lying there when Bolan entered the room, kneeling on glass fragments without seeming to notice.

The Executioner didn't bother to tell those out in the office that the situation was under control. He didn't have the time. Local law enforcement would be on its way by this time, and he'd rather not have to deal with their bureaucracy. Raising the tiny digital camera provided to him by Aaron Kurtzman, cybernetics mastermind for Stony Man Farm, Bolan's sometimes base of operations, he quickly nudged over the body of the gunner and snapped his photo several times. A single push of a button took a half dozen digital images in various configurations, which Kurtzman's imaging software would be able to dissect for an immensely detailed computer image. It took him just seconds to photograph the second gunner. Then he moved to the fallen man in the suit. He knelt and without apology turned him onto his back.

"What the hell are you doing?" McCord asked.

"Collecting information."

"He's not one of the killers!"

"I'm aware of that."

"Who are you?"

They heard the sirens finally. The heavy soundproofing had muffled the noise until the Arlington PD was right outside the office mall. Bolan knew they'd evaluate the site of the obliterated van and the three sprawled masked men and quickly come to the conclusion that the call had been genuine. He hoped they'd stay out of the building for several minutes, at least, until they were sure the scene was safe.

"You're not a cop," the woman said accusingly.

"Go tell your people that the situation is under control."

She glared at him with a mixture of amazement and incredulity. "Under control? You call this under control?"

"Safe for the moment," Bolan said, in a tone that allowed no argument. The woman seemed to snap to reality. She nodded and stood, walking out of the office. She never noticed that Bolan had been aiming the digital camera in her direction as he spoke to her. He took his photos of the corpse in the suit and quickly scanned the mess of papers on the desk, finding little that might be of value. He grabbed a piece of letterhead and tucked it into his pants pocket, then strode into the main office area, ignoring the stares of the office workers. Many were sobbing on each other's shoulders. Others regarded him with a mixture of awe and fear. The woman from the office was on the phone.

"Hey, you. The police want to know who you are."

"John Smith," Bolan said as he retrieved the fallen and untouched H&K.

"What agency are you with?"

Bolan didn't answer that.

"They say you should come out with your hands up."

"Is there a north entrance to this building?" he asked Al Zeller.

Zeller nodded mutely, then said, "Go out the main entrance, down the stairs."

"Thanks."

Bolan pushed through the front door. Behind him he heard the woman from the office shouting at him. "They say they'll shoot if you don't come out quietly!"

As soon as the main entrance to the office suite was behind him, Bolan found himself in a deserted waiting room. He descended to the second level, raced down the hallway and emerged into the stairway he'd used as an entrance. He went to the third floor and up the emergency roof exit. By this time he was sure the Arlington PD was going to have been alerted to his attempts to exit on the north side of the building.

He'd save himself a few hours of headache if he could get himself away from the scene without allowing himself to fall into their hands.

The Executioner emerged on the roof and strolled to the corner. Police were on the streets but this side of the building was momentarily deserted, as far as he could see. He had to take his chances, and it would have to be now. He grabbed the rain gutter and lowered himself quickly down the building, falling the last eight feet and landing in a crouch on the cobblestones before crossing to the next building and slipping inside. A minute later he had passed into the third building, grabbed his pack and emerged on the street, heading for his car, his hardware stowed out of sight.

HEADING WEST out of the nation's capital, U.S. Highway 29 joins up with U.S. Highway 15 for several miles, soon crossing over Interstate 66 and intersecting with U.S. Highway 211. Following 211 west, the scenery becomes more mountainous and less civilized by the mile, until the road begins to climb into the Blue Ridge Mountains and passes through the border into the Shenandoah National Park. Here, about eighty miles outside the city limits of Washington, D.C., 211 intersects Skyline Drive, a road popular with vacationers and sightseers for its beautiful vistas.

One of the highest points along Skyline Drive is Stony Man Mountain, named for the noble profile that can be made out on its flank. Nearby is Stony Man Farm, a somewhat isolated agricultural estate whose orchards are said to produce some of the highest quality peaches outside Georgia. But, although the locals like the produce, they've never been able to get too friendly with the proprietors. In fact, no one in the area is too sure who owns the farm.

Bolan entered the Farm at the main gate and drove to the center of the large farm plot, where a main house and a few auxiliary buildings stood. Farmhands barely glanced at him, though he was under constant surveillance. They were busy working on some of the equipment and seemingly couldn't be bothered with his arrival.

Even to a man of Bolan's talents the cover was a good one. He had barely noticed the string of proximity detectors and batteries of cameras that had been watching him since before he'd turned into the Farm. He was hard-pressed to spot the guns on the farmhands, who were trained personnel from all divisions of the U.S. military.

When he parked and approached the main building, it was like walking up to a large, well-maintained farmhouse. That impression vanished inside the front door, the first of several coded steel access doors that allowed entrance to one of the most sophisticated and secret antiterrorist special operations bases on the planet.

Bolan knew the place well. In fact, he had helped found the organization, years ago, with the help of Hal Brognola, a high-ranking official in the Justice Department and the Farm's liaison to the White House.

As if smelling it in the very air of the converted

farmhouse, Bolan knew that things were at a low ebb. The Farm's action teams were temporarily inactive.

Bolan headed to the computer room, which was always alive with the hum of state-of-the-art computer systems. A young Japanese man was sitting at one of the consoles, wearing headphones wired into the minidisk player strapped to his blue jeans pocket. He was thumping his thigh with his hand and staring at a screen, where a jerky animated sequence showed a naked blond woman enjoying her own company.

"Hard at work, Akira?" Bolan asked.

"Mack," Akira Tokaido said, turning to face the soldier and dragging off the headphones. "I'm eavesdropping on an Internet session by a few intelligence guys in the Turkmenistan secret service. They've been accessing the same hard-core video site over and over again for weeks."

The elevator in the corner chimed as the doors parted and a large, brawny man in a wheelchair rolled out quickly, his big hands maneuvering the ungainly steel chair precisely. With his barrel chest and bodybuilder arms, Aaron Kurtzman had earned the nickname "The Bear," and he fit nobody's image of a disabled person. But he had been locked inside his rolling cage for years, since being wounded during an attack on the Farm.

He didn't let it slow him down.

"Mack!" he said with a smile, rolling to a stop at Bolan's feet and taking the Executioner's hand in a firm grip.

"Bear."

"It's good to see you. Things have been pretty dull around here for days."

"So you're trying to make your own entertainment?" Bolan asked with a half-smile, nodding at Tokaido.

Kurtzman glanced at the screen his resident hacker was watching and shook his head. "Internet neophytes. When those Turkmen guys find something they like, they stick with it."

Bolan held out the camera. Kurtzman took it without a word and spun his chair neatly to one of the smart consoles tied into his central system. Within twenty seconds he was downloading the graphical data Bolan had retrieved.

Tokaido was watching him, and Kurtzman gave him a nod. A moment later the images started pulling up on both screens. The young man got to work as Kurtzman opened several windows on the monitor, revealing the faces of dead men.

"Give me a clue," Kurtzman said.

"These men are all employees of what I believe to be a large illegal arms trading organization. I got wind of their activity yesterday and tracked them down when I realized they were about to launch some kind of a raid or attack. I followed them this morning to an office complex in Arlington. They broke into the offices of this company." He extracted the piece of letterhead stationery from his pocket and smoothed it out on the desk in front of Kurtzman.

"Lipetsk Enterprises," he said, then read out loud the Beacon Street address and suite number. A quick glance at Tokaido told him the young computer wizard was already working on uncovering more data on the company.

"This man was their vice president of technology, Serge Gordetsky," Bolan explained. "The other dead men were his attackers. I also neutralized a couple of guards and a driver. Only one of the drivers got away."

"A live one," Kurtzman muttered as he pulled up the image of a very frightened and beautiful young woman.

"I didn't catch her name, but she's an employee of Lipetsk Enterprises and maybe had something going with Gordetsky."

"Arms dealers don't usually get involved in terrorist-type activities," Kurtzman commented. "They just sell to people who do."

"Exactly," Bolan said. "So what were they doing going after this Gordetsky guy?"

"I thought maybe you knew."

Bolan shook his head. "I don't even know what Lipetsk Enterprises does, and the Arlington PD showed up before I had the chance to scrounge up a copy of their annual report and mission statement."

"Well, that's easy enough to clear up," Kurtzman said. His fingers flashed over the keyboard, pulling up one of his many customized search routines. He tapped in the company name and watched as results windows began to open one after another. Whatever the company did, it was no secret. Summaries were included in many of the databases Kurtzman's Stony Man system stored or had access to. He chose a window and brought it to the front.

"'Lipetsk Enterprises, research and development/ consulting firm specializing in portable magnetic generation equipment for mining and drilling applications,'" Kurtzman read aloud.

"How would you use portable magnetic generation equipment for mining and drilling?" asked a feminine voice from across the room. The honey blond woman standing in the door wore faded jeans, a white cotton blouse with turquoise stitching and cowboy boots. The outfit accented an athletic, trim figure.

Barbara Price looked like the ranch foreman's beautiful young wife—the one who knows how to knock around the hired hands when they drink too much whiskey and raise too much hell on Saturday nights. The comparison wasn't too far from the mark. Price was the mission controller for Stony Man Farm. Recruited by Hal Brognola from a secret arm of the National Security Agency, she was highly incisive, expert at sifting through massive amounts of data for the one tiny fact or pattern that made for a successful operation. She was capable of controlling and commanding missions taking place anywhere in the world, with the help of Aaron Kurtzman and the rest of the Stony Man cybernetics and communications team.

She gave Mack Bolan a smile and touched his arm as she stood beside him, then looked at Kurtzman's display.

"Good question," Kurtzman replied. "I think I've heard of research being done to use magnetic pulse generation as a kind of radar. You point it at the ground, send a pulse and measure the signals that bounce back. If you can analyze the signature of the bounced signals you can theoretically come up with a precise mineralogical survey of what's underground."

"How far underground?" Price asked.

"Maybe several miles," Kurtzman said.

"The economic potential is easy to imagine," Bolan added.

"Sure," Price said. "You could locate oil or gold or water in a few minutes. Currently you'd have to drill a well or excavate a mine."

"Or you can take seismic readings from carefully placed explosive charges," Kurtzman stated. "It's all pretty inexact. The promise of magnetic pulse generation is getting a list of all subsurface mineral deposits and their depth."

"Not too useful to an arms dealer unless he's planning on changing to a more legitimate trade," Bolan commented.

Nobody replied to that. Kurtzman leaned over the screen to read the small print on the database window he'd pulled up, then straightened and magnified the text for everyone to read. It was a list of top executives and research personnel with the company.

"Nicholae Dinitzin," Kurtzman said. "Serge Gordetsky. Alex Kardarma. Anton Aktumisyk. I think I see a theme here."

"All Russian," Price said. "Even the company name has a Russian ring to it."

"Anything more on the company?" Bolan asked.

Kurtzman quickly began to scan and close the other results windows. "Not really. They all say more or less the same thing. The company's a couple of years old. No products on the market. No sales. Privately held."

"Investors?" Price asked. "Where's their capital coming from?"

"Several private investors from around the world. Mining equipment companies," Kurtzman said.

"I'm sure they've dealt themselves in for rights to the technology in exchange for research funding."

"Which must be promising if they're floating a company without a product for a couple of years at a time, including a staff of twenty or thirty employees," Bolan stated. "Do they have patents or trademarks? Other facilities? Anything to indicate they're ready to start actual production?"

"Not a thing," Kurtzman said.

They were mulling over the facts when Tokaido spoke from across the room. "Catch."

"Okay," Kurtzman said. A new window pulsed open on the screen. Bolan recognized the face instantly as one of the men he had shot down in the office in Arlington.

"Yves Castres. Born Limoges. Served in the French army. Records show he beat the hell out of his commanding officer and went AWOL ten years ago. Since then has popped up as a mercenary during Mexican and South American jobs. No exceptional accomplishments. No strong ties or loyalties. Current employer unknown."

"Not too helpful," Price commented.

Kurtzman went through the profiles one after another. They were mercenaries, all of them, with military backgrounds. But they all had different national and cultural backgrounds. None was known to be working for any specific organization on a regular basis. None had been known to engage in overtly political activities or causes.

"Sorry, Mack," Kurtzman said finally. "I haven't given you much to go on."

Bolan was looking at Price, but his thoughts were

miles away. "Keep looking, Bear," he said. "Get the IDs on the other dead men."

"The Arlington Police Department should have photographed and fingerprinted the corpses by now," Kurtzman said. "We'll drop in on their attempts to perform their own identification and extract all the information we can."

"This is going to be a high-profile event," Price commented. "I wouldn't be surprised if the FBI insinuated itself in the investigation."

"All the better for us," Kurtzman added. "They'll put more information in their system than a local police department would. Akira can get at all of it."

"Also, find out whatever you can about the company principals and Gordetsky. I'm going to try to get some firsthand knowledge about this Lipetsk Enterprises."

"From whom?" Price asked.

"From her. Stephanie McCord." Bolan touched the screen, where the window still showed the corner of the face of the young woman.

"She's very pretty," Price said, giving Bolan a touch of a smile.

Bolan didn't take the bait. "At this moment, she's the only lead I've got."

CHAPTER THREE

The scrawny, short man looked like a gawky teenager in his shorts and T-shirt, although his lined face and graying sandy hair gave the impression of a man in his early fifties. The small man reminded the tennis pro of one of those child television stars from the sixties—when you saw them on talk shows these days they always look like kids with bad senior citizen makeup jobs. That was the impression he got of Roger Kabat.

"Morning, Mr. Kabat," he called across the court. "Ready to start the lesson?"

"Okay."

"Have you played much?"

"Here and there. It's been a long time. I bet I'll need some pointers."

"Fine. Why don't we play a game and I'll get an idea of your strengths and weaknesses? Then I'll know the best areas to concentrate on during our sessions."

"Okay."

The guy even talked like a kid. How'd this guy possibly make enough money to buy a membership at a country club like Nordic Fields? And how would he have impressed the current membership roster enough to extend the invitation? This was the kind of person the Nordic Fields businessmen used as stepping-stones in business.

The tennis pro gave Kabat an easy serve. The man was standing there waiting for it like a geeky adolescent standing in the loser's corner at a high school dance. He seemed confused when the ball sailed across the net and bounced nearby. He jumped at it and managed to get his racket behind it. The stroke looked pretty good, though, and the ball flew at the pro. He got behind it and lobbed it back to Kabat, who stepped into it and tapped it over the net with a higher degree of precision.

Smart ass, the pro thought. He backhanded the ball across the net and dropped it inches from out of bounds on Kabat's left. The little man had somehow placed himself in a perfect position for a strong backhand that jumped the net and landed as far away from the pro as possible without being on the line. The pro scrambled, reached and managed to tap the ball just inches from the ground. More luck than skill was involved in getting it over the net, and even then it was a weak effort.

Kabat was waiting for it, choosing his moment and his position. When his racket hit the ball it rocketed over the net and slammed into the court and skipped away. The pro didn't even attempt to chase after it. There was no way he could hope to reach it.

ROGER KABAT REVELED in being underestimated. People had been doing it all his life. By the fourth game he had the club tennis pro exhausted and dispirited, and that was exactly how he liked his opponents.

He'd been sixteen when he came to the realization that he was going to grow up to be a small, insignificant-looking man. He wallowed in self-pity for a few years, then came to the conclusion that, although he couldn't change his physical stature, he could change everything else about himself.

He had begun to redefine himself as a well-respected, highly skilled and powerful man in every sense of the word, and he had succeeded spectacularly.

He was about to exceed even his own standards for success. In a few short weeks.

Kabat checked his watch. He'd have good news waiting for him by the time he got back to the house.

The phone in his gym bag rang as he was about to serve. The tennis pro dropped in relief and went for a towel as Kabat answered it.

"What?" he demanded acidly, then looked around to make sure no one had overheard him. He said more quietly, "How did that happen?"

"I'm still not sure," Frank Parmley replied. "Only one guy made it back."

"One!" Kabat grated.

"The rest are dead. They got hit by some kind of special forces team."

Kabat digested this bit of unpleasant information. "How did a special forces team get called to the scene so quickly?"

"According to the survivor, the team was on the scene almost immediately. Before the shooting even started."

"Impossible."

"He said the first he heard of the special operations guys was when they shot the two stationed guards and grenaded one of the vans. Then he got the hell out. After he left, the SO team must have hemmed in our men on the third floor of the building and taken them out one after another. Not before they assassinated Gordetsky, though.''

Well, that was one tidbit of good news. But the implications were what concerned him. ''If there was a special operations group on the scene when our men were deploying then they knew we were coming,'' he declared. ''That means we've got a leak.''

''Not necessarily,'' Parmley protested.

''Give me a scenario in which a highly trained team capable of taking down seven out of eight militarily trained mercenaries would just happen to show up within one hundred twenty seconds of the outset of that operation.''

''Maybe one of the locals saw something and called in the Arlington SWAT.''

Kabat laughed derisively. ''SWAT doesn't deploy on the whim of the locals. And no matter how well-trained they are, they're not going to arrive on the scene in two minutes, Frank. More importantly, SWAT are police. They'd start yelling for surrender before they started shooting. Even FBI would call for the surrender of our men before they started cutting them down.''

Parmley was silent.

''We've either got a leak, or these mercenaries attracted attention to themselves somehow.''

''We're tight, Mr. Kabat, I swear it. I know all my men personally. I worked with them for years. They're loyal, and you're paying them too well for them to be tempted by outside offers.''

"So you're blaming the mercs?" Kabat demanded.

"Yes."

"I knew you would."

Kabat clicked off the connection before his second-in-command could defend himself, then stuffed the phone in the bag and waved away the pro, who was waiting for him to rejoin the game. He'd finished showing up the tennis pro. Now there were other, more important people to deal with.

And dealing with them wouldn't be nearly as pleasant.

STEPHANIE MCCORD STOOD in her front doorway and couldn't decide whether to scream or cry.

The dark killer was sitting in her living room looking at her, calmly assessing her, his blue eyes piercing her thoughts as if he were reading her mind. He was dressed casually in dark slacks and a worn brown leather bomber jacket. He didn't smile.

"The police are looking for you," she said finally.

"Come in."

"You going to kill me next?"

"I don't harm innocent people."

"So why'd you run before the cops arrived at the scene today?"

"I'm not exactly an authorized law-enforcement officer."

"So what are you?"

Bolan didn't answer that. After a few moments of silence, McCord closed the door behind her and slumped into the couch opposite him, her face red from crying. She was exhausted. "What do you want with me?"

"I want to know why a highly skilled team of mercenaries armed with military-grade weaponry would attack Lipetsk Enterprises."

"I'd like to know that myself. So would the Arlington police and the FBI."

"They targeted Serge Gordetsky specifically," Bolan told her.

McCord's eyes reddened and she looked at him hard. "Why would they want to kill Serge?"

"You tell me."

"Why should I tell you anything?" she demanded.

"Because I saved your life this afternoon."

McCord glared at him, unwilling to concede the point. She realized she should be afraid of this man. As far as she knew he was just another killer, maybe somehow in competition with those who had murdered Serge. But just now she was too exhausted to be afraid.

"Another good reason to talk to me is this—whoever was behind the attack had more than one target in mind," Bolan added.

"What do you mean by that?"

"I mean they were pros, clearly not on a personal vendetta. I assume whatever motivated them to cut down Gordetsky had something to do with Lipetsk Enterprises."

"What? How can that be?" She was pleading with him, as if he could change that reality. "We don't even do anything. We're just a research firm."

"Researching what?"

"Mining technology, for God's sake!"

"Mining technology so revolutionary that it might threaten Middle Eastern oil concerns? Or South African diamond mining monopolies?"

"No, dammit! It's still experimental technology—"

"So why kill for it?" Bolan asked, probing.

"I don't know!" she retorted, infuriated.

Bolan stood. "If you can't help me, I'll find someone who will."

"Wait!" McCord got to her feet, as well. "You have to tell me who you are."

"My name is Mike Belasko."

"Not your real name," McCord stated. Bolan didn't deny it. "I mean who *are* you? What's your role? You CIA or something?"

"Something."

"If you're Central Intelligence then you know all about Lipetsk Enterprises, right? So why are you asking me?"

Bolan changed his tack abruptly. "Where is Nicholae Dinitzin?"

McCord glared at him. "Is he in danger, too?"

"Until I know differently I'll assume he is."

"On his way home from South America. He's in-flight now. He doesn't even know about the attack yet. FBI agents are going to meet him at the airport. I told them I'd be there, too. I just came home to cool down for a couple of hours."

"Why are all the corporate principals Russian?"

The question made McCord stop and blink. "Everybody knows that."

"I don't," Bolan said.

She told him.

BOLAN PULLED OUT his phone as he took the antique elevator from McCord's second-floor apartment.

When Aaron Kurtzman came on the line, he said, "What have you got for me?"

"Lots of data, none of it useful," Kurtzman said. "For one, I have IDs on all seven corpses in the Arlington morgue. How that's going to help you out I don't know."

"Not much unless those IDs point to some sort of linked political inclination or tie them to any group with a known agenda."

"They don't."

"Any of them Russians or from the former Eastern Bloc?"

"No."

"Any of them potentially Russian agents?"

Kurtzman snorted. "Not too likely. Why do you ask?"

"I've got some new information."

"Talk to me."

Bolan unlocked the driver's door and got into his vehicle, a rented Blazer. Nice and inconspicuous. "Ever hear of Soviet science towns?"

Kurtzman repeated the phrase thoughtfully. "Science towns. I have, yes. An old USSR initiative. They'd get a whole bunch of scientists together and move them into one area, along with their families. They'd live and work together. The intention was to drive accelerated research and technology development. I think that in the early eighties there were as many as sixty or seventy of them in existence."

"Yeah," Bolan agreed. "Was their focus on weapons development, Bear?"

"Not at all. Well, I'm sure some of them were doing weapons research, knowing the Soviets, but they were geared to all kinds of avenues of research.

Agricultural and genetics research, medical advances. Whatever. It was a highly touted program when it was first developed. It was thought the very focused research would come up with world-class advances in science that would make the USSR a leader in many high-tech fields. They gave the concept a whole Communist ideological slant, as well. They saw it as a way to achieve the same levels of research success as being employed by for-profit Western and Asian corporations."

"How well did the approach work?" Bolan asked.

"Very well, in some cases. Not so hot in others. The Soviets tried to claim a high degree of success for the towns without actually offering evidence of such success. The proof is in the pudding. After the demise of the USSR, Russia allowed the towns to disintegrate. Why this course of inquiry by the way, Striker?"

"Because one of those Soviet science towns was named Lipetsk Nov."

There was a moment of silence on the other end of the line as all kinds of puzzle pieces started fitting together in the mind of Aaron Kurtzman. "Of course!" he said. "Everything makes sense now. Lipetsk Enterprises is a corporate continuation of a Soviet science town."

"Exactly."

"The reason all the people involved in the corporation are Russian is that they are all scientists from Lipetsk Nov. They immigrated to the U.S. and started the company to continue the line of research started in the eighties in Russia."

"That's how I figured it."

Kurtzman immediately used the information to determine his next course of action. "So if I can access old Soviet databases on the science towns, I might be able to come up with extensive background on the direction of the research, principal members involved, their backgrounds, all kinds of stuff."

"How much of that sort of information was digitized by the Soviets?" Bolan asked.

"Not much," Kurtzman admitted. "On the other hand, a lot of it has been declassified by Russia. Well, not so much declassified as not aggressively protected, unless it included evidence of the USSR involved in atrocities or weapons research. If Lipetsk Nov was truly involved in mining research methods—especially technology the Russians never considered to have marketable potential—the files might be available."

"Find out what you can for me, Bear."

"Where are you headed?"

"Dulles. Nicholae Dinitzin, the president of Lipetsk Enterprises, is en route from São Paulo as we speak. Sorry, but I don't know the airline. Can you provide me with a flight number and arrival time?"

"Piece of cake," Kurtzman said casually. Bolan heard the quick clicks of his fingers flying over his keyboard. "Varig 303 is scheduled to get into Dulles at 8:08 p.m. In fact it's running ten minutes ahead of schedule. Activity at Dulles is normal, so it'll be landing without delay and is scheduled to disembark passengers at gate C-8. Dinitzin is traveling in 2-B. First class aisle seat. He had the vegetarian platter for lunch."

"Show-off," Bolan growled.

"Anyway, he's in front so he'll be one of the first ones out."

"I'll get there about the same time he does."

"What's on your to-do list tonight?"

"I have a feeling the FBI is about to get in over its head. I'm going to give them a hand."

"The FBI hates it when you do that, Striker." Bolan could hear the grin in Kurtzman's voice.

"If they don't screw it up, they'll never even know I'm there."

THE FBI SCREWED it up big-time.

Because the Feds sent their entire escort force, other than their driver, into the terminal to collect Dinitzin, they never saw the pair of Lincoln Town Cars with blacked-out windows circulating through the loading zone. One of the cars always stayed on station as the other left and circled, reentering the loading zone from the rear. Bolan noticed them their first time through the loading zone, became suspicious the second time through and called in their plates the third time they moved through the loading zone in ten minutes. Carmen Delahunt, a vivacious redhead on the Stony Man Farm cybernetics team, intercepted his call and reported back in sixty seconds.

"Both sets of plates are off stolen private livery vehicles, Striker. An old Rolls and a white stretch Caddy."

"Thanks for confirming my suspicions, Stony," Bolan said, clicking off as he spotted the Feds emerging from the terminal building with a rather shocked-looking older man held tight in their circle. The older man had to be Dinitzin. The Feds either hadn't had time or had been too shortsighted to see the need for less obvious attire. The men were all in dark suits.

Even the female agent was in a strict, formal jacket and slacks. They might as well have been wearing their hard probe windbreakers—the navy blue jackets with the letters FBI emblazoned in five-inch white letters on the back.

Bolan was sure Nicholae Dinitzin had received little in the way of an explanation, but the Feds had to have given him enough to know he would be in danger of imminent attack. His eyes were skimming the crowds of travelers wildly. The agents were doing their best to look casual and bored, but it was too late in the day for sunglasses, and their eyes were likewise scanning all movement at the busy pickup spot. Bolan was leaning against a concrete pillar in the vicinity of a few tired business travelers. The Feds never suspected he was out of place.

Lincoln number one had started to leave its place at the curb, but when the Feds and Dinitzin emerged it braked to a halt at the head of the line of limousines and taxis waiting to pick up arrivals. Lincoln number two was at the very rear. Nicely done, Bolan thought. Their simple but well-conceived strategy and a little luck had put them in position to expertly hem in the FBI car, a dark blue Chevrolet van without extra windows. The Feds remained oblivious as they piled into the van and maneuvered away from the curb. With all the limos and taxis coming and going, the fact that Lincoln number one, forty feet ahead of them, pulled away at the same moment didn't seem unusual.

As oblivious as the Feds were to the pair of Lincolns, the limousine drivers were just as unaware of the presence of the Executioner. He strode into the road when Lincoln number two started after the van,

looking straight ahead with his hands in his pockets
as he strolled into the path of the big car and heard
the squeal of the tires.

He jumped as if startled, then stood there looking
at the hood of the big car as if scared stiff by the
close encounter.

The driver gestured and honked the horn, yelling
at Bolan. The words were unheard. Bolan's face
grew angry, and he started to yell at the driver.
"Watch where you're going, you stupid moron! Did
you get your chauffeur's license off a cereal box or
something?"

The driver's impatience was growing exponen-
tially as the FBI van pulled farther away. He honked
while Bolan played the irate pedestrian to the hilt,
shouting back angrily, refusing to budge. The driver
revved the engine and squeaked forward a few
inches, knocking his bumper into Bolan's legs.

Bolan swore at the driver. "You asshole! Come
out here and try something like that! I'll show you a
thing or two! Who the hell do you think you are!"
He slammed his fists hard into the Lincoln's hood,
leaving two dents in the metal. The driver slammed
the car into Park and pushed open the door.

"You want me to come out and show you a thing
or two, motherfucker!" he shouted, stepping onto the
road and pulling open his jacket to display the handgun holstered there.

Then he froze as Bolan's hand snapped inside his
own brown leather bomber jacket, extracted the silenced Beretta 93-R and snapped it into target acquisition. The driver went through a moment of sudden realization. He'd been set up for a hard fall, and
he'd taken the bait. He was a dead man. The 93-R

triggered a single coughing round that cored him through the heart and dropped him on the pavement.

Bolan ignored the screams of eyewitnesses as he strode to the side of the car and leveled the big handgun at the passenger. The man was already lining up on Bolan with a sawed-off shotgun, and the soldier reacted with his feet, slamming the door shut as the passenger squeezed the trigger. The huge 12-gauge blast filled the interior. The buckshot crashed into the bulletproof glass and ricocheted throughout the vehicle's interior. Bolan yanked open the door again and found the man clawing at his face and screaming. The Executioner fired a single shot through the man's skull, sending him slithering as if boneless to the floor of the front seat.

The back seat of the Lincoln was empty. Bolan let the driver lay on the pavement where he'd fallen, slipped behind the wheel, put the vehicle into Drive and stomped on the gas. The big Lincoln powerhouse thrummed to life and squealed the tires as Bolan swerved around a limo trying to pull out and chased after the FBI van.

"Come in, Isaac!"

Bolan grabbed the radio from the seat and punched the Transmit button briefly. "Here."

"Where the hell've you been?" someone demanded. Bolan spun the wheel hard in a nearly instantaneous lane change when he spotted the blue FBI van and, a couple hundred feet ahead, the first Lincoln. "Close in!" the radio squawked. "Be ready to come up hard on their ass on my signal. Got it?"

"Got it," Bolan replied into the radio. If they were depending on some sort of security verbiage, he'd be tagged as an impostor almost instantly. There was nothing to point to that so far. He drove the big engine hard to close the gap between himself and the van, then slowed to pace the Feds when he was about fifty feet away. The FBI van was cruising along at sixty-two mph, the Feds utterly inconspicuous on the expressway heading into the city and utterly oblivious to the pincers closing on them. Bolan didn't waste time haranguing the Feds in his head for their dismal lack of awareness. He had to be prepared to cooperate in the attack on them long enough to avoid raising the suspicion of the gunmen in the other Lincoln—then react fast enough to take down the vehicle without getting himself shot to pieces by the Feds. It would be a tricky maneuver, and he contemplated getting in touch with Stony Man Farm. They could relay a message to the Feds and keep them off his back. Before the thought could be acted upon he ran out of time.

"Close, Isaac, close!" the radio buzzed. The gunmen had chosen a moment when the expressway was clear between the vehicles. The lead vehicle slammed hard on the brakes and skidded across the lanes of traffic, the driver exercising extraordinary command of the computer-controlled braking system to steer the vehicle into the path of the van, despite the FBI driver's attempt to avoid the impact. The Lincoln driver spun sideways at the last moment, bringing the skidding automobile to a sudden halt directly in the path of the van. The squealing of the van tires ended with a sudden crunch as the nose caved into the door of the Lincoln. The driver of the car already was out his door and lying across the roof of the car with a sawed-off shotgun aimed square at the van. Another gunner emerged behind him and took up a position with the weapon aimed over the hood of the car. Anybody exiting on either side of the van was already targeted.

Bolan was watching the situation develop as he braked hard within twenty yards of the rear of the van, then stomped on the pedal again as the gunners took up their positions. The rear doors of the FBI van swung open, and a pair of dark-suited men with handguns leveled their weapons at Bolan's vehicle. The determined look on their faces transformed to confusion when they realized Bolan wasn't trying to hem them in—he was accelerating and twisting the wheel to carry his vehicle around the van. He stood on the gas and leaned into the swoop of the big car as he steered it into the parked Lincoln. The gunners' faces gaped in shock in his windshield, but they didn't have time to avoid the collision. The tonnage of the car slammed into the other's flank and shoved it sideways across the pavement, pushing the body of the vehicle into the gunners. The driver received a body slam that sent him flying over the pavement, flopping through a backward somersault and finally dropping him on the asphalt in a facedown sprawl. The man with the autorifle was luckier. The front end of the car moved less, and he was sent flipping over the hood. With a judo twist that evidenced years of martial-arts practice, he rolled through it and crashed to the pavement on the opposite side of the hood, next to the front tire of the van. He pushed himself to his feet in an instant, grappling for the automatic rifle and sweeping it across the front end of the van as he squeezed out a full-auto burst. Bolan didn't bother to duck. The rounds pinged off the bullet-resistant glass of his vehicle.

He was about to jump out of the Lincoln when he felt a thumping in the air. Leaning far over the steering wheel, he was able to see out the front of the big Lincoln, where a large black helicopter was descending almost on top of him. The aircraft was almost totally unlit, and its underside glowed like the belly of a lizardlike beast in the lights illuminating the expressway.

The man with the autorifle aimed his weapon at the van with one hand while snatching a radio out of his jacket pocket, backtracking for cover behind the repositioned Lincoln number one. Bolan listened to the man's voice erupt from the still-functioning receiver mounted on his dashboard.

"Target the rear of the van—they'll make a break for it. There they go!"

He'd heard enough. He was out of his vehicle in a moment, wishing like hell he'd brought the Heckler & Koch G3-TG3. But it would have been impossible to keep a piece of hardware that substantial out of sight during his airport surveillance. All he had was his handguns and the shotgun that had clattered onto the pavement. Now the black chopper tilted on its nose, its headlights coming on bright as spotlights, and unleashed a deadly barrage of high-caliber machine-gun fire at the van. He watched a pair of FBI agents, one of them the conservatively dressed woman agent, get swatted to the pavement by the barrage as they attempted to exit the rear of the van. He saw them die as if in slow motion, a sudden cold anger igniting in his soldier's belly.

He fired the sawed-off 12-gauge at the helicopter, watching one of the headlights shatter and darken. He dropped as the other ground-based gunner targeted him with his autoweapon and peppered Bolan's vehicle with the remainder of rounds in his magazine.

"Take him down! Take him down!" the gunner shouted into the radio, and Bolan heard the sound in stereo from the man himself and from the radio in his own vehicle.

"Is that Isaac?" said a voice over the radio from the helicopter.

"No! It's another Fed! He must've hijacked Isaac's car!"

"So where's Isaac?" the helicopter demanded.

"Just take him down!"

Bolan crouched beside the car door and waited for the helicopter to swing its machine-gun barrel onto him. He heard the change in the rotor pitch, then stood, coming face-to-face with the nose of the chopper from a distance of less than a dozen feet. The pilot and copilot registered surprise upon seeing him, but the copilot grabbed for his gun controls. The Executioner fired the shotgun, shattering the windshield of the aircraft, obliterating the other headlight. The helicopter recoiled, and the copilot fired, drilling a torrent of machine-gun rounds through the air above Bolan's head. The soldier pumped the big shotgun and fired again, directly into the chopper. The buckshot pinged off the body harmlessly. The copilot and the pilot were getting synchronized and the helicopter nodded at Bolan again, ready to direct the machine-gun fire into his unprotected body.

Bolan sped away, spinning alongside the car he had been driving and around the side of the FBI van. The path took him directly under the helicopter, and he was lost from the sight of the pilots. He jumped into the van's interior, finding himself facing a hand-ful of terrified federal agents and the shocked face of Nicholae Dinitzin. The interior of the van was set up with padded vinyl bench seats along the walls. Within a few paces on the asphalt lay the bloodied remains of two agents.

"You a Fed?" one of the agents asked.

"Yeah," Bolan said. "Is this vehicle driveable?"

"I don't think so."

"You," Bolan ordered. "Keep an eye out the front."

The agent turned to look out the front windshield. "I can't see anything," he protested.

"There's a gunman on the ground," Bolan stated.

"I don't see him!"

"What about the chopper?"

The agent leaned forward over the abandoned front seats. "It's ascending," the agent reported.

Was the ground-based gunner moving in on the van? One way to find out. Bolan jumped out of the open rear of the van and dropped to the ground, land-ing on his side and pivoting on his shoulder with the shotgun held in front of him. He saw the movement of feet as the gunner approached alongside the van, and he fired. The blast of buckshot from just five feet away flayed through the shoes of the gunner and ripped his flesh to the bone. The hardman dropped to the pavement, screaming. Bolan crawled to the shouting man and ripped the autorifle out of his hands. The gunner opened his pain-filled eyes when he came suddenly to the realization that his weapon had been taken away from him. He raised his hands in protest of what he thought would be the killing shot, but Bolan ignored him, crawling back to the rear of the van as he felt more than saw the monstrous bulk of the helicopter maneuver awkwardly over him. When he was inside, the agents stared at him incredulously.

"What happened to the gunner?" one of them asked, a man in his fifties with hideously bloodshot eyes. The man in charge.

"He's going to need handicapped parking plates," Bolan said.

"What are you doing now?"

"We can't get out of here while that thing is waiting for us."

"They won't stay long," Agent Red Eyes declared. "We radioed for reinforcements and the state police will be on their way, too."

"We can't wait for them to get fed up and leave," Bolan said. "Any second they'll start gunning this van. They came here to kill Dinitzin, and they won't care if they take down a few more Feds in the process."

"How do you know that?" Red Eyes demanded.

"They're assassins," Bolan said. "They wanted to neutralize Dinitzin when they visited the office in Arlington this afternoon. Bad luck for them he was out of town."

Red Eyes' mouth became a hard line, and in seconds his face began to match his eyes. "You're the gunman who was on the scene in Arlington this afternoon!" He didn't wait for confirmation from Bolan. "You're under arrest!"

"I don't think now's the best time," the soldier said, listening more carefully to the unseen activity of the helicopter than the fury of the FBI agent.

"Give me that gun!" Red Eyes suddenly lunged

at Bolan, grabbing for the autorifle. The Executioner snapped the rifle butt into the agent's forehead, sending him sprawling on his back down the aisle between the seats. Bolan was watching the ceiling. None of the other FBI agents moved.

Then the great black bulk of the helicopter lumbered into the sky, the shattered windshield dangling from the frame like a single eyeball hanging from a bloody socket. The faces of the pilot and copilot were contorted with anger.

There was nowhere for the occupants of the van to flee to. The machine gun was going to burst to life and fill the interior with flesh-shredding metal like the inside of a motorized meat grinder. Bolan jumped out of the van and bolted directly toward the chopper. The pilots spent a full half second watching him, caught by surprise. The autorifle in his hands chattered to life, cutting into the unprotected pilot, stitching him across the face and chest, then chewing across the interior of the helicopter into the fast-acting copilot, whose finger closed on the machine-gun trigger as the rifle rounds slashed into his chest. The machine gun unleashed a handful of rounds that seared the air just inches from Bolan's body, slamming into the steel shell of the van.

Time stood still for the Executioner as the two weapons fired, twin streams of bullets flying back and forth between the van and the interior of the helicopter. The soldier could do nothing more than fire a continuous burst into the copilot. Suddenly, rounds severed the copilot's nerve center and his entire body went through a spasm that wrenched his grip off the firing mechanism. At the same moment, the pilot slumped out of sight and the helicopter tilted sharply. Had the machine gun still be firing, it would have traced a deadly path across Bolan's body and across the occupants of the van.

The helicopter carried itself out over the grassy field that separated the eastbound lanes of the expressway from the westbound, then the engines stalled. It slid to the ground like a stone, slamming nose-first into the grass, crumpling the fuselage, shattering the rotors and smashing the landing gear. Unencumbered all of a sudden, the engine accelerated to revolutions far beyond its design tolerances, spinning an empty shaft and billowing white smoke. It overheated and locked up with a sudden loud screech of protesting steel.

Bolan strode to the side of the van where the wounded gunner lay on his back, breathing quickly and shallowly and staring at the sky as if looking for an afterlife. The soldier grabbed him by the collar and dragged him into a sitting position.

"Who hired you?"

"Fuck you." The voice was little more than a distant hiss.

"You're dying. If you give me the information I want, I'll take you to a hospital. You'll be alive. Otherwise you bleed to death."

The gunner's eyes looked away from the heavens and focused hazily on the face of the Executioner. "Kabat."

"What?" Bolan demanded.

"The man's name is Kabat."

"All right. Good enough. Come on."

Bolan was going to make good on his bargain, but by the time he had dragged the wounded gunner to the Lincoln he was beyond the help of any doctor.

The soldier left him there. The FBI would deal with him. They were already yelling for him to stay where he was and put down his gun.

Bolan let the autorifle clatter to the pavement, then he eased behind the wheel of the Lincoln and drove away.

CHAPTER FOUR

It took Bolan fifteen minutes to ditch the Lincoln on a city street and grab a taxi back to the airport. Then he was in his rented Blazer, talking to Stony Man Farm on a scrambled cellular connection.

"Kabat is his last name," Barbara Price told him. "First name Roger. Born in London and raised all over the U.S., with business interests that are mostly based out of Malaysia."

"What kind of business?" Bolan asked.

"According to U.S. arrest records, he's dabbled in everything over the last two decades. His entry into big-time crime came when he ran a prostitution ring that circulated women around Mediterranean tourist spots. He owned a kind of floating brothel that would pull into various ports, do a couple of wild nights of business, then leave town before things got too hot. Eventually the French shut it down and the ship's business manager served some time behind bars. Kabat avoided serving jail time over it, mostly because he stayed out of France for years afterward. Then he graduated to drug smuggling. Nobody knows how well he did, but it all came to an end eight years ago with a major bust. Once again, Kabat managed to avoid prison. Since then he's been living well on nobody-knows-what income. The investigations that have been able to dig up anything on him show a growing propensity for arms dealing.''

"So why's he trying to assassinate Lipetsk execs?" Bolan asked.

"He must believe it'll give him access to their technology, somehow," Price suggested.

"Yeah. But Stephanie McCord told me the company is nowhere near having a marketable product," Bolan said, chewing on the implications.

"If Kabat wants to get his hands on this technology, why would he be wiping out the Lipetsk developers now?" Price asked. "Why not wait until the technology is ready, then move in?"

There was silence over the line for a long five seconds.

"Here's a hypothesis," Bolan said. "When McCord told me the company is nowhere near having a marketable product, she meant a perfected device for mapping geologic strata using magnetic pulses. Not a device for causing the destructive magnetic pulse that Kabat needs to construct an effective weapon."

"Of course," Price replied, seeing the answer suddenly. "Lipetsk Enterprises is trying to create a highly sensitive instrument. All Kabat needs is a cheap, effective piece of destructive weaponry."

"If that's what he wants, and if he knows Lipetsk Enterprises already has the capability to make such a device, then he's got a pretty good line on their research and development progress," Bolan continued. "That translates into inside information."

"He's been either watching Lipetsk carefully and managed to recruit an employee from the inner circle, or someone on the inside saw the opportunity to make a quick buck and approached him," Price concluded. "Who?"

"I think I'll try to find out. Meanwhile, I need all the information I can get on Kabat."

A masculine voice came on the line. "Aaron here, Striker. I've been listening on speaker. For what it's worth, I think you're on exactly the right track. I've got a truckload of stuff on our boy Kabat. It's downloading to you now."

Bolan glanced at the notepad computer sitting on the passenger seat, connected to a cellular modem. The screen was filling a directory with incoming files. "Thanks, Bear."

"There's also a bunch of information coming in on the old science town of Lipetsk Nov," Kurtzman added.

"Anything I should know right away?"

"One fact that might be pretty important—only half the senior research team from the original science town ended up joining the corporation that was set up in the U.S. in 1998. They went their separate ways over the years. The head man in charge of Lipetsk Nov, incidentally, is living in São Paulo now. A guy named Andrei Sheknovi."

Bolan instantly made the connection. "Dinitzin just returned from São Paulo," he said. "Think this man Sheknovi could be the insider who's in deep with Kabat?"

"Yeah. But what does that mean?" Kurtzman asked.

"I don't know yet."

"Something else you should know, Striker," Price interjected. "We called in some favors from Langley to get our Lipetsk Nov research accomplished. Everything we needed was in the Kremlin vaults. But our researcher didn't get far. Seems there was an internal investigation going on in Moscow at the same time, trying to access the same collection of files.''

''So Moscow is interested in the research of their old science town, after all these years.''

''Doesn't seem like a coincidence,'' Price mused.

''No, that'd be pretty damn unlikely,'' Bolan said. ''I think I'll be on the lookout for strangers with Russian accents.''

''I think that'd be a good idea, Striker,'' Kurtzman agreed.

ALEX FRUDKIN WASN'T a man who frightened easily. But when he saw the ghost in the garden he just about jumped out of his skin.

He'd been standing guard over the home of Lipetsk Enterprises president Nicholae Dinitzin for hours. Getting this lookout post had been ridiculously easy. The neighbors were out, on holiday or something. He'd picked the lock and walked in the back door, then found the upstairs window with the best view of the Dinitzin house. A half hour later the FBI arrived. They'd been too stupid to send an advance team to watch the neighborhood before setting up their perimeter guard. Anyone in place prior to their arrival went unnoticed.

Sure, they'd rung the doorbell. Agent Frudkin didn't answer it, and pretty soon the FBI went away.

After which Frudkin was free to observe the house undetected. The room was a second-floor office and he kept it dark, so the FBI who were watching the neighborhood never saw his field glasses or his laser listening devices, aimed at the Dinitzin residence. He spied with impunity.

His respect for the FBI returned as he regarded their on-the-job professionalism. They were clearly at a high level of awareness. There were guards in the open, guards hidden, all coordinated through constant radio communications. Nobody was going to move on this street of big homes and professionally landscaped yards without the FBI knowing about it. Certainly nobody was going to sneak past them into the home of Nicholae Dinitzin.

Then the ghost appeared, a flash of blackness among the shades of a decorative shrub. A malevolent face materialized in Frudkin's field glasses and was gone a moment later, melted into the black. That was no FBI agent. What the hell was it?

Not what. Who. It was human. It had to be. But how had a human being slithered among the FBI agents without being noticed? And where had he disappeared to?

He saw it again, emerging from the shadows just long enough to jimmy one of the windows on the first floor, raise it smoothly and step into the house.

There was no sound of alarm. No sign of awareness among the FBI. But surely it wasn't the FBI. So who was he?

And what should Agent Alex Frudkin do about him?

"WHO ARE YOU?" Nicholae Dinitzin demanded, looking terrified and backing into the tall antique French buffet that stood against the wall separating the formal dining area from a small parlor.

"Belasko?" Stephanie McCord asked, as if she couldn't believe her eyes. "What are you doing here?"

"You know this man?" Dinitzin demanded. His thinning silver hair was disheveled, his eyes dark with worry, and his mouth drooped with fear. Dinitzin looked older than his sixty-something years. He looked ancient.

"Nick, this is the man who killed the attackers that came to the office."

That seemed to snap Dinitzin's awareness like a jump into a cold lake. He stared at Bolan with more amazement than fright, and then his expression became hard. "Who are you? Why have you involved yourself in our affairs?"

"I'm Michael Belasko," Bolan said, as if that was more than sufficient identity. "I involved myself because I discovered someone intending to kill innocent people. I thought it would be a good idea if somebody didn't let that happen."

Dinitzin frowned. "You're American, but you're not FBI," he stated. As he became slightly less tense and fearful, his Russian accent noticeably diminished.

"No."

"Private enterprise?"

"No."

"Then who are you?"

"Who I am really doesn't matter, Dinitzin. What matters is that you're in a great deal of danger, this very minute. I think I know why."

"What? You didn't tell me that before!" McCord protested.

"I've learned quite a bit in the past few hours.

With your help I can fill in several of the blanks that remain, and start trying to determine how to neutralize the danger to you. And—'' he nodded to the doorway behind Dinitzin ''—to your family.''

A thin, striking woman in her late fifties stood in the doorway, watching the conversation. She looked regal—a proud, strong woman, despite the fact that she was suddenly, inexplicably, living in fear.

''What's going on?'' she asked, directing her question at Bolan. ''Have you learned something more?''

Bolan was silent, looking at Dinitzin. The woman clearly thought he was just another FBI agent. There had to be eight of them on the grounds, and she couldn't have met them all.

''He was about to tell us, dear,'' Dinitzin said.

''Well, what? What is it?'' she demanded, stepping toward Bolan. From closer proximity, Bolan could see the cracks in the dike. She was a strong woman, but the attack on her husband, the danger she felt, were compromising a wall of self-control built over a lifetime.

''Susan,'' Dinitzin said firmly, ''please make us some coffee while Agent Belasko explains.''

Mrs. Dinitzin nodded and retreated to a small coffee bar. Stephanie McCord pulled out a chair and touched Nicholae Dinitzin's arm as he lowered himself wearily into it. She sat next to him, moving her body near to his. ''Speak, please, Mr. Belasko.''

Bolan remained standing. Susan Dinitzin was giving him piercing looks as she comforted herself in the familiar task of brewing a pot of coffee. ''Someone is after your magnetic pulse technology,'' he stated simply.

"I told you this afternoon that can't be," McCord protested. "It's a good eighteen months away from being perfected."

"Eighteen months away from being a viable tool for mapping the geology underground. Ready immediately, I assume, for use as a powerful, portable magnetic pulse generator."

Dinitzin said, "Yes. Yes! You're saying someone wants to get access to the technology now for use as a weapon."

"Exactly."

"But why would they go to such violent ends to get it?" McCord asked. "It's not that good a weapon. I mean, it might do a lot of damage. But look at all the damage they've done just today. They must have their own supply of weapons of all kinds." Her voice belied her frustration.

"Of course," Susan Dinitzin agreed. "They had automatic weapons when they came to the office today. That's how they killed poor Serge, isn't it? And they had rifles or machine guns or something when they attacked my husband at the airport. What good would something like our Lipetsk device do them?"

"We're not talking about a single weapon," Bolan answered. "These people are arms traders. They want the technology. They want to launch a new industry."

"Oh, God," Dinitzin muttered.

"You're not serious?" McCord asked.

"Deadly serious. The man behind the attacks today is thought to be an international arms trader. He's a global businessman. Seriously wealthy and connected, and out to make a name for himself among those who don't know him already. I think he's decided to obtain a large cut of the worldwide arms trade by gaining a monopoly on one of the most innovative weapons since the Gatling gun.''

''But it isn't designed to be a weapon!'' Dinitzin protested. ''It's an instrument of exploration and analysis.'' His Russian accent was slipping in again.

''It doesn't matter what you intend it to be. What matters is what the worms of the earth corrupt it into,'' Bolan stated. ''If you let them.''

McCord was shaking her head. ''Wait. This still doesn't make sense, Belasko. They attacked Serge without provocation. They never approached him for the technology behind the pulse generator.''

''That you are aware of,'' Bolan said.

''I would have known,'' she stated flatly.

''Unless Serge knew there was a real danger and was trying to insulate you from it, Stevie.'' Mrs. Dinitzin spoke up.

McCord looked at the older woman, and her expression became limp and blank. ''I suppose so.''

''I'd believe it,'' Dinitzin admitted. ''Serge Gordetsky was our vice president of technology development. If there was one person to start with to access the engineering behind the pulse generator, it would be him.''

''All right,'' Bolan said. ''Let's assume they approached Gordetsky and he refused to cooperate. They knew they needed to convince someone else in the ranks to come up with the technology for them. Someone highly placed. How would they go about it?''

''Money,'' McCord said. ''They'd try to buy one of us off.''

Bolan shook his head and asked Dinitzin, "Would that have worked?"

"No," the company president said. "We're a community. The senior staff of Lipetsk has been together for two decades. Our families are bound together. We're more than just a company. We're really one big family. I think one of us would no more sell out the others than you would sell out your brother, Belasko."

Bolan nodded, suspicion confirmed. "That's what I thought. And that's the same conclusion Roger Kabat came to after he tried to buy Gordetsky. He knew he had to change his tactics. Instead of trying to work against the natural order of the Lipetsk family, he tried to capitalize on it."

Susan Dinitzin was standing at her husband's shoulder, and she nodded with grim understanding. "Of course. A man would never sell out a member of his own family. But to protect them from harm he would give up all his wealth and possessions. Even if he was asked to give up the thing that originally brought the family together, he would do it."

Dinitzin nodded, staring at the floor. "My wife is correct, Belasko," he said. "Lipetsk came together to work on this technology, but now the Lipetsk community is more important to me than that technology. I will give it up to this Kabat person if it means saving this community from more harm."

"If you do, you'll be helping perpetrate the deaths of thousands," Bolan warned.

"You don't understand. I can't do anything that might harm my people."

"You're wrong. I do understand. I know the position you're in and I'm not judging you, Dinitzin.

But, as difficult as it is, you have to understand the consequences of your actions.''

His Russian accent was thick and his shoulders were stooping as if he were growing more elderly by the moment. ''God in heaven knows how well I understand the consequences.''

But, as difficult as it is, you have to understand the consequences of your actions.

The Russian secret was hot, and the shooters were looming in the very growing pulse pace in the industry. 2000 a Russian history have won support getting that competition.

CHAPTER FIVE

By 5:00 a.m. the FBI had pulled out all but two pairs of agents. One pair was posted on the street in a dark Buick sedan. The other was walking the neighborhood, checking in occasionally with the security guard who manned the small brick booth at the gate into the exclusive community.

Bolan had watched the bulk of agents leave. They'd told Dinitzin that the attack would come right away if it would come at all. Otherwise they would just have to wait and see what happened.

At 6:00 a.m. the agents on foot had left the scene, leaving just the pair of guards, two men in suits smoking cigarettes and sitting in a parked car on the street. Not too obvious.

But the neighborhood was quiet. A few early risers were already heading off to work. A fast-walking housewife in a pink fleece jogging outfit hurried by on the sidewalk, large blue weights encircling her wrists. Bolan watched the FBI agents check her out as she passed.

Around him, the house was silent. Stephanie McCord was asleep on the couch in the living room. The Dinitzins had finally been able to get to sleep around three in the morning.

Bolan didn't enjoy the long, monotonous hours of the stakeout, but here he was anyway, relieved Nicholae Dinitzin had been too shaken up to demand some sort of official identification. McCord's confidence in him had been enough to convince her employer to trust him. He wandered from room to room in the large suburban home, staring out the windows for activity that never occurred. He felt uneasy. The consummate warrior, capable of adapting to any environment and circumstances, felt vaguely displaced in the comfort and quiet of a family home.

He shrugged it off mentally. So he wasted a few hours on guard duty. No great loss. He hadn't been able to figure out a line of investigation that would have served him any better. And he had been bothered, all night long, by a gnawing sense of danger. Some warrior's impulse, perhaps, told him to stay right where he was.

He couldn't explain it, even to himself, but he had learned to trust those instincts over the years. That trust had saved his life time and again.

This time, though, they'd been wrong. The sun was up, and the night had been peaceful. He was tired. It had been more than twenty-four hours since he'd slept.

He noticed someone crossing the street about a block down and trained his binoculars on the person, angling them to overcome the glare of the difficult angle from the bedroom window.

It was the fast walker in the pink fleece jogging outfit. She was crossing the street, but suddenly tumbled to the pavement, most of her head gone.

AGENT ALEX FRUDKIN had dozed on and off in front of the window in the neighbor's home. He'd watched the FBI team trail away in small groups until just the pair in the sedan was left. He watched the neighborhood lights wink off one by one as the dawn broke with soft light. He had never seen the strange, dark figure leave the Dinitzin house and assumed the man was still inside. But the FBI had checked in on the family a dozen times since the man's arrival. The stranger had done them no harm.

He checked with his teammates every hour on the hour. They reported the coming and going of the FBI and the few late-night stragglers returning to the neighborhood. Parked in a municipal building lot across the street from the entrance to the gated community, they had a clear view of the small security guard hut, windowed to give the security guard a three-hundred-sixty-degree view. Street lamps thoroughly illuminated the area. The young black man who worked the shack concentrated on a textbook of some sort most of the night.

At 5:56 a.m. an Asian man arrived and parked at the brick guardhouse. He and the black man exchanged words for a few minutes. They both laughed at some joke as the night guard crammed his book into a backpack, then got into his car and drove away with a wave. The Asian man slumped into the chair in the guard shack, then stood again almost at once as a van turned into the drive and stopped inches from the gate.

The Asian man smiled and leaned out the window of the guard shack to talk to the driver of the large Ford van.

Across the street, the Russian agent watched through his binoculars. He made out some sort of landscaping logo on the side of the vehicle. These rich people had all kinds of service vehicles coming and going.

The Asian man seemed to be waiting. Then he raised his fist and knocked on the window of the van. There was another pause.

The Russian agent squirmed in his seat and pressed the binoculars harder into his eyes. Something wrong? He waited. He hardly noticed a woman in a pink jogging outfit appear down the street, a half block beyond the guard hut.

The van window rolled down.

The agent watched the Asian recoil into the interior of the guard hut at the same moment the windows transformed from clear glass to pink opaqueness.

Then the barrel of a weapon appeared from the window and was aimed at the camera that videotaped all arrivals to the gated community. The camera silently exploded into pieces that dangled from frayed wire.

The Russian shouted for his partner, who awoke in the passenger seat and blinked his eyes to clear his vision. He spotted the guard shack, its interior splattered with blood. The wooden gate snapped as the van forced its way through.

The first agent tossed the binoculars into his partner's lap and twisted the keys in the ignition, then shifted the car quickly into Drive and shot over the grassy divide, over the empty road and past the guard hut. The agent in the passenger seat was straining his eyes through the binoculars as the van screeched to a halt just a few paces from the unsuspecting woman in the jogging suit. She looked at the van, startled by the noise, and recoiled suddenly. The muzzle of the gun protruded from the driver's window again. When it fired, without a sound they could hear, it seemed to halve her skull at the nose bridge.

BOLAN CROSSED THE ROOM in a few long strides and pounded on the door to the Dinitzin bedroom. "Up and out," he ordered. Even before he reached the stairs he heard the door behind him open.

"What's happening?" Nicholae Dinitzin asked.

"They're on their way," he said over his shoulder. "Meet me downstairs in sixty seconds."

At the base of the stairs he saw Stephanie McCord pulling on a sweatshirt. "What's going on?" she demanded.

"Someone's coming."

"Did you warn the FBI?"

"The FBI agents will have to take care of themselves."

"We should try to escape out the rear," McCord suggested.

"That way's too open. We'd be gunned down." Bolan had evaluated the rear escape route potential during his reconnaissance the night before. The ground to the rear of the house, which sat on two and a half acres, was mostly bare, well-kept grass. Open. Nothing more than decorative shrubbery for cover. The back edge of the grounds touched a narrow road that separated the residential community from a private golf course. More flat, manicured terrain. There was no effective cover for hundreds of yards.

Dinitzin and his wife descended the stairs quickly

and found Bolan at the rear of the house. He gestured for silence.

They gazed in horror at the monstrous automatic rifle slung over one shoulder, its muzzle pointing at the ground at knee level. In his hands was the strangest-looking handgun they had ever seen—a big, two-handled weapon. Another black handgun was holstered under his left arm.

"No time for questions," Bolan stated, interrupting Dinitzin's words before they were uttered. "Do just as I say. Is that understood?"

"Yes," the man said. The women nodded fearfully.

Bolan opened the door to the garage.

FRUDKIN WAS TEMPTED to run down to the first floor as soon as he got the frantic radio message from his fellow agents. But he waited, standing still at his best window watch post, for a long 120 seconds. His patience was rewarded when he saw the activity through the window of the garage on the Dinitzin house. There was the man himself, his wife and the woman. Leading them was the familiar black-suited figure—the ghost Frudkin had spotted in the darkness hours before. They passed in front of the window and were gone, presumably inside one of the Dinitzin vehicles.

Now what was Frudkin supposed to do? The man in there clearly wasn't FBI, but he was protecting the Lipetsk people. His first goal would be to escape whoever it was that was coming for the Dinitzins. Having witnessed the failure of the FBI, the man's next step would be to get the Dinitzins and the rest of the Lipetsk staff into hiding.

Frudkin couldn't allow that to happen.

He raced down the stairs of the empty house, jerked open the door and ran into the yard, hugging his SIG-Sauer P-228 pistol close to his chest and wishing he'd taken the chance of sneaking in an assault rifle. His adversary was armed with far more than a single handgun.

But one shot was all it took to bring a man down, and Frudkin had the advantage of surprise. As he quickly radioed his position to his comrades, he snaked through the formal garden that covered half the front grounds of the big estate. He could see the FBI car. The remaining two agents were sitting inside, oblivious to the sudden activity. Maybe even asleep. The intruder's vehicle was in view, approaching at a speed that wouldn't arouse suspicion. Frudkin wondered how long the Dinitzins' protector would wait inside the garage. He would be watching out the small Plexiglas windows set in the garage door, waiting until the time was right for flight.

BOLAN PEERED OUT the small window in the garage door as the others waited inside the Saab convertible. The neighborhood was silent, seemingly peaceful, as far as his limited perspective could see. That was an illusion that couldn't last. The women were in the back seat, Dinitzin in the driver's seat. The top was down.

The large Ford van appeared on the street, moving slowly, then pulled to a stop in the street, next to the parked FBI vehicle.

"Let's go," Bolan commanded, and yanked swiftly on the garage door as Dinitzin started the Saab. Opening it manually instead of using the automatic opener made it slightly quicker and quieter. They needed every advantage they could get. As he shoved it above his head, he spotted movement to his left and trained the Beretta 93-R on the spot in the bushes. Anything might come out of those bushes. A dog. A local kid on his way to school.

The man who emerged was clutching a police handgun to his chest. The race began, but it was an unfair competition. Bolan was far more practiced with his weapon. The single suppressed shot took the man through the right upper arm. His handgun plopped into the grass, and he grabbed his tattered biceps. A rattle of automatic gunfire erupted from the street. The FBI were going down in a merciless hail of fire. Bolan sprinted to the Saab and vaulted into the passenger seat. "Drive and don't stop for anything!"

Dinitzin gunned the engine and the Saab's tires chirped on the shellacked ceramic tile floor of the garage, boosting the vehicle quickly down the fifty-foot driveway. Bolan laid the big Heckler & Koch G3-TG3 rifle on the open windowsill and triggered a long spray at the rear doors starting to swing open on the Ford van. The doors shut again quickly and the figure in the front passenger window ducked out of sight. Dinitzin pulled the Saab into a hard left and stomped on the gas, and for a fleeting moment Bolan thought they were on their way to safety.

Then disaster struck. A green Maxima came out of nowhere, nearly airborne over the suburban street. It screeched to a halt and twisted at the last minute, skidding sideways over the pavement. Dinitzin swerved but didn't have the skill or time for a tricky maneuver. The front end of the Saab slammed into the front corner fender of the Maxima with a crunch of buckling metal.

Bolan didn't give the Russian businessman time to deal with the impact shock. "Get it started again!" he ordered. He stood in his seat, slammed the G3-TG3 onto the top frame of the windshield and watched the sudden terror in the faces of the Maxima's occupants. They ducked behind the dashboard as the soldier triggered a blast of 7.62 mm rounds that slashed the windshield and rained a torrent of glass pieces over the vehicles.

"It's dead!" Dinitzin said, grappling with the ignition.

"Get out!" Bolan said, twisting at the sound of the van ripping over the grass in a full-throttle U-turn and gunning onto the street again. Bolan thumbed a 40 mm high-explosive grenade into the HK79 grenade launcher mounted on the rifle. The grenade sight was useless on a target that close. He fired the round on pure instinct and placed it on the asphalt five feet in front of the van. The impact slammed into the front end, transforming the windshield into a deadly hail of crystalline shrapnel mixed with streaks of orange fire. The driver and front-seat passenger simultaneously experienced a sudden flaying of all exposed skin and a blast of flesh-melting heat.

The van lurched onto the sidewalk on its rims, leaving flying glass and melting rubber in its wake. The rear doors flew open and a screaming man danced onto the street, twisting and waving his arms before flopping onto the ground.

Bolan didn't have time to put the man out of his misery. He hit the pavement and circled the Maxima.

His first and only goal was to put both sets of attackers on one side of himself. He ripped open the driver's door and dragged the first bloody man onto the street. The man was staring at him with grim contempt, and the soldier didn't like the obstinacy in the man's face. Somebody with that much attitude might be tempted to make a chancy grab for a weapon. Bolan stepped into him and rapped him across the temple with the butt of the rifle. The man went limp.

The second man had his hands in the air. He'd held them up as he tried to escape Bolan's gunfire blast, and they were now ripped and bloodied, with at least two bullet wounds. The blood was streaming into his jacket cuffs.

The soldier dragged him to his feet by the collar and flung him onto the pavement. "Behind this car!" he ordered, scanning the smoking battleground. McCord and the Dinitzins scrambled behind the disabled Maxima and crouched on their heels.

"Get that man's gun," Bolan ordered, pointing at the unconscious driver. "Then if either of them moves, shoot him in the head. Understand?"

"Got it," McCord said, yanking at the lapels of the driver and dragging out a .38.

There was a rattle of fire. Sure enough, there was at least one survivor out there somewhere. The soldier had expected the van to drop off a gunman or two before making its charge. He crouched as a long volley of rounds chopped through the fenders of the Saab and the Maxima.

Bolan waited for the pause, then vaulted to his feet and targeted the stand of small bushes that was the origin of the gunfire. A dozen rounds ripped at the greenery before the soldier retreated to cover again.

"We just want Nicholae Dinitzin!" the gunner in the bushes yelled. "Then the rest of you can go free."

Bolan said nothing, his warrior's senses suddenly buzzing. Why was the man trying to talk to him? To distract him? If so, from what?

"Watch for movement," he whispered. "There might be more closing in on us."

The gunner in the bushes tried a new tactic. He gauged his moment, then stood in plain sight and directed his next barrage underneath the Maxima. Bolan heard the rattle of the rounds bouncing off the pavement and thrashing around underneath the vehicle, just a few feet away from their bodies. The gunner was firing from a bad angle, but any moment one of the rounds might ricochet into them.

The Executioner had a grenade in the launcher, and at the moment the rifle fire let up, he stood. The gunner was hidden again behind the bushes, but that didn't matter. He triggered the HK79 and dropped a grenade into the shrubs. The deadly bomb exploded, and tiny metal shards sped in every direction, shredding the bush to its skeletal branches in an eye blink and cutting into the gunner like countless tiny whirling razor blades. The man went into instant shock, never experiencing the pain of the wounds that covered him head to toe before he was suddenly dead.

"There!" McCord shouted, pointing to the side of a house. Bolan saw it. The muzzle of a weapon appeared around the corner and then was gone again. It was to their side, just a little behind them.

"This way!" Bolan said, pointing to the other side

of the street. Then he stopped cold. Another gunner was coming from between a pair of big houses. The attacker's eyes met Bolan's and he triggered his weapon. The Executioner jerked to one side and squeezed hard on the G3-TG3's trigger, his mind racing for overlooked options. But there was none. He was hemmed in on two sides.

At the moment his rounds outraced the gunner and ate into his knees and crotch, Bolan heard the echo of automatic fire from behind him. As the gunner in front of him curled like a wounded bug and collapsed, the soldier whirled. Dinitzin was already falling onto the cold, hard street. Stephanie McCord was jumping in front of his bloodied wife, firing her appropriated handgun, and Bolan's finger squeezed the rifle's trigger as he wrenched the Beretta from its holster on his right hip and leveled it on the second gunner, issuing a triburst just as the G3-TG3 fired on empty.

The second gunner was suddenly very dead, his torso blasted to scarlet ribbons of flesh and his face obliterated.

Susan and Nicholae Dinitzin had been hit by only a couple of rounds each.

But they were just as dead.

CHAPTER SIX

Bolan left McCord lying where she was, between the bodies of the husband and wife, and grabbed at the conscious man from the Maxima. Hoisting him onto his stomach and bending low, he pushed the man's head against the pavement.

The man gasped for breath.

"Who are you?"

"FBI!" the man wheezed.

The Executioner pressed the Beretta against the back of his prisoner's head.

"No more lies."

The man's eyes were wide open as he writhed and squirmed like a half-crushed earthworm. "Russian Intelligence," he gasped.

Bolan let go of the agent's head and grabbed his wrists, securing them, then his ankles, in disposable plastic handcuffs. The agent struggled briefly, quickly realizing the more he moved the tighter the cuffs became. The soldier checked the second agent, the unconscious driver, and realized the man wasn't unconscious, after all. Bolan had to have applied too much force behind the blow to his head.

A third stranger had to be dealt with. He jogged to the Dinitzin house and found the man with the shot biceps leaning over a smoke-blackened body. With his good hand he was pressing his handgun against the burn victim's temple.

"Put it down," Bolan commanded.

The gunner stood up slowly over the burn victim, his P-228 pistol hanging limply at his side. "Don't even think of it," Bolan growled.

The movement was quick and deft. The man had only to move the muzzle of the handgun a few inches to redirect its aim at the burn victim. He fired in the same instant Bolan triggered the 93-R. In the next half second the burn victim died of a shot through the heart, then the P-228 bounced on the corpse's bloodied chest.

The gunner gasped and fell into a sitting position, staring at his freshly tattered hand. He glared malevolently at Bolan, and he could only gasp when the soldier pushed him on his stomach and yanked his wrists behind him, snapping them into plastic handcuffs. His ankles were next.

Agent Alex Frudkin was completely powerless.

Bolan reached the Dinitzin garage in a few strides and entered the house. He grabbed the key from the key rack and started Nicholae Dinitzin's big BMW, popping the trunk then pulling into the driveway. He hoisted Frudkin into the trunk as if he were loading a cord of firewood onto the bed of a pickup truck. The cry of emergency vehicles was closing in.

His next stop was for McCord. He guided the dazed woman into the front seat. The second Russian agent went into the trunk, then Bolan closed it on the wounded men.

He left the dead Russian lying where he was. Along with the Dinitzins. Someone would take care of them. Obviously he wasn't in the position to do so.

WHEN THEY PULLED into the parking lot, McCord registered a moment's surprise. They were in Arlington, at the Lipetsk Enterprises offices.

"Why'd we come here?" she whispered.

"It's Saturday. We'll have some privacy."

Bolan backed Dinitzin's BMW into the small loading dock, which McCord opened with her building pass card. Bolan found a battered steel cart used by the building maintenance staff to transport garbage cans and brought it to the edge of the loading platform, dumping the Russian agents onto it, one on top of the other. The agent with the mutilated face was enraged and shouting for his freedom. The agent with the wounded arm and hand was staring blankly into whatever was in front of him, his eyes unfocused.

"He's shocky," McCord said, slowly coming out of her stupor.

"Yeah."

"He might die without medical help," she protested weakly.

"Not before he answers some questions, I hope."

Bolan wheeled the cart to the elevator, McCord following because she didn't know what else to do. She was in a state of bewilderment. The scenes she had just witnessed were replaying like an unreal silent movie in her head. She wasn't able to believe she had just seen her friends being gunned down.

Bolan watched her slow movements as she unlocked the office doors and knew she needed activity to keep her thinking straight. He was sure he was going to need her. She had to be alert enough to be useful.

"I need an Internet connection on a computer with a camera," he said. "Does this office have an online conferencing system?"

"Yes," McCord said, somewhat surprised at the request.

"Come on, Stephanie," Bolan urged. "I need your help."

She looked at him and nodded and said quietly, "Stevie. Nobody calls me Stephanie except for my mother."

They got set up in Nicholae Dinitzin's office. McCord brought the PC to life, and they were instantly tied in to the company's T1 lines. A tiny digital camera was built in to the monitor, and a browser screen opened on the monitor. In the lower corner was a four-inch-square window that showed the office interior as viewed by the digital camera.

"Give me the URL."

Bolan gave her one of the hundred domain names operated by Stony Man Farm, and an instant later a complicated, multiframed page blossomed on the browser. It claimed to be the home page for a small-scale Internet service provider operating out of Washington, D.C. In fact, it had no customers other than Stony Man Farm. And, after Bolan exposed it to Stevie McCord, it would have to be shut down and wiped off the Net to maintain Farm security. But for now Bolan got behind the desk and used his access code to enter the web site, then issue a series of commands that directed the server to record the images on the screen onto Internet servers Stony Man operated. Whoever was on staff at the Farm would be watching the incoming images with curiosity, launching whatever information searches they could based on the intel Bolan was about to provide them. The soldier knew it would almost surely be Aaron Kurtzman. He rarely left the compound. They would also be prepared to respond when Bolan initiated communication.

Bolan moved the tiny camera onto the desk until it was focused on the battered bodies on the flat garbage cart. The browser page swam with video streaks before it focused. The soldier hoisted the two agents into side-by-side sitting positions.

"Talk," Bolan said, standing behind them.

"Fuck you," said the man with the mutilated face, trying to turn to see his tormentor, and failing. One of his eyes was glued shut with clotted blood.

Bolan spoke to the PC. "Striker here. Give me profiles for these men."

The browser pushed a new page into the screen. It had been just two minutes since the Farm had first viewed their faces, and already a complete profile had been accessed either from the Farm mainframes or from whatever various international agencies might keep such information. Bolan was sure the Farm was accessing secret Russian databases to get what came through on the pair.

"'Alex Frudkin,'" Bolan read out loud. The face was clearly that of the man with the wounded hand and arm. "'Mosty Sigulda,'" he announced at the second photo, showing the other agent from a time when he had a complete face.

Frudkin was aghast at the rapidity of the destruction of his supposedly airtight identity. He'd been operating in the U.S. for eight years without a single slip to his cover. Now it had been wiped away within minutes. "Who are you?" he demanded.

"I'm the man who is going to execute you for the murder of Nicholae and Susan Dinitzin." The simple declaration carried deadly weight.

"We did not kill Dinitzin!" Frudkin tried to turn and face his questioner, but the pain was too great.

"I hold you responsible," Bolan said. "You deliberately interfered with our escape."

"You were stealing Russian secrets!"

Suddenly, Frudkin's arms were hooked and pulled out from behind him. Frudkin toppled backward with a cry, his hands slipping off the edge of the steel cart and crumpling against the floor, stretched by the handcuffs and bent against the wounds. He screamed, but the sound was cut off when a strong hand locked on to his throat and pinched his windpipe shut.

Now he saw his torturer: blue eyes as piercing as steel; dark hair and darkened skin; a powerful jaw set rock hard. Frudkin was an experienced agent, but he quailed when he was face-to-face with the Executioner.

Bolan spoke quietly. "There's no reason for you to live. You've just killed two innocent people, and as far as I'm concerned your life is forfeit. I have no compunction about killing you as soon as your usefulness to me is done. If you expect to live to see the U.S. prison where you're going to spend the rest of your days, you had better start giving me reasons not to kill you right now."

"We're not telling you anything!" Sigulda stated. "You have no right to hold us..."

Bolan never looked away from Frudkin. His fist slammed into Sigulda's jaw, knocking him off the cart.

"Well?" Bolan asked.

Frudkin started to talk.

"YOU WERE RIGHT, Barb," Bolan said into the phone five minutes later. "The Russians have been keeping an eye on the residents of Lipetsk Nov ever since they started to seek financing for research and incorporation."

"What are the Russians after?" the mission controller asked.

"Even they don't know," Bolan said. "They were suspicious of the success of Lipetsk Enterprises, but until a few days ago they were planning on only making a grab for the technology through international legal maneuvering. Either that or by simply stealing back the technology. They were intent on waiting for it to be fully developed, since they didn't have the resources to develop it themselves."

"The attack yesterday changed their minds," Price guessed.

"Exactly. They still don't know as much as we do about the usefulness of the technology. All they know is that if somebody wants it bad enough to kill for, they should want it, too. They're trying to find a lead to the technology and figure out who's after it and what they plan to do with it. Their first priority is to keep the U.S. or anybody else from getting the technology before they do."

"So what are you going to do with them?"

"Good question," Bolan said. "My first inclination was to get them out of my way. But there are more Russians in the vicinity keeping an eye on the situation. Kind of a backup team."

"Russia's pretty hard up for income," Price said. "They must see this as a potential cash cow."

"The backup team will step in if Frudkin and Sigulda are taken out of the picture."

"You want to keep me around, American." Frudkin spoke suddenly, raising the head that had been dropped on his chest.

Bolan said, simply and without emotion, "Why?"

"Because I know what you do not. What I have not told you."

Bolan put down the phone and flipped on the speaker so Price could listen in.

"Tell me now."

Frudkin grimaced. "When you have released me from these handcuffs I will tell you."

"No."

"I have intelligence your people cannot provide you."

"You have no idea what my people are capable of," Bolan replied.

"But this is valuable information about Kabat's intentions," Frudkin protested.

So the Russians had a line on Roger Kabat. Bolan wondered idly how much more the Russian was going to tell him while refusing to tell him anything. "I will not bargain with you."

"How can you say that when you do not know what I have to say?" Frudkin demanded. "Why not ask your superiors what you should do?" He nodded at the illuminated red light on the speakerphone.

"I have no superiors," Bolan said. "We just work together from time to time."

Frudkin laughed, although he could see Bolan was serious. "What does this mean, you have no superiors? Who is your commander?"

"No one."

"Are you some kind of a rogue? Are you outside the law?"

"I'm just about done wasting my breath on you, Frudkin," Bolan said. "Spit out what you've got."

"I want to be a part of any operations you take against Kabat," Frudkin demanded.

"Striker," Price said from the speakerphone. Bolan took it off speaker and held the receiver to his ear.

"Yes?"

"Maybe you should form some sort of an alliance with the Russians," Price said. "I think it'll help us gather some high-grade intelligence."

"Such as?"

"Such as the true potential of this weapon, and what Russian intentions are if and when they get their hands on it."

Bolan considered that. It was clear there was some sort of strategy taking shape on the other end of the phone line. He'd get the details on that later.

"Better the devil we know," Bolan said for Frudkin's benefit. "They'll report to their superiors that they're still on the job. They can make up whatever kind of excuses they want to keep themselves in the shining light with their Russian commanders. But I'm keeping them with me."

"How will you know they aren't telling their commanders that?" Price asked.

"My Russian isn't half bad, and my new assistant speaks fluent Russian," Bolan explained.

"Stephanie McCord?"

"Yeah. She more or less coached most of the upper management through their advanced English lessons during her years with them. She'll be helping me monitor the Russians. Until I see evidence of a second Russian team at work here they're coming with me, whether they want to or not."

"And where are you headed, Striker?" Price asked.

"To visit Mr. Kabat," Bolan replied, "and see what he has to say for himself. How can you help me out on that front?"

Price gave a short laugh. "Bear's been champing at the bit to tell you all about it," she said. "We had an idea you'd be visiting our friend at his home."

"I thought you'd never ask," Kurtzman said, coming on the line suddenly. "We managed to get a peek inside the man's home just about an hour ago. Had to call in a few favors at the Pentagon, but what the hell. Are you on a private terminal?"

"Yes," Bolan said, spinning the PC so that the monitor faced him alone. On the other side of the office, McCord was busy bandaging the wounded Russian agents, who had yet to be released from their cuffs. Mosty Sigulda was still out cold.

Bolan regarded the thermal satellite image that appeared on the screen, then watched as an outline of the building was superimposed over it to make the rooms and features easier to see. "Looks like a beach house," he told Kurtzman.

"It is. It's on the Outer Banks."

The Outer Banks of North Carolina was a string of narrow islands that extended in a long half-circle into the Atlantic Ocean. Most of it was designated national seashore. A few bridges connected the islands with the mainland, and the low elevation made the land especially vulnerable to incoming water. In some places the great, 125-mile-long stretch of land was just a mile wide. Most of the land mass, especially on the northern Hatteras Island, was heavily developed with vacation homes. The homes were uniformly wooden, with living areas held aloft on wooden stilts above ground-level carports—out of the water that flooded the islands under hurricane conditions, which were common enough that far out in the Atlantic Ocean. It took three minutes for Bolan to make an intensive evaluation of the layout from the on-screen image.

"What kind of reception can I expect here?"

"Heavy," Kurtzman said. "Our thermal image scans counted upward of twelve humans inhabiting the building. Unless Kabat was having a social gathering at the moment the satellite moved overhead, he keeps a small army of staff. But you'll have the Russian agents giving you a hand," Kurtzman suggested less than seriously.

"Would you like some more dependable assistance?" Price asked.

"Yeah," Bolan said. "Who's available?"

"Everybody. I can also offer you the blacksuit team," she said.

"I don't think we'll have the freedom to cause that much havoc," Bolan said. "I don't want to panic the locals." He considered his options, mentally reviewing the staff profiles. He was familiar with the capabilities and personalities of every member of both Stony Man Farm action teams. "Send me Gadgets and Jack. And a chopper for reconnaissance. I'll rendezvous with them in Rodanthe. I'll be in touch when I'm on the scene, in about six hours."

"When's the last time you slept?" Price asked.

"Several hours last night," Bolan told her. "Can you set up a safehouse?"

"Already done. Sleeps a dozen," Price said. "Think you'll need it long?"

Bolan considered that. "No. With Gadgets, I can get in quietly, take down Kabat, and get out in a hurry. With any luck, we'll put a stop to this business for good, before it escalates further."

CHAPTER SEVEN

North Carolina

They were driving into Rodanthe in midafternoon, pulling into the safehouse at almost the same instant a four-bladed Bell 430 helicopter, painted with the logo of a nonexistent high-tech marketing firm, made a beauty pass over the Atlantic Ocean and descended onto the concrete helipad placed in the sandy soil within a stone's throw of the shore. As the helicopter powered down, a figure emerged, waving briefly to Bolan, who was busy perusing the property.

Stony Man had made a good choice in the house. On an island crowded with vacation residences, there were probably few spots this private in the residential districts. The house was stationed on a small outcropping, its seaside grounds blocked off from the mainland by the house itself. The carport was enclosed, a unique feature on the island, and it added to the privacy and kept public eyes from the grounds. This wasn't the ideal place to practice military maneuvers by any means, but the isolation was sufficient for their current short stay.

The pilot stepped out of the silent helicopter. He put his hands on his hips, evaluated the layout and smiled broadly. "All right!" he exclaimed and followed his passenger. "Striker, you know how to live."

Bolan shook hands with Hermann "Gadgets" Schwarz and introduced him as Jorge Mentia to McCord and the Russians. Frudkin and Sigulda had finally been freed of their handcuffs. Frudkin's arm and hand had been stitched and bandaged by McCord, but he had refused a trip to the hospital in lieu of participation in the probe. Despite their battered condition, the Russians were showing a high level of awareness of their surroundings. Bolan could see the wheels turning in their heads as they made quick work of observing faces and locations. He watched Frudkin memorize the ID numbers on the rear of the chopper. All this, Bolan was confident, would be reported to his superiors in Moscow at his first opportunity. Let him. It was all wasted effort. Stony Man Farm was expert at covering its tracks.

Schwarz smiled slightly as he took McCord's hand. He moved with quiet, unconscious grace, and McCord knew he was the kind of man who could effortlessly sneak up on a room full of Dobermans and steal their bag of kibble without raising a growl.

The pilot was a tall man, thin almost to the point of being gaunt. He had a wide, quick smile, and the laugh lines around his eyes spoke of a congenial personality. "Bill Geogh," Jack Grimaldi said when he took her hand. "Pleased to meet you."

McCord found his face so friendly and open it never even occurred to her that both these men must be using fake names. But she was wondering who they were, how they fit into the growing puzzle picture being painted by this strange man, Mike Belasko. Where did they all come from? Were they actually FBI or CIA or something? They sure didn't act like the FBI she had always heard about—arrogant attitude and look-alike suits.

What else was there in terms of U.S. protection agencies? she wondered. The Secret Service was one. They mostly handled protection of politicians and counterfeiting cases. More likely these people were from some military agency. SEALs or Rangers or who knew what.

"So what's on the itinerary?" Grimaldi asked of Bolan. "A few hours on the beach? Did we remember to pack limes for the margaritas?"

"Sorry, flyboy. I don't think you're going to have much time for R&R on this visit."

"Dinner, at least?" the man asked. "You aware Kill Devil Hills has some of the best seafood restaurants on the planet?"

"Maybe we can send out," Bolan replied.

BRIEFED BY STONY MAN, Schwarz and Grimaldi were well aware of the status of the two Russian agents. They were to be treated as equals—and watched at all times for suspicious behavior. There was no doubt in Bolan's mind they had more in the works than assisting him in the neutralization of Roger Kabat and his plan to stock the world armies and terrorists with a new and better weapon. He knew they wanted the technology for themselves.

Bolan wasn't a political animal. He didn't know the details behind the transformation of the Lipetsk Nov science town into the Lipetsk Enterprises corporation, and he didn't care. Ownership of the technology was up to some sort of international court to determine.

What he did know, and what he did care about, was the ultimate disposition of the Lipetsk technology and the protection of the innocent people who would almost certainly be victimized by it.

The ruse began with the planning of the probe of the Kabat residence at Kill Devil Hills. Using large-scale schematics of the home, they laid out a detailed strategy for the probe. Schwarz had been briefed en route as to Bolan's plan to change small but important details. The most vital: the probable location of Kabat's data center. If the satellite imagery could be trusted, the top-floor southeast corner was a hotbed of electronic hardware, with temperature extremes thought to come from heat-generating information hardware and the extra environmental cooling designed to keep that hardware within optimal parameters. If Kabat kept his records electronically stored, this was the most likely place to find them.

But on the doctored structural blueprints, Stony Man had indicated a bottom-level, northwest corner as the probable information technology center.

Bolan's plan called for Alex Frudkin and Mosty Sigulda to secure the bottom level while he and Schwarz entered from above. The Russians agreed with obvious eagerness. The soldier wondered what their ploy would be. When would they spill the intelligence they were keeping from him? And would that intelligence be worth the price of their participation?

He wasn't used to or comfortable with being at an intelligence disadvantage.

But if the ploy would give him the edge on putting

a stop to Kabat and preventing the deaths of hundreds, then he could be patient.

AT 0400 HOURS, the night sky was littered with small gray clouds. The sea shushed onto the rocky beach, an omnipresent rush of sound that washed away most of the lower noises of the night. The tossing of the wind never stopped.

The small rowboat bounced on the breaking surf and spun sideways when hit by a two-foot surge of white foam. It tilted wildly, flopped into the trough of the wave and finally ground into the soft sand. The next wave rushed under it and drove it farther up the beach, where it lodged in the sand when the tide began to go out. No one was there to pay attention to the rowboat.

The big beach house was silent, and only a lamp over the carport illuminated the grounds. If there was anyone awake in the house, they were keeping well out of sight.

A pair of shadows emerged from the depth of the rowboat and slunk over the side as if they were boneless sea creatures. They crept over the sand until it turned grassy. A small square of the grounds around the brick patio was manicured, but the dark figures waited in the long grass at the edge of it, watching for any sign that their approach had been noticed.

There was nothing.

Bolan's and Schwarz's faces and hands were darkened by combat cosmetics and they wore blacksuits, twin shadows in the night. They packed heavy firearms, but they were going in armed with the simplest of lead weapons. Schwarz sported a Ka-bar fighting knife, while Bolan's combat netting was stuck with a trio of balanced Randall throwing knives.

Knives were always quieter than firearms, no matter how well-suppressed.

"Steamroller Base?" Bolan whispered into the tiny microphone on his headset, using the designation they had agreed on for Stony Man headquarters, from which the probe would be organized. There was no need to clue the Russians in on who they were dealing with. Doubtless a complete debriefing of these events would take place as soon as the agents returned to their supervisors.

"Stand by, Steamroller One," Barbara Price replied.

"We're at our starting point, and we're splitting up," Bolan said.

"Understood."

"You reading me, Steamroller Base?" Schwarz asked into his mike.

"Loud and clear, Steamroller Two."

Bolan rose out of the tall beach grass just long enough to send a weighted rope flying over his head. It tightened and swung around the wooden railing of the second-floor balcony that encircled the house. The rope overlapped and the tiny surgical-steel hook on the end dug into the wooden rail. The rope was as secure as if it had been knotted to the supports. Bolan lowered his weight onto the rope, then began a quick hand-over-hand ascent to the balcony. When he reached it he paused long enough to peer onto the balcony with his eyes at floor level. It was deserted. He had chosen this entry point because, according to the schematics supplied by Stony Man, it was one of the few places no windows looked directly out onto

the balcony. Hanging from the balcony edge by his
fingers, he gave himself an extra ten seconds to find
a video monitoring system. The camera was mounted
on the roof, peering down onto a wide stretch of
balcony and a wider stretch of the grounds on the
south side of the building.

The soldier hung by one hand and withdrew a
clamped device from his webbing, closing the jaws
of the device on one of the narrow wooden rail supports. He flipped it on. A tiny red laser light shone
on the side of the building. Bolan adjusted it quickly
to direct the laser into the lens of the video monitor,
then tightened the lock-down screws. The camera
would receive nothing more than a polarized swarm
of cloudy images. It was unknown if a security detail
was on-staff. If there was, they might not notice the
sudden scrambled image. Regardless, they weren't
going to witness Bolan's incursion.

He slipped over the rail and hugged the rough,
unfinished wooden exterior wall. Through the floor-
to-ceiling windows he saw a small bedroom, dark
and empty, and within seconds had pulled a set of
picks and managed to jimmy the sliding glass door.
It slid open easily on well-lubricated slides. The air-
conditioned air wafted in the soldier's face, and he
waited for a response. The glass showed no signs of
alarm system hard-wiring, and no audible alarm
sounded. He entered the home of Roger Kabat.

"Steamroller One here. I'm inside."

"You just got somebody's attention," Schwarz
answered over the headset. "I have a light on the
bottom floor."

"Activity?"

There was a pause, then Schwarz answered. "One

head just went by the window. That's not a definitive count.''

"Understood."

Bolan waited by the door. Even as it opened, he heard Schwarz adding to his report. "More company coming your way, Steamroller One. Two or three."

Bolan digested that information with one part of his mind as the figure stepped into the room and flipped a switch. His quick sweep of the tidy interior revealed Bolan's presence, and he shouted an alarm as he leveled a .38-caliber revolver. The sound died in his throat as a Randall throwing knife buried itself in his throat. The .38 bounced on the bed as Bolan fisted a second knife and struck blind at the mere impression of a body coming through the door on the heels of the first man.

A grunt of surprise turned to a shout, and the body backed away from the entrance. Bolan yanked the door open and in the light from the small bedroom spotted a figure with a Browning handgun staggering backward in a short hallway, the knife protruding from a beach ball stomach. He collapsed on his posterior, staring at the anodized handle that was smeared with his own red blood. A long, low moan escaped from his throat and echoed in the house like the moans of the dead though a catacomb.

Somehow, the obese figure had the presence of mind to bring the Browning into play. Bolan didn't waste time with his third knife. The time for silence had abruptly ended. He raised the suppressed Beretta 93-R in his left hand and fired a single round into the prone form's hand, knocking the Browning out of its acquired target. The Browning went off with a wall of sound that filled the hallway and reached every corner of the waking beach house. The second 9 mm Parabellum round from the 93-R took the fallen gunner in the forehead and put his brains on the wall behind him.

"Striker, here. I blew it. They know we're here," he said into his headset.

"Understood," Schwarz answered. "I'm moving in."

"Russian team," Price said, "make your entrance."

"Understood, Steamroller Base."

"Steamroller One, let me know if I should deviate from my entrance plan," Schwarz stated quickly.

"Understood, Steamroller Two," Bolan answered. The soldier wouldn't call for backup assistance from Schwarz unless it was absolutely necessary. Now that he had the attention of the guard staff of the Kabat beach house, Schwarz would have a much easier time getting to the arms smuggler's war room unnoticed.

Bolan's mental image of the interior of the house flashed inside his head. Schwarz was coming in via the stairway that led to the ocean, an indispensable feature on any Outer Banks beach house. The least Bolan could do was lead the chase through the house in a different direction and keep the pressure off his companion. He made his decision in a heartbeat and made for a stairway that would take him through the middle of the house.

He took the two flights that headed to the third story in a few long strides and listened to the thumps of approaching footsteps below. There were angry shouts—confusion seemed to be slowing the guard staff. Time to get their attention.

Bolan tucked away the suppressed Beretta and pulled out a piece of hardware with a bigger voice. His large Desert Eagle pistol was the U.S.-made version, assembled in the .44 Magnum configuration and fitted with a six-inch barrel. He triggered the weapon at the first head to appear just a dozen feet below him at the bottom of the stairs. The Magnum round crashed into the gunner's skull with the impact of a brick dropped from a skyscraper, pulping his brains so instantaneously he never knew he was dead, but simply flopped against the wall and onto the steps. Bolan didn't wait to get a clear shot at the dead man's companions, but hurried onto the stairs and fired into the quiet hallway before stepping into it and finding it deserted.

The soldier had two goals. One, keep the gunners busy while Schwarz found his way to the communications and data center and initiated the download of Kabat's records. Two, find the big man himself, if he was here. Stop the monster before its real rampage of death commenced. If Kabat was in residence, then his guard staff would be all the more enthusiastic about getting up to the third floor—and all the more likely to ignore other security issues.

The largest suite of rooms was four paces from where he stood.

FROM HIS GROUND-LEVEL vantage point, Schwarz could see precious little of what was happening on the raised first floor of the mansion-size beach house. After issuing his report to Bolan, he moved away from the building. He'd done what little he could. The Executioner was on his own.

Not that Schwarz was worried for the big man. If

there was one man on the planet who could handle himself well in a lone-wolf battle, it was Mack Bolan. Besides, Schwarz had other items on his to-do list. He ran in a crouch through the waist-high tangle of beach grass and creepers until he reached a rise in the sandy soil before it started down again to the beach. Over the ridge, where he would be best hidden from the house, he crossed to the north until he came to the stairway that led into the raised first floor of the Kabat residence. Nearly every beach house on the Outer Banks had such a stairway-walkway that led directly to the shore.

It was just about the most dangerous approach possible. He'd be entirely exposed, a perfect target.

He'd take his chances. With a few strides he made it to the top of the stairway and performed a quick assessment of the house. The sound of gunfire was oddly muffled and dulled by the rush of the surf behind him. The open walkway between his position and the house was almost 125 feet.

Schwarz sprinted, keeping his footsteps light and his eyes open, fighting his way forward with his M-16 combo gripped in both hands. Lights were coming on throughout the house.

The house and grounds and the entire walkway were suddenly bathed in brilliance, turning the dark starlit night into near daytime. Schwarz couldn't have been more visible, and he still had sixty feet of wooden walkway to cross. He watched for any sign of life. Just because the lights were on didn't mean the attention of the house had been pulled away from the battle Bolan was leading.

To the Able Team warrior it seemed to take fifteen minutes to reach the house, where he flattened against the exterior wall, listening to the sound of gunfire within.

"Steamroller Two?" Price said over the headset.

"I'm at the house, about to make my entrance."

"Steamroller One is out of contact," she reported in a level, emotionless voice.

"He sounds busy," Schwarz replied. "I'm going in."

Schwarz was on the opposite side of the house from Bolan's access way, and he made his entrance with less finesse. The butt of the M-16 cracked into the thick glass of one of the sliding glass doors, and it disintegrated with a noisy crystalline crash. He stepped inside a small sitting room and exited the door, finding himself in a back stairway, as expected. Two floors directly above him, if the Farm's analysis was correct, would be the communications and data center. Alone and unnoticed, Schwarz moved quietly, directly up.

At the third-level landing he heard the sounds of the battle that was raging in the hall. He wondered briefly if Bolan was under siege. Schwarz fought his urge to join the battle and help his friend. He had a job to do. He stepped quickly across the open area from the stairs to the room that was thought to be the communications center, pulled open the door and slipped inside.

His eyes didn't bother to register the wall-mounted cabinetry containing a data server and the three terminals spread around the room. His gaze focused on the man sitting at one of the terminals. A shoulder holster rested on the table next to the keyboard. The 9 mm handgun had been removed and placed on top of the leather for quick access. The man's attention snapped on the intruder and he made a grab for the pistol. Schwarz stepped away from the door, to save the equipment behind the man, and triggered a single round from the M-16. It tossed the man off his chair before he could fire the gun, slumping him in a limp wreck against the far wall. Schwarz was satisfied to see that the terminal he'd been manning was still functioning.

He shut the door behind him, which had no lock. As he took his turn behind the monitor, he had no intention of allowing himself to be caught off guard like the dead man on the floor. He placed the M-16 combo on his lap, aimed into the doorway and typed with his left hand while he gripped the weapon.

"Stony, this is Able. I'm in the comm center."

"Copy that, Able," Price said. "We're standing by for your signal."

Schwarz grabbed an automated modem from his pack and had it plugged into the terminal within seconds. The battery-operated cellular unit was entirely independent, and at Schwarz's signal Stony Man dialed into the unit and began its exploration of the system.

"We're inside," Aaron Kurtzman said over Schwarz's headset. "I've got Akira downloading the contents."

Schwarz's next move was to grab the desk telephone next to the computer. He stabbed at the buttons and heard ringing at the other end, followed by a quick series of electronic noises. Stony Man Farm was in control of the communications system. All calls that went out on this line had to go through the Farm first.

"How's Striker doing?" Schwarz asked.

"No word," Price stated.

CHAPTER EIGHT

Stephanie McCord pressed the headphones harder
into her ear, listening to the mumbling on the other
end.

"They're complaining about their lack of intelligence on the probe," she reported into her microphone.

"Are they staying put?" asked the voice in
McCord's opposite ear.

"For now. I have a feeling they're getting rest-
less."

"We won't let them stew for long."

The equipment provided by Stony Man Farm for
the Russians had been doctored to serve a special
purpose. Despite what the controls at the user end
suggested, the Russians' microphones were always
on and the transmitters always operating. Stony Man
Farm was listening in on the Russians' conversation
during the probe, even when the Russians thought
they were conversing privately. McCord's task was
to translate that conversation and keep her contact at
Stony Man Farm, a pleasant, faceless woman called
Carmen, up to date on what was said. Carmen was
serving as McCord's liaison with the probe team.

McCord was enjoying her role as a member of the

team. She was nervous and excited, but mostly she was eager to bring down the men who had murdered her lover.

For most of the time, however, she was doing little more than serving as a spectator. She heard the woman at headquarters who was strategizing the probe order in her charges, Frudkin and Sigulda. "Russian team, make your entrance."

"Understood, Steamroller Base," Frudkin replied.

"COME ON," Frudkin said under his breath, leading his companion into the brick drive that curved in front of Kabat's beach house. But they had advanced barely twenty paces before the lights came on throughout the house, as well as the pole-mounted floodlights.

"Shit! We're exposed," Sigulda said under his breath.

"Hurry!"

"The Americans are feeding us to the wolves."

Frudkin didn't bother to argue the point with his embittered companion. "Come on, dammit!"

They raced across the long, contoured lawn of coarse grass, slowing suddenly at the stairway to the front entrance. They crept up the stairs as silently as they could move on the creaking wood, then paused at the front entrance to the house, both relieved they had made the run through the open without being spotted.

Sigulda dropped lightly on all fours, putting his eye close to the floor. Frudkin realized he was staring through the gaps in the planks into the carport beneath. They'd been unable to get a good look into the carport from their stakeout position. Their U.S.

liaison had reported that Kabat typically drove an open-topped Land Rover while staying on the island.

"It's gone," Sigulda said. "Kabat's not in residence."

"So what?" Frudkin demanded. "It's the Americans who care about Kabat. Let's get inside." Frudkin had his left hand laid flat against the door, feeling for the vibrations of nearby residents. There was only the distant thunder of a gun battle above them in the middle of the house. The longer that situation continued the better.

Sigulda felt the front doorknob and shook his head. Frudkin nodded and gestured with his gun. When Sigulda stepped back, he leveled the handgun and triggered it into the knob. The metal knob jumped in its socket as its mechanism shattered. Sigulda shouldered the door hard and fast, before the inhabitants had an opportunity to react, on his knees while his companion covered the room above his head. If there had been anyone within the foyer, he would have required lightning-fast reactions to save himself.

There was no one.

"Up," Frudkin said shortly, and the two men headed for the center of the house, starting up the main staircase. Above them they spotted gunners busily engaged in the third-floor gun battle.

"Think we can get past them?"

"Let's take them out!" Sigulda suggested.

"We'd never get all of them before they turned on us. Then we'd be stuck. Let's get to the comm room."

The Russian agents waited until a barrage was launched by the gunners on the stairs, their attention solidly focused away from whatever was behind them. Then they climbed quietly from the first floor to the second, ducking out of sight into the second-floor hallway as the barrage just a few paces away came to a halt with a sudden silence.

"Steamroller Base here, Frudkin. What's your situation?"

"We're on the second floor, Steamroller Base," Frudkin reported.

"Have you reached your target?"

"One minute, Steamroller."

Frudkin evaluated the empty hallway. Three doors, all closed. Any one of them could be hiding a small army. Flanking the last door in the hallway, they waited just long enough for a quick listen. No sound came from beyond it. They pushed it open and entered with their weapons leading the way, Frudkin high, Sigulda low.

There was no one there.

"It's a bedroom," Frudkin said as if trying to understand it.

"They screwed us." Sigulda spit the words out.

Frudkin ripped open the wooden closet doors, as if he thought the closet might somehow house the information center they were looking for. Nothing was in there except a few items of clothing on hangers.

The Russian stormed out of the room and carelessly tore open another door in the hallway. It was another bedroom, but no one was in residence. He swore vehemently and pushed through the last door in the hallway.

It was an empty washroom.

"Talk to me, Russian team."

"Fuck you, Steamroller Base!" Sigulda retorted into his mike.

"They screwed us!" Frudkin said.

"You never should have trusted the Americans," Sigulda declared accusingly.

"We had no choice!"

"You know what they've done," Sigulda said bitterly. "They've sent their own man to the IT equipment instead of us. Now they're getting all the data on the Lipetsk system."

Frudkin stared at his companion, then slammed his fist into the wall with a burst of fury. "Then let's take it!"

"STEVIE HERE. You on the line, Steamroller Base?" McCord said.

"Carmen here. Go ahead, Stevie."

"The Russians aren't happy. They've just come up empty on the second floor where they were expecting to find the computer room. They feel they've been double-crossed."

"Understood."

"Uh-oh. Steamroller Base, the Russians are going berserk. They're going to try and take the data from our side."

Carmen, the faceless voice on the other end of the line was cool as ice. "Understood, Stevie."

BOLAN WAITED OUT the barrage of autofire until he heard the weapon come up empty, then exposed himself momentarily in the doorway, quickly placing a big .44 Magnum slug into the ceiling over the stairway. Then he ducked to ride out a volley of handgun fire. He was getting the enemy increasingly angry, which meant they would stay on-site, eager to get at him and take him down. The longer they were in that state of mind, the longer Schwarz was safe.

"Steamroller One," Price said over the line with the slightest inflection of excitement, "we've got trouble with the Russians."

"Copy that." Even as he replied he heard a blast of autofire from below, and he emerged into the hallway long enough to evaluate the situation. Kabat's enforcers were suddenly scrambling up the steps to escape the autofire onslaught from below. A pair of them were stitched across the chest as they stood their ground and triggered down the stairwell. They collapsed out of sight. The remaining pair of guards retreated quickly.

An angry, wordless shout erupted from below, and one of the running men straightened to his full height abruptly as he came to the top of the stairs, a trio of red stains appearing across his back, and then he collapsed. The final man retreated from the stairwell, eyes wide in horror, and stopped only when his back was against the wall. He held his handgun, a .38 revolver, in front of him like a shield.

He spotted Bolan with a startled expression and turned the revolver toward the hallway, but the soldier stepped back into the small room that had served as his bunker. He heard a pair of blasts from the revolver, then a shout of terror and streams of fire from an autoweapon. When he looked again, the last gunner was being nailed to the wall by autofire as Frudkin walked calmly up the stairs, his fingers locked on his trigger.

He spotted Bolan and turned the weapon without a pause in the firing, the rounds chomping a trail of ruined wall paneling in the Executioner's direction. Bolan triggered the Desert Eagle before the rounds reached him, but Frudkin descended below the third-floor level and the Magnum round sailed over his head.

"You fucked us, American!"

Bolan heard the movement of feet on the stairs and knew instantly what the plan was—to keep him occupied and get one or both of the Russians onto the third floor to search for the real communications-information room. He wasn't going to allow that to happen. When he reached around the door, he saw Frudkin covering Sigulda.

Frudkin shouted something in Russian as he spotted Bolan. In the same instant Bolan fired, Sigulda reacted, dodging into the wall. The round from the Desert Eagle clipped his right arm instead of coring his torso. Sigulda shouted and dropped to the floor, but Frudkin was already laying out a fresh torrent of gunfire at Bolan from the stairs.

The Russians were angry. Despite their training, they were allowing their anger to propel their actions. Bolan knew he had just a fraction of a second to wait. Then the fraction of a second expired and the weapon in Frudkin's hands was allowed to cycle dry. Bolan emerged from the hallway, leveled the Desert Eagle at Frudkin's surprised face and triggered it once. Frudkin's head jerked violently when the round slammed through the bridge of his nose, then he disappeared down the stairs like a rabbit down a hole.

Sigulda was gone. Bolan was in the company of only corpses.

"Steamroller Base, has the Russians' radio reception been terminated?"

"Of course, Striker," Price replied. With the Russians locked out and McCord receiving only the Russian transmission, there was no more need for the special code names.

"Able, Sigulda's looking for you and he's not a happy man."

"Understood."

GADGETS SCHWARZ WAS PREPARED to defend the computer system as if it were an innocent child until Stony Man Farm completed its data download. Then it was just scrap plastic as far as he was concerned.

There was a thunder of footsteps coming closer, and another few blasts from Bolan's .44 echoed through the beach house. More of Kabat's men. Where the hell were they all coming from?

That didn't matter. What mattered was buying some time. Sigulda would want to protect the system as long as he thought he could get data out of it. But what if he thought the Americans were accessing the data first? He might feel it was more important to keep the information out of the hands of the U.S. than getting at it himself.

But he never had to know the Farm had made it as far as this room. Schwarz went into hiding.

MOSTY SIGULDA REALIZED the handgun was about to drop from his fingers. His right hand was losing feeling and strength. He grabbed the weapon with his left hand and covered the long hallway behind him.

There was a rumble of noise from below. New arrivals. Kabat's reinforcements were quickly making their way up through the beach house. The American soldier came into view, and Sigulda was forced to make a lightning-fast decision. Who would he rather have at his back? The American warrior or the arms traders' hired guns? He chose the hired guns, and that translated into sudden strategy. If he was to drive the American warrior away from the stairs, he would allow Kabat's reinforcements to come up to the third floor. They would engage the American. Until they spotted Sigulda, the gunners would believe it was one of their own they were protecting. They'd have no reason to believe the team that had penetrated the house had experienced a falling out.

Sigulda emptied half the handgun's magazine at the top of the stairs, then retreated before the American, the man called Steamroller One, could retaliate. The gunfire had attracted the enforcers from below, and in seconds Sigulda was pleased to hear an exchange of gunfire between Steamroller One and the new arrivals.

He was on his own for at least the next minute or so.

The Russian staggered from one doorway to the next, pushing through them with careless abandon. He was on the verge of getting killed, but the exhilaration and blood loss seemed to make that fact of marginal importance. What was clear was that there was no time for cautious maneuvering.

When he found the computer center at the end of the hallway, it was unoccupied. The system was powered up but inactive.

Without any time to waste, Sigulda plopped into the chair and quickly evaluated the operating system. It took him seven seconds to figure out how to dial out. He typed savagely at the keys with his less-dexterous left hand. It was eight more seconds before he was in contact with the Russian computer system expert at the other end. The hacker was trained and waiting for just such an eventuality. Thirty seconds after Sigulda had entered the room he was feeding a high-bandwidth data stream to his fellow operatives. He grabbed his gun again and watched the door. The battle might reach him at any moment.

He wondered how he could manage not to be here when that happened.

"HE'S DIALED OUT through us, Able," Price reported over his headset. Schwarz didn't respond. Above him through the honeycombed floor panels, four inches from his face, Sigulda's feet rested on the floor. "All right. We've got a lock on his receiving system. We're sending them a bunch of junk. Gigs and gigs of it."

Sigulda stood suddenly, wheeling the chair away from the terminal. Schwarz twisted his head. In the close cable-strewed quarters of the false floor, in which he had crammed not only himself but the recently deceased systems operator, he could barely wriggle. "Sigulda is on the move," Schwarz whispered.

"His connection is still active," Price replied. "Let him go, Able."

"Understood," Schwarz said through gritted teeth. He wasn't thrilled with hiding under the floor like some moron and allowing one of the bad guys to make an easy exit. But if that was the best way to handle things… He reminded himself the Russian still had a forty-foot drop to make to get to ground, and it looked like his right arm was hanging uselessly. Maybe he'd take a big plunge. The thought made him smile.

"He's out the window," Schwarz reported as Sigulda vanished. He pushed the floor panel away and jumped out of the hole, peering cautiously out the window. He spotted Sigulda swinging carelessly from the planking into a second-story window.

"He's bypassed the activity and made it to the second story," Schwarz reported. "I'm guessing he'll try to make a clandestine escape."

"Let him. We're still on him," Price reported.

"So tell me I can go give Striker an assist!" Schwarz demanded.

"Go."

BOLAN HAD BEEN LISTENING to the exchange on his headset, barely conscious of the words but fully aware that he was no longer on his own—and aware his stall tactic had endured long enough. He waited for a pause in the fire from Kabat's reinforcements, then whirled into the hallway, firing the Desert Eagle in his right hand and the Beretta 93-R in the left. The first unaimed blast from the big .44 crashed like a swung hammer into the edge of the wall and sprayed the gunners with wood splinters. One of the men grunted and collapsed with shards imbedded in his face at the same moment the 9 mm Parabellum triburst cut through his companion. The two of them, one dead and one wishing he was, collapsed in a ruin that bowled through the tangle of fleeing gunners below them. Bolan skidded to a halt at the top of the stairs with Schwarz stepping to his side. They mounted a deadly barrage, shoulder to shoulder, that stilled the writhing mass of humanity at the base of the stairs. The screaming that had erupted soon stopped. Only one figure was glimpsed fleeing, and a moment later they listened to him slam through the entrance and down the steps to the ground.

CHAPTER NINE

The beach house looked like a real-estate open house. Roger Kabat noticed the glow of the shrubbery and the extra illumination spilling onto the drive from a quarter mile away. Immediately he was suspicious, and he pushed on the clutch and released the accelerator on the ancient, perfectly preserved Mercedes.

His hesitation as the near-priceless automobile slowed to a crawl lasted all of three seconds.

"Dial home!" he demanded.

A tiny green light set into the hand-rubbed oak lid next to his seat blinked, and a series of orange and white lights flickered around it. The speakers hidden in the dashboard played the sound of a connection and then the ringing at the other end. Nobody answered. By the time the line rang for the fourth time, the Mercedes had come to a halt on the asphalt of the street.

"Disconnect," Kabat declared. "Security system status."

"Off-line," the electronically generated female voice answered almost instantly.

"Shit." He slammed the Mercedes into first and accelerated, trying to look like normal traffic and craning his neck as he rolled by the house. It appeared peaceful. But the lights were a big problem. Why would the house be fully illuminated except in the case of some sort of major security breach?

"Scanner," he demanded.

The sound system had been playing a Vivaldi piece broadcast by a Charlotte classical station, but the sound of strings dropped off at once, replaced by the staticky hum of the local emergency frequency. The dispatcher was radioing her report to a local officer in Hatteras. Something about a man with a Virginia driver's license having one speeding ticket on his record. Nothing more was said.

So the police weren't in it, whatever had gone down. Kabat continued to drive past the house at reduced speed, looking for any clue. Looking for any of his men. Where the hell was everybody?

He reached the end of his private drive and turned back the way he had come in. He genuinely didn't know how to respond to this. He sure wasn't going to enter the grounds of his house until he knew everything was safe.

"Dial Melissa." The scanner static was instantly gone, and the voice of Kabat's no-nonsense secretary at his British corporation answered during the first ring. It was the beginning of the workday in London.

"Yes Mr. Kabat?"

"Shit!"

"Pardon me, sir?"

Kabat didn't hear her. He was craning his neck and stomping on the gas. In seconds he had jerked the gearshift into reverse and backed up ten feet.

The well-lit interior made the broken window at the far north side of the house obvious. As plain as day was the great, splattered stain of blood that covered most of the glass that remained in the window-frame.

Somebody had died inside that room. The blood was still streaming down the window in thick rivulets.

Somebody had died very recently. Like within the past few minutes.

Kabat crammed the stick mercilessly into first gear and popped the clutch, ripping the rubber on the pavement. "Call the airport and have my plane ready in five minutes!" he shouted to his secretary. "I have to get off this island right now!"

INSIDE, THE BEACH HOUSE looked like the interior of a train car after a high-speed derailment. There were two survivors.

"This house is clean," Schwarz quipped.

"Talk to me. Striker, Gadgets?" The soothing voice of Price betrayed just the slightest twinge of concern.

"We're done," Bolan reported. "How's Bear's data?"

"Looks good at first glance. Akira's rummaging through the system for any bits and pieces we may have missed. Can you confirm the status of our Russian friend Frudkin?"

"Dead," Bolan stated.

"Sigulda is on the run," Schwarz added. "You're still getting a transmission from him?"

"Yes. He's not speaking, but we're getting background noise. He's breathing hard and I assume he's trying to put some distance between himself and you guys. Our GPS on him is fully operational."

Kurtzman broke into the conversation. "I know just where he is. Down to the centimeter. Carmen and Stephanie McCord are watching him closely. And here's some good news."

"Tell me," Bolan said.

"Hunt Wethers was watching the Russian data probe when Sigulda put them on-line to the Kabat system. Since they were channeling their phone link through the Farm they never even knew Hunt was there. He managed to get a toehold on the inside of their system. He's exploring their system now."

"Won't they figure out they've got a snoop?" Schwarz asked.

"Maybe not if he pulls out his probe before the Russians finish their download of the Kabat system. Since they're actually downloading from us, we can keep feeding them junk data until we're done exploring. We'll stay sharp."

"THE ELECTRONIC HARD PROBE paid off big-time," Hunt Wethers reported over the conference audio link Bolan established with the Farm from the safehouse fifteen minutes later. "We extracted lots of high-quality information on the original Lipetsk Nov science town research efforts. The science towns were one of the few nonbureaucratic areas in which the former USSR invested in computerization in the early eighties. Part of the optimization of scientific development they hoped to get out of the towns. The result is a mother lode of on-line data. And now we've got all of it."

"You did good work," Bolan said.

"It wasn't just my doing. Everybody had a hand in this one," Wethers answered in an appreciative but modest tone. "We've already started poring over the data, and I'd like input from your able-bodied companion there."

"I was hoping to tag along with Steamroller One," Schwarz said with a shrug. "But I'll go where I'm needed."

"What have you got for me?" Bolan asked.

"Maybe a strong lead on Kabat's strategy," Kurtzman stated. "He's put a lot of resources behind tracking down the original members of the Lipetsk Nov science town—and I'm not talking about the individuals who went on to form the corporation. I mean all the scientists involved. Kabat tracked them down, accessed their government and military records, followed the careers of those who left Russia, even went to great lengths to confirm the deaths of those who have been reported deceased."

"How many others?"

"As near as we can figure, there were at least twenty-four PhD-level researchers involved in forming the original Lipetsk Nov," Kurtzman explained.

"And only ten of them were involved in Lipetsk Enterprises," Bolan added. He glanced at McCord for confirmation of that fact. She nodded. She was only half-listening to the conference call. Her attention was still on her headphones as she and her liaison, Carmen Delahunt, listened in on the flight of Mosty Sigulda.

"It's not going to be easy tracking down fourteen scientists," Schwarz said.

"We won't have to," Kurtzman replied. "Kabat's intelligence prioritizes the likely targets. We can start at the top of the list."

"Give me a name," Bolan said.

"Andrei Sheknovi," Wethers suggested. Before he was asked, he added, "São Paulo."

"What's his background?"

"He was a member of the Communist Party throughout the seventies and developed a solid reputation as a loyal Communist," Wethers explained. "He had all the right friends in the Kremlin. He helped develop some of the science town concepts and was instrumental in procuring funding for them, especially for his own pet project, Lipetsk Nov. When the research failed to achieve what he had promised in the accelerated time frame he had promised it, his standing became shaky. After the USSR dissolved, he left Russia in disgrace, turning over the reins of Lipetsk Nov to his assistant, a by-the-book, apolitical scientist who you've met—Nicholae Dinitzin."

"Since then?" Bolan asked.

"Sheknovi left Russia for good in 1994 to take on various international corporate research projects. He's still got a good reputation as a solid research scientist in certain circles, and he's making a good living. Seems disinclined to return to Russia."

"Can't be of much use if he's been uninvolved in the Lipetsk research for a decade," Schwarz said.

"Sure he can," McCord told them. "Keep in mind that Lipetsk research came to a halt when the science town was dissolved in 1989. It only started up again a few years ago, and there was a lot of catch-up work to be performed just to verify the old research and quantify the hard data that had been abandoned to the Russians. Also, Nick Dinitzin tried to recruit Sheknovi to the company just four or five months ago. He knew the research would proceed at a faster pace if an expert like Sheknovi came aboard. And he felt obliged to allow Sheknovi to share in the wealth. Nick was convinced the company was going to become very profitable very quickly."

"So he brought Sheknovi up to speed on their research," Bolan said, guessing.

"In detail. Flew down personally to São Paulo with a laptop full of test data, prototype CAD files, all kinds of stuff. Sheknovi was impressed with the research and he even gave Dinitzin some good leads on new avenues of scientific investigation, but he had no interest in being a part of the corporation. Dinitzin was down there again this week to try to get Sheknovi interested again."

Bolan nodded. "If I wanted to build the portable magnetic generation equipment but didn't have access to the Lipetsk research databases, would I start with Andrei Sheknovi?"

"You'd start with him," McCord said, "and you would end with him. You wouldn't need to go any further. He knows it all."

The decision was made as fast as the flip of a switch in Bolan's brain. "I'm going to São Paulo. You with me, Jack?"

"I am if they let me." Jack Grimaldi spoke for the first time. "Steamroller, if you provide us with a ride to Brazil I'll do the driving."

"Copy that," Price said. "I'm working on it."

"Something nice," Grimaldi added.

"I'll see what I can do."

"Damn," McCord declared suddenly, pulling off her headphones. "We lost him."

"Looks like Sigulda ditched his headset, and the clothing and armor we provided him," Price said a moment later over the speaker. "We're out of contact."

"I'm not all that worried about the Russians," Bolan stated. "They're a step behind us, and they'll be hesitant to act on U.S. soil again soon. They know we'll be watching for them."

"Still, I'd like to get my hands on that son of a bitch," Schwarz stated emphatically. "I hope letting him go was worth the intelligence we gathered."

"It was," Kurtzman told him.

Bolan was thinking about the Russian agents and the mayhem they had caused. They had murdered innocent people. The Dinitzins hadn't been a threat to the security of the Russian state, and yet Mosty Sigulda and his partner gunned them down. Now Sigulda would face the consequences of those murders: the Executioner's justice.

But that justice would have to wait.

"Sigulda will get his in the end," Bolan said quickly, but loud enough for Schwarz to hear. With that quiet declaration, Mack Bolan had just issued a death warrant. Schwarz nodded, satisfied.

São Paulo, Brazil

ANDREI SHEKNOVI FROWNED, his forehead becoming a mass of wrinkles. "Who is this?" he demanded.

"My name is Stephanie McCord. I work for Lipetsk Enterprises, Mr. Sheknovi."

"I never heard of you."

"I was engaged to marry Serge Gordetsky."

Sheknovi thought about this. "Why are you calling me, Ms. McCord?"

"I want you to know that I've been working with

a group that has been investigating the killings of Serge and the Dinitzins. In fact, I was with the Dinitzins when they were killed. I barely got away myself."

The woman sounded genuine, but the impression of sincerity meant nothing. "You're working with the FBI?"

"There are several federal U.S. agencies involved in the investigation, Mr. Sheknovi. Yes, I'm working with them."

"So what do you want with me?"

"All I want to do is to warn you, Mr. Sheknovi. The men responsible for killing Serge and the Dinitzins know where you are, and you're on their list. All I want is for you to protect yourself."

"I've been in contact with the FBI several times over the past few days, Ms. McCord," Sheknovi protested. "Why isn't Agent Levins calling me with this warning?"

"The FBI isn't exactly up to speed on all the most recent developments. I won't go into it. Suffice it to say we've identified who is behind the attacks. They want the pulse technology for weapons development."

"This doesn't make sense," Sheknovi protested. "If you're with a U.S. agency, why would they have you call me? Why not an official representative of their agency?"

"Listen, I'm not asking anything more than that you protect yourself!" McCord stated, the exasperation potent in her voice. "You are in danger. These men won't hesitate to kill you or the people around you to get the technology for the pulse."

Sheknovi gripped the phone with his shoulder

against his face and began manipulating his computer mouse furiously, a sudden chill of fear dancing down his spine. Within seconds he had opened his browser and navigated to the system he had set up in his home. The opening page showed a child's playroom—deserted. Silence came through the PC speakers. He clicked an arrow on the browser screen and the image switched within a few seconds to a large kitchen decked out in rich Italian ceramic tile and stainless-steel appliances.

There was a slim, tall woman standing at an island in the kitchen chopping celery, a mane of rich ebony hair flung over one shoulder. At about twenty-five years old she was less than half Sheknovi's age. As the photo reloaded, he watched her put a celery piece into a tiny hand that appeared over the side of the counter.

"Are you there, Mr. Sheknovi?"

"My family is safe," he said, as much to himself as to the woman in the U.S.

She seemed to realize he'd just verified that information for himself. "Only for the time being," she warned.

"I'll make sure they stay that way." He hung up on Stephanie McCord.

JOSÉ OLIVEIRA LEANED against a tree trunk in the woods and watched the quiet house some thirty paces from where he was hiding. The afternoon was cool in the trees, but the sun was shining on the lawn. A collection of new-looking toys, all brilliant colors of plastic, was scattered in the yard.

Oliveira was looking for a dog. A dog might notice their approach long before the people did. Even a little dog could make a racket. If there was no dog, this job was going to be much easier.

It had been half an hour and he'd seen no signs of an animal. The child had been in the yard when Oliveira arrived with his men, and the mother had emerged long enough to herd the boy indoors. Surely the dog would have shown itself by now. Oliveira decided there wasn't one.

He pulled the walkie-talkie out of his blazer jacket and pressed the button. "We're moving," he said.

He didn't listen for confirmation from the others. They would come. He started to make his way quietly through the woods. The moist compost that made up the ground and the springy green undergrowth made a silent approach easy. Not that a great deal of care was needed. The woman certainly wasn't aware she was in danger. The neighborhood—mostly wealthy expatriates from throughout Latin America working for Brazilian subsidiaries—was a quiet place with lots of trees and space between the homes.

Hardly the kind of job that called for a team of skilled mercenaries armed with automatic weapons. But that's what the client paid for and that's what he was getting.

Oliveira paused at the edge of the trees, his body hidden behind a small wall of fern growing wild at the decorative fence. Nobody on the lawn. No sign of dog shit. There was no sign of movement through the windows, but the watch out front had reported nobody leaving. Deolinda Sheknovi and her kid were still in there.

Suddenly, Oliveira felt very stupid. What the hell was he expecting? What was with all the covert operations crap? The woman was a mindless trophy wife, and the kid was hardly old enough to be toilet trained.

But Kabat had specifically requested a heavily armed team for both operations, despite the lack of danger and despite the fact that neither of the Sheknovis had military experience. Oliveira's employer had agreed to do what Kabat asked.

"Let's go," he growled into his walkie-talkie, feeling mildly embarrassed.

He pushed through the curtain of ferns at the same moment four of his men stepped out of the woods at various points around the sloping expanse of lawn. Out of sight, along the sides of the building, were three others. Two men would be approaching the front entrance under cover. No need to alert the neighbors. They were only there as a safety measure, just in case Mrs. Sheknovi made a break for it out the front of the house. Oliveira was determined not give her that opportunity.

"José, we've got police on the street!" an agitated voice said through his radio.

"Get to cover!" Oliveira ordered. He bolted for the house and flattened himself against the back wall. Around him, his men vanished like vermin squirming into their holes.

"Report," he commanded into the radio.

"They're checking out the street," his man answered.

Oliveira jogged along the side of the building, ducking under windows, reaching an eight-foot wooden fence covered in ivy in the rear grounds. He stooped and pushed his finger through the ivy, peering into the front of the house just in time to spot a police vehicle rolling slowly down the street. There were two officers inside—a rarity in São Paulo, where the beat cops often didn't ride with partners. The cop in the passenger seat was peering intently at the Sheknovi house.

Then the car was out of sight, leaving Oliveira to think about what he'd seen.

"It's turning," radioed his watchman in the front. A moment later the police car was in view again, and Oliveira watched the driver now, wrinkling his brow as he examined the Sheknovi mansion.

"What the hell was that all about?" Oliveira demanded when the car passed from his field of vision. "Somebody get careless and get spotted by one of the locals?"

"It wasn't us," one of his men protested. "I'd bet my life we haven't been seen here."

Oliveira knew that was the truth. "Who had the best view of the police?" he asked into the radio in a low voice.

"Probably me." Ricardo Carlos's voice answered.

"Were the cops keeping an eye on the Sheknovi house specifically, or were they making a neighborhood patrol?"

"Hard to say. They didn't seem to give this house extra attention."

"I need you to make a judgment call, Carlos," Oliveira said. "It makes all the difference."

Carlos had some trouble with the hard decision. "I would have to say I think it was a neighborhood sweep," he answered finally.

Carlos wasn't inspiring Oliveira's confidence. He was doing some thinking himself.

Why had the police come? If Oliveira's men had been spotted, they most certainly would have done more than just drive around the neighborhood peering into yards. So maybe they were just doing a sweep. Maybe these rich expats rated better law-enforcement protection than most of the city, and this sweep had occurred coincidentally during Oliveira's infiltration of the Sheknovi grounds. Coincidence or not, it bothered him.

"What happened to the cops?" he asked finally.

"Left," Carlos reported. "They went down the hill."

"Is that the only road into this neighborhood?"

"Yeah."

"Carlos, you watch it. If those cops come back, I want to hear about it."

"I understand, José."

"Okay. Let's get the bitch."

CHAPTER TEN

The building was a brick, three-story box dating from the late 1980s. It had the mirror windows and sterile architectural lines that would have made it at home in just about any office campus in the U.S. or Europe. The parking lot was full of mid-grade and expensive cars, the grounds well-maintained and clean, marred only by a chain-link fence separating the grounds from the road. The young Brazilian in the guard shack smiled and waved through a pair of cars before he faced the man in the stretch Lincoln.

The driver rolled down his window and smiled. "Here to pick up Mr. Smith," he said in Portuguese.

"I don't have you on my schedule sheet," the guard answered. He didn't need to check the schedule. "Are you sure you are at the right office?"

The driver shrugged. "Ask him," he said with a careless thumb to the back seat. The rear window opened with a whir of the motor, and the guard had to lean down at the waist to see the occupant. When he had his head level with the window opening, he realized he was staring down the muzzle of a handgun suppressor. Before he even grunted in surprise, the weapon fired with a burst of noise that filled the limo interior but didn't travel far outside it. The round drilled through his forehead and into his brain, killing him instantly.

The driver quickly opened his door and grabbed the guard by the material of his shirt before the body collapsed to the ground. The rear door opened and a figure emerged, took the guard by the arm and walked the corpse into the back seat of the car. The doors closed and within twenty seconds of their arrival they were on their way again. A battered, open-topped jeep followed close behind.

Incongruously, the next vehicle to pull through the front entrance was a school bus.

THE LINCOLN LIMOUSINE pulled to a stop across several parking places. The driver and two men from the rear seat exited, heading into the front vestibule where a pretty young woman sat at a low, circular desk, wearing a headset as she worked the phone system. The company was a U.S.-based research firm farming out its expertise to the expanding Brazilian industrial infrastructure. The linen skirt the receptionist wore would have been far too short to be acceptable in an office in the U.S., and the daringly cut white cotton blouse fit far too snugly. The all-male contingent of U.S. expatriates running the Brazilian division of Oak Development Limited joked among themselves that they didn't want to step on any toes culturally by addressing the issue of office attire with their young receptionist.

The smile she gave the men was professional and lifeless. "Can I help you?" she asked.

Henrique Goncalves had examined the reception area closely as he entered. There were two entrances into the building's interior. One was a hallway, and its doors were closed. The second was a stairway to the second-story offices. The doors at the top of the stairs were also closed. One man waited on a leather sofa in the reception area, absorbed in a celebrity magazine.

He finally answered the receptionist's question as he extracted the silenced 9 mm handgun from his belt behind his back.

"No," he said, leveling the weapon at her chest. She arched her back when the bullet slammed through her sternum. The round managed to stay in one piece as it destroyed her heart and penetrated the padding of her office chair. When it hit the steel frame of the chair it made a loud metallic click. The receptionist flopped back in the chair, dead even as the gasp left her body, her head rolling back and to the side.

The salesman dropped his magazine and got to his feet with a look of slack-jawed terror in his drooping features. The briefcase that had been on his lap crashed to the floor. He tried to back away from the murderer but collided with a coffee table and sat heavily on it, sending a ceramic ashtray to the floor.

The suppressed weapon targeted him.

"No!" he protested.

When the weapon fired he raised his arms as if to ward off a blow, but the bullets pushed him onto his back, sending a lamp off the coffee table with a small crash.

"We're in and the front door is secure," Goncalves said into his cell phone.

"Right behind you," the bus driver answered.

Goncalves glanced out the front entrance to see the bus roll slowly to the far edge of the parking lot, where a handful of men jumped out. They would circle the building, guarding the rear as a precaution in case anyone managed to make a break for it. Another four gunmen, including the man driving the bus, would guard the front entrance. The remainder of Goncalves's small army of mercenaries would fan out through the building.

Goncalves waited, and his men were silent. They knew the wait would be short. Just long enough for the men on the outside to get into position.

"Let's move," Goncalves said finally.

He led the way through the door. The first person he spotted was a young man in a lab coat over a red T-shirt. The lab assistant never stood a chance. Goncalves targeted him with his assault rifle and cut him down with a merciless burst of rounds. The sound carried throughout the bottom floor of the building, and suddenly screams filled the lower level. People started stampeding from the gunner.

Goncalves's mercenaries moved among the cubicles and offices like water flowing around rocks. Nobody escaped them. Bursts from their smaller caliber, Brazilian-made assault rifles were fired into the floor and kept the people moving. After the brutal killing of the young lab assistant, no further lives were taken. Goncalves didn't want to risk getting Sheknovi by mistake.

Above him, he heard the muffled chatter of more rifle fire as his second and third teams gathered workers in the management offices and research labs. Everyone was to be gathered on the second floor, where there was enough space to bring them together into a single room.

"What do you want from us?" one of the sobbing women screamed suddenly, becoming hysterical.

"Shut up," ordered a mercenary, gesturing up the stairs with his weapon.

"What do you want? Tell me!" She was becoming red-faced. Suddenly she lashed out at the merc with her clenched fists, pounding on his face like she was pounding on a closed door. The merc twisted and shoved, sending her to the floor hard. For a moment she was silent, the breath knocked out of her. Before she got it back the mercenary straddled her, jammed the muzzle of the weapon into her abdomen and fired.

The people on the stairs began to scream and cry, nearly paralyzed with the horror of what they had just witnessed.

"I want quiet, or another of you gets it," Goncalves announced. He waited. They wouldn't shut up. Goncalves was a pretty good judge of group panic dynamics and he was confident there would be at least one among them too unhinged to cooperate. That was fine with him. Sure enough, one of the older men kept babbling and sobbing, unable to silence himself.

Goncalves moved up the first few steps, the crowd scattering from him, and grabbed the babbler, a black-haired, mustachioed man in his fifties. He reminded Goncalves of his father. He grinned when he shoved the man in the chest. The man tripped and landed full-length on the stairs. His mouth opened wide in a silent scream of pain.

Then he froze, staring into the muzzle of Goncalves's weapon. The mercenary leader sported an FN FAL .308 Light Automatic Rifle. He chose the weapon for its uniqueness. He liked having a weapon that was one of a kind among his mercenary outfit. It set him apart from his men. Using the folding-stock version of the weapon gave him added maneuverability when he needed it.

The terrorized man on the stairs didn't know or care about the weapon. He knew only that it would easily destroy him.

"Who among you wants me to kill this man?" Goncalves demanded in Portuguese. He looked from face to face. At least a couple of the people were American. He didn't bother to translate his words into English. They'd know what he was saying.

"Please don't hurt him," a small older woman begged.

"I need cooperation from you people. If I get cooperation, nobody else gets hurt."

"We'll do whatever you say."

Goncalves hardened his brow and glared at the woman, then allowed his gaze to travel from face to terrorized face. Finally, he backed away from the fallen man.

"Get upstairs. Do what my men tell you and go where my men tell you to go," he said. "They have my permission to shoot at will if and when they don't get your full cooperation. Understand?"

The people nodded and murmured, then started up the stairs again.

Goncalves grinned. He had them right where he wanted them, and it had cost him no more than a couple of murders.

"STRIKER, WHAT'S your situation?"

"We'll be in the air in thirty seconds," Bolan answered into the radio as he clicked his seat belt. "What's up?"

"We've lost contact with Oak Development," Price reported. "Stephanie McCord tried to reestablish contact with Sheknovi."

"He didn't answer?"

"The company didn't answer. We tried every ingoing line."

"Hold on," Grimaldi warned as he fed fuel to the rotors and propelled the rented chopper off the tarmac at the São Paulo airport. It was a Bell 430, with a forty-two-foot rotor span. The Allison 250-C40 engines generated 800 horsepower at takeoff, and within seconds Grimaldi had the 9,000-pound aircraft ascending at its maximum rate of climb of just under 1,900 feet per minute—an ascent rate that would have left a typical passenger searching for the little paper bags. Bolan had been through too many tricky airborne maneuvers to be affected by it, especially with a pilot at the stick in whom he had the highest level of confidence. Jack Grimaldi was perfectly at home behind the controls of almost any aircraft.

"We're airborne," Bolan notified Stony Man Farm. "Maybe the problem is with the Brazilian phone system."

"That's a negative, Striker. There's a single set of phone lines going into the building, and their Internet servers are still working. The data lines wouldn't remain active if the telecom lines went out. They're just not answering."

"What's the size of the building?" Bolan asked.

Price described the building. Fifteen to twenty offices on the third floor. Twenty smaller offices and cubicles on the first floor. Extensive product development laboratories on the second floor.

"Is there a way in through the roof?" Bolan asked.

"Unknown. We don't have blueprints."

"How about an eye in the sky?"

"Negative. There's no satellite available for over an hour, and I don't know if we could finagle access in that much time."

"We'll make do," Bolan growled.

There was a moment of silence. "That's a large building. There have to be dozens of people working there, Mack," Price said reasonably. "They'll have put a lot of men on the scene in order to extract Sheknovi."

"I'm aware of that."

"It's pretty risky to go in against such large numbers," she continued. "Even for you."

"It's even riskier for Andrei Sheknovi if I don't."

Price didn't reply to that. She wouldn't argue with Bolan. He was his own highest authority. If he was determined to get in and help the Russian scientist, her words wouldn't change his mind. She wouldn't waste time with the effort.

"Did you get through Brazil customs with all your luggage?"

"Yeah. Our diplomatic passports saved us from having to make any declarations. We're well-equipped."

"We put your ETA at eight minutes. Good luck."

Guided by the Bell helicopter's global positioning systems, finding the building they wanted was effortless and, at the rate Grimaldi was pushing the chopper, it was just five minutes later when they spotted it. Another minute brought them thrumming over the roof of the building, just a hundred yards above it.

"We have their attention," the pilot stated as he swung the Bell in a quarter-mile circle that carried them over the grounds to the front of the building. They counted three men with automatic weapons running in their direction. More were appearing from the rear of the building.

"Let's keep them interested," Bolan suggested.

"You got it, Sarge." Grimaldi descended over the grounds, just outside the perimeter fence, swinging sideways to give Bolan easy access to the rushing targets. The soldier stuck a hand out the window and fired the big Desert Eagle into the ground, knowing that even over the rotor thrum the sound of the .44 Magnum rounds would reach the mercenaries.

The mercs numbered a half dozen, and as they came to within firing distance of the Bell they sought cover among the sparsely planted trees. Bolan continued to fire sporadically. Grimaldi wobbled the Bell as if he were having problems maintaining his static offensive position. In reality, he was maintaining a distance of a few hundred yards, hoping to stay out of the range of the automatic rifle fire. Keeping himself faced away from the fire, Grimaldi was safe, and Bolan was staying behind the cover of the window-frame.

"We're moving them away," Bolan said. "Another hundred yards and they'll be gathered at the perimeter fence."

"All of them?"

"There's just one pair remaining at the building,"

Bolan answered. "There's seven on the ground at the fence. We can cut our odds considerably."

"Give the word. I'm ready when you are, Sarge."

Bolan emptied a second clip at the gunners at the fence, deliberately missing. They perceived the attackers in the helicopter as impotent, unskilled cowards. Their overconfidence was about to cost them. As the Bell chopper hovered just at the edge of automatic gunfire range, Bolan picked up the G3-TG3/HK79 resting on his lap.

"Let's go in, Jack."

"You got it." Grimaldi grinned and snatched at the controls, tilting the helicopter on its nose and jumping into quick acceleration. Bolan could almost hear the cries of surprise coming from the edge of the grounds of the development firm. Before the enemy had time to bolt for the building, the Bell circled them and dropped like a falling rock, coming to a sudden stop less than fifty feet above the ground. The gunners dropped flat, the more quick-thinking among them seeking new cover behind the trees.

But that was a useless maneuver when they realized the extent of their antagonists' firepower. Bolan directed the big G3-TG3/HK79 through the door of the helicopter and triggered a 40 mm grenade from the HK79 launcher.

The Executioner met the gaze of one of the gunners over the vastness of space separating them. He witnessed the man's momentary confusion, then a heartbeat of understanding as he recognized the flash and the sound for what it was. He knew that he had made a grievous error. The helicopter, this mercenary and his companions were suddenly discovering, wasn't what it had pretended to be.

The high-explosive 40 mm grenade landed in the midst of the men, outracing their sudden flight in all directions. The blast cratered the earth and slammed into their backs, ripping into their bodies and driving them into the earth with the force of its concussion.

Two of the mercs scrambled to their feet again, only to meet the withering fire from the Heckler & Koch G3-TG3 automatic rifle. Bolan allowed the momentum of the helicopter to carry the deadly stream of rounds across the mercenaries at waist level, slamming them to the ground again.

"Three o'clock, Jack," Bolan said calmly.

"You got it." Grimaldi's hands maneuvered the helicopter with the fine control of a highly talented musician, bringing the aircraft in a ninety-degree turn and sliding it forward as if it were on a track, adjusting slightly to compensate for the erratic flight of the three remaining panic-stricken mercenaries.

Bolan loaded another grenade and waited a few seconds for the fleeing prey to gather. Two of the gunners came to within several paces of each other. They were running on the same course, and the man in the rear was faster than the man ahead. Bolan knew they would be shoulder to shoulder in just seconds, and he judged the conditions ideal for killing two birds with one stone.

"Steady, Jack."

"Okay, Sarge."

Grimaldi finessed the controls, doing an expert job at keeping the Bell even in her position and consistent in her speed. Bolan shouldered his weapon and triggered another grenade.

The soldier's aim and compensation were impeccable. The high explosive arced through the air and landed on the ground less than a yard in front of the running men at almost the instant they were shoulder to shoulder. The blast tossed them away in pieces, like scraps of confetti in a strong wind.

One mercenary remained on the run. Grimaldi chased him down as Bolan triggered a steady stream of long-distance automatic rifle fire, watching the small disturbances where the 7.62 mm rounds ate divots into the grass. The runner's eyes were wild and white when he stared at the encroaching chopper, and then he saw the gunfire coming at him, eating its way through the ground like some deadly subterranean creature that would strike at him from beneath the soil. He screamed and threw his gun away, then the Executioner's fire caught up to him and slapped him down.

"The two at the front?" Bolan asked.

"They circled around the back when we turned the tables on their friends," Grimaldi said.

"Drop me off, then you can distract them and keep them busy while I make my way inside. Don't let on that you're alone. They'll probably be reporting to their people on the inside."

"Understood."

Grimaldi rushed the Bell toward the three-story laboratory, descending and slowing suddenly when he was over the roof. At five feet from the surface Bolan pushed through the door and dropped out without a word of goodbye, landing in a crouch as the Bell banked away with a roar of engines.

THE SECOND FLOOR was a sprawling room with an eleven-foot ceiling, divided into several sections with large racks, pieces of equipment and cubicle walls serving as dividers. The front end was dominated by a single large box made of dull, textured metal. A steady low-pitched thrum came from the air-conditioner-like cube of machinery leeching onto it on one side. Goncalves could hear it and feel it under his feet at the same time. He noticed several of the lab workers sporting headphones around their necks.

The third floor had been emptied, and the building's occupants were coalescing in the middle of the second-floor lab. His second-in-command, a youthful-looking man named Cerrera, gave him a satisfied grin and a wave as he approached. He shouted when he was within a few paces, his voice muted and drowned by the thrum of the test chamber.

"Piece of cake," Cerrera said in English. It was a phrase the street punks of São Paulo and Rio de Janeiro had picked up from the latest action movie. Cerrera kept in close touch with his roots. "I spotted our man right away." He jerked a thumb at a grungy, defeated-looking man slumped between a pair of Cerrera's men, his wrists bound with hemp rope that looked heavy enough to tie down a fishing trawler in a heavy storm. Goncalves stepped up to the prisoner. The old, unshaven man refused to meet his eyes. It didn't matter. At a glance the mercenary leader could tell this was the same face he had seen in the photo Kabat faxed to him. This was the Russian researcher, Andrei Sheknovi, alive and well and in his hands.

Goncalves laughed and clapped Cerrera on the back. "We'll live high for a year on this one, my friend!"

"I think I'll invest my cut," Cerrera said. They both laughed at what was an old joke among them.

"Let's secure these people and put some distance

between ourselves and this place," Goncalves said. His eyes fell on the big steel box at the end of the lab. "Put them in there."

Cerrera nodded and began to issue rapid-fire orders. Goncalves and his valuable prisoner left the room along with the Russian's guard. They kept their weapon trained on him at all times, but the Russian was as meek as a mouse.

This was too easy.

CHAPTER ELEVEN

Grimaldi spun the helicopter so that it skidded sideways a hundred yards, giving him a revolving view
of the far side of the building. The two remaining
guards were plastered against the side of the building, their eyes wide as they witnessed the chopper
swing into view almost directly over their heads.
They pointed their rattling automatic weapons in the
direction of the chopper, and Grimaldi heard the impact of the rounds against its metal belly. He backed
up and away in a hurry, once again striving for an
illusion of caution. Grimaldi was staying out of the
thick of the action, but the one thing he could accomplish was to keep these two from joining their
comrades inside the building and give Bolan better
odds at coming out intact.

He got an idea. It was a simple plan, but it just
might work. It depended on the gullibility of these
two, and the extent of their familiarity with vertical
takeoff aircraft. He started fluctuating the fuel feed
to the helicopter, steering it through a series of wild
pendulum swings as he brought it closer to the
ground. He chose a spot carefully, blocked from the
view of the gunners by a small grouping of young
trees, planted in a perfect triangle by the landscapers.

He found a slight incline and raced the Bell down to it, slowing for a gentle landing only at the last minute, and facing away from the office.

Then he sat and waited.

He was beginning to think the ploy wouldn't work when he spotted the pair of gunners coming across the lawn, their automatic rifles trained on the idling helicopter and moving cautiously. Grimaldi couldn't allow them to get close enough to plug holes in the vital components of the Bell. But he would wait until they got within a hundred yards. By then they would have a long walk back to the building.

It was a ploy similar to the one they'd used earlier. And maybe it wouldn't work. What the hell. It wasn't like he had anything better to do while he was waiting for Bolan's call for extraction.

Craning his neck to peer at a sharp angle through a rear window, he could barely see them coming down the long, shallow slope from the building. Then he spotted a vehicle coming around the front of the building and heading down the slope after the gunners. It was the military jeep the Stony Man pilot had spotted parked at the front of the building, manned by a driver and a gunner.

Grimaldi laughed out loud. "Come and get me, assholes!" he shouted, well pleased with himself. Two more mercenaries chasing him outside meant two less gunners after Bolan inside. Even better, their presence might indicate the mercenaries had failed to catch Bolan's drop-off, so they weren't all that concerned with the activity inside the building. They considered the entire threat to be outside.

"Oh-oh," Grimaldi muttered as he saw the jeep accelerate down the incline, racing at the Bell at highway speed. The passenger was getting to his feet and pulling a large, deadly-looking firearm from behind his seat. Grimaldi raced the engine on the Bell and fed speed to the rotors, lifting into the air when the jeep was less than seventy-five feet away. There was a rattle of machine-gun fire and the jeep maneuvered to follow the movement of the helicopter. Grimaldi swore bitterly when he heard a series of impacts, so close underneath him he could feel them in his feet. As soon as he was far enough off the ground, he tilted the chopper on her nose and raced ahead, fleeing the jeep. He didn't forget to waver the steering and throttle the fuel unsteadily, hoping to continue giving the perception of a less-than-healthy aircraft. As he spun to the left, he craned his neck to glimpse the jeep. The passenger was waving frantically, and the jeep was coming after him at top sped. Behind it the foot soldiers were running to catch up. They wanted to be in on the kill.

"You will be, suckers," Grimaldi announced, then brought the Bell to a halt at a spot just twenty feet from the flat earth. They were off the property owned by the research laboratory, and underneath him was dank grassland, a swampy, boglike area—unpleasant but not enough to slow the jeep, which raced through the puddles with torrents of flying brown water.

As Grimaldi grabbed the pack behind his seat, he raced the engines and spun the aircraft in a complete three-sixty. The show was working. The jeep was coming straight at him as if the occupants expected him to plop to the ground at any second. Grimaldi grinned and brought the chopper to a sudden halt, stock-still and steady, at an angle to the oncoming jeep. The passenger, standing with his machine gun, and Jack Grimaldi suddenly locked gazes at 150 yards.

"Enjoy the show?" Grimaldi asked with a grin. The machine gunner couldn't possibly hear him, but somehow, something told the man that all wasn't as it seemed. He triggered the machine gun, waving it wildly in the general direction of the suddenly under control chopper and shouting at the driver. The jeep came to a halt.

Grimaldi found what he wanted in the pack. He reached out of the window of the Bell as if he were tossing an empty fast-food cup on the freeway and he dropped the fragmentation grenade. The passenger spotted the tiny egg as it rolled out of the sky almost directly on top of him, and he screamed at the driver, slapping him wildly on the shoulder. The driver yanked the jeep into reverse and popped the clutch with an impressive display of driving skill, coaxing a tremendous burst of reverse speed out of the jeep before the grenade hit the earth and detonated.

Grimaldi didn't see what happened, but when he twisted the Bell into a tight spin and looked down again, the jeep had halted on the grass. The headlights were obliterated. There was obvious damage to the sheet metal, and the windshield was still disintegrating.

But Grimaldi's effort had failed. The driver and the machine gunner in the passenger seat were still alive and conscious. They were covered in blood, but they were moving too rapidly to have been seriously wounded. The gunner leveled his weapon at the attacking Bell as the driver struggled to get the vehicle moving again.

Grimaldi piloted the helicopter into a high rate of

speed across the driver's field of vision, then pushed it into a twist and a sudden dive to come directly behind the stalled vehicle. The gunner's mouth was opening and closing like a fish on dry land, berating his driver to get them moving, as he awkwardly maneuvered in his seat with the big machine gun. Grimaldi knew what it was like to manipulate a big weapon like that. The man was barely able to get his barrel lined up on the Bell before it was on top of them. The passenger leaned backward over the frame of the windshield, laying on the trigger and spewing a steady stream of machine-gun fire, but he could not catch up with the dive-bombing helicopter. As the roar of the rotors reached a thunder pitch just yards over their heads, the jeep came to life and the driver carelessly lurched forward. The passenger sprawled sideways out of the vehicle, cursing the driver.

Neither of them had time to see the small hand grenade that arced out of the chopper's window and deposited itself onto their rear bumper. The jeep detonated with a sound like a crash of falling machinery. The burst of metal shrapnel ripped through the back of the driver's skull and into the upturned face of the sprawled passenger, opening his face and neck in a dozen large wounds. The blood flooded out of his body in a river that stopped only when he was long minutes dead.

Grimaldi pulled up the chopper and focused his attention on the two foot soldiers. They had come to a halt upon witnessing the sudden demise of the men in the jeep and couldn't seem to understand what their next course of action should be. The Stony Man pilot decided it for them by swooping toward the ground, cutting them off from the office building.

There was no way they were getting back to their comrades without going through the sleek, innocuous-looking, but unbelievably deadly Bell 430 helicopter. So they ran.

BOLAN BLASTED AWAY the lock with a single suppressed shot and wrenched open the service door from the roof into the interior of the building. When he descended into the dark interior he found himself inside some sort of small service room. He waited half a minute for the sound of his incursion to elicit a reaction. None came, and he opened the door and found himself in a plush office suite. The place had been deserted in a rush. Papers littered the floor. Computers waited in the middle of functions and documents for their missing operators. Coffee was cooling on desktops. Bolan moved as quickly through the offices as silence would allow until he determined that the top floor was completely abandoned. Knowing the elevator was a death trap, he made his way catlike down an emergency exit stairway to the second floor, finding himself in a large room whose walls were coated with acoustical foam insulation. The room was dominated by a refrigerator-size metal-and-glass box. Inside, a small, articulated robotic arm was moving in spurts from place to place, its drill-like tip gouging tiny bits and pieces out of a sandy resin block in its center. Already the shape of a complex gearing system prototype was beginning to emerge from the resin.

He crept to the sealed doorway and peered through a small, three-paned window. His field of vision limited to just a few desks, he saw no sign of life. During the lulls in the grinding of the prototyping tool, he didn't hear a sound from outside the room.

Bolan opened the door into a narrow section of a room. One of the walls was the rear end of some sort of steel-walled enclosure. As he moved around the enclosure, he spotted the hostages, twenty of them, inside the chamber. They were milling about, looking at one another with faces filled with terror. Many of them, men and women, were weeping. Facing front, toward the door, none of them spotted the Executioner.

Then insanity seemed to spring upon the prisoners like a sudden, simultaneous frenzy. They screamed and dropped to the floor of the chamber, writhing in an orgy of suffering, grabbing at their ears and squeezing their eyes shut. At the same instant, Bolan heard and felt a penetrating squeal that set his teeth on edge, cutting into his brain like a frozen scalpel. One of the prisoners pounded and yanked at the door. A face appeared on the other side of the glass and laughed at the suffering old man.

Bolan gritted his teeth and pushed himself away from the window as a river of cold descended into his gut as if he had swallowed a heart of ice. He moved to the front of the chamber, finding himself in a large, long room filled with machinery and equipment for all kinds of testing operations. He didn't notice it. His main goal at that moment was to find the laughing face on the other side of the window.

Two men stood at the computer monitor and membrane switch panel on the side of the chamber. They had a chair wedged against the door to jam it shut. Both looked up in surprise when they saw the

Executioner, and it took them a full two seconds to come to the realization that he wasn't one of them. By that time it was too late.

Bolan's gaze locked on the man who had laughed, and at the same instant he triggered the G3-TG3 in full-auto, chopping his companion from shoulder to hip in one deadly swath of fire that dropped him in a bloody pile.

The soldier stepped forward, slamming his foot into the gunner's gut just as the man was bringing the Executioner into target acquisition. The guy folded to the floor in an untidy heap.

Bolan took the time to look around. A pair of hardmen hustled into the room, looking concerned, and he triggered a deadly figure eight that they couldn't avoid. They danced under the torrent of 7.62 mm rounds, then dropped hard.

Bolan kicked at the chair that was wedging the door shut, whirling it across the room. As the door flew open, he was hit with an onslaught of sound that seemed to cut into his brain like a cold steel knife. It was the kind of sound that might drive a person insane. The sound was turned off with the opening of the door by some sort of automatic cutoff, and it died quickly as figures began staggering and flopping out of the chamber like souls escaping from purgatory.

Bolan glanced over just long enough to determine that there were those among them who were still conscious. They would have to take responsibility for those who were in worse shape. The soldier had other duties to perform.

He waited until the chamber was empty, then he

grabbed the laugher by the shirt collar and dragged him into the chamber.

The man was clutching his stomach, so transfixed with pain he didn't notice what was happening. Then he opened his eyes, looking around him as Bolan shut the door.

The laugher came to his feet, eyes wide with horror.

Bolan spun the controls.

Even through the walls he could hear the metal onslaught of sound that filled the chamber. Before the prisoner could grab for the door, Bolan jammed the chair back in place.

The victims of the laugher were watching Bolan with a kind of amazement and curiosity as they tried to recover from their torture. Maybe one of them would feel pity for the mercenary and let him out. But it wasn't going to be Bolan. As far as the soldier was concerned, the gunner could wait inside that chamber until his skull exploded.

He glanced through the window one last time. The laugher had his eyes squeezed shut and his mouth wide open.

But he wasn't laughing now.

CHAPTER TWELVE

Bolan couldn't find Andrei Sheknovi among the chamber victims. He also failed to find anyone among the lucid victims who seemed to know where Sheknovi was or to be aware that the Russian was the target of the mercenary attack. They were too dazed to know much of anything.

Another pair of gunners hurried from the doorway at the rear of the expansive laboratory, and Bolan took cover. They peered at the huddled collection of victims from the sound chamber, concerned and unable to determine why they were free.

Bolan showed them why. When they reached the cabinet that served as his hiding place he fired, point-blank, without mercy. The torrent of rounds cut through the first man, brought him down, then ate into the second man. The two gunners collapsed like a single butchered animal in a messy heap.

There was a rattle of something collapsing at the same moment, and Bolan caught a flicker of movement in his peripheral vision. He swung his weapon toward the sound, identifying a gunman who had skidded to a halt, knocking over a rack of electronic laboratory test equipment and trying to reverse himself through the doorway. He never made it. The instant it took the Executioner to identify him as one of the mercenaries and translate that realization into a burst of automatic rifle fire was like the blink of an eye, and the gunner collapsed with a shattered rib cage.

A sudden blast of gunfire flew through the open doorway—panic fire, meant to slow pursuit. Bolan waited for the fire to stop, then stepped into the doorway, catching sight of a mercenary as he disappeared around the corner.

HENRIQUE GONCALVES HEARD the gunfire and ignored it. It was just his mercenaries taking out prisoners.

Then he cocked his head, bringing his men to a halt with a gesture. In the circular front drive to the building, where the limousine and school bus were parked and idling, everyone froze. Even Andrei Sheknovi was held where he was, one foot inside the rear of the limo, his arms gripped by two mercenaries.

Goncalves heard more shots, as quiet as taps, from deep inside the building. Those weren't potshots. That was the sound of battle.

"They're under attack," he declared.

"How's that possible?" Cerrera demanded. "How could anybody know we're here?"

Goncalves's head spun. "Where's Cimaron and the others?" For the first time he realized their jeep was missing.

Cerrera shook his head, then glanced at his watch. "They were scheduled to report." He grabbed the cell phone from his pocket and dialed it with a thumb. "Cimaron doesn't answer."

"Fuck! Kabat's been less than straight with us. He's got us into something a lot bigger than he's let on."

Cerrera shrugged. "Maybe it's just security guards we missed on the way in. Can't be a big force."

"Why not?" Goncalves demanded.

"They didn't leave anybody out front. They would've if they'd had the people." He grinned. "We'll take them."

A figure slammed through the doors of the lobby, stumbling and falling onto the ground. The mercenaries reacted skillfully and quickly, and in a second eight weapons were drawn on the newcomer. But he was one of their own, a new recruit from the Brazilian army. He got to his feet and raced to his comrades, holding his weapon like a club.

"What's going on?" Goncalves demanded.

"I don't know, but they're dead!"

"Who?"

"All of them!"

Goncalves looked at his men and did a rough count. "How do you know?"

"I saw the bodies! He cut them all down!" The ex-soldier righted his Brazilian autoweapon and was covering the big, open lobby with it, as if he expected the enemy to appear at any second.

"One man?"

"That's all I saw!"

Goncalves considered this for a second. "Okay. Let's get out of here."

"We can't go," Cerrera stated. "Our men are here somewhere."

"They're dead, I'm telling you!" the soldier retorted.

"Shut up. We can't go without our men, Henrique."

"And if he's right?" Goncalves asked.

"We take out the guys who did it."

Goncalves agreed with a nod. "Get him in the car," he ordered to the figures flanking Sheknovi. "Move it away from the building and be ready to head out. We take these guys down but we don't waste time doing it, understood?"

Cerrera raised his hand sharply, palm out, staring at the sky. "Shit! We got a chopper in the vicinity!"

The easy raid had become complicated in a big hurry, Goncalves thought. He heard the thrum of the helicopter, coming closer. He bolted for the bus, hugging it. The chopper appeared over the top of the building, moving slowly at three hundred feet. It was black, with some sort of logo painted on the side.

"Can you ID it?" Cerrera asked.

"No. It doesn't look military. It must be a private aircraft."

"So who's flying it?" Goncalves demanded.

Something small, black and oblong arced out of the helicopter and tumbled end over end. Goncalves watched it with interest that transformed to shock.

"Grenade!" he shouted as he broke from the bus, tearing across the lot and scrambling for the cover of an employee car. He was half behind it when the grenade touched the concrete and blew. Goncalves crouched in a duck-and-cover position, expecting to be pelted with debris, but the blast receded and the rattle of shrapnel never reached him. When he got to his feet he was shocked to observe the reason. The grenade had missed the bus. It had never even been aimed at the bus. It had been directed into the mass of mercenaries collected several meters away, waiting at the front of the building. The mercenaries had spread in all directions, and not one of them had made it far enough to escape the blast. They lay in a jumble on the concrete, some of them half-obliterated, others simply torn up. Three were dead. The other two would be soon.

Suddenly, during that two-second period of observation, Goncalves took on a much greater degree of respect for his unseen enemies.

"JACK," BOLAN SAID into his radio, "stay away from that limo."

"I'm ahead of you there, Sarge. I spotted them shoving in their prisoner during my flyover. Is that Sheknovi?"

"Affirmative."

"Here comes trouble," Grimaldi said.

Goncalves was on his feet, running for the limo and sweeping the sky with automatic weapon fire. Bolan spotted Grimaldi pull up farther and watched a starlight pattern appear on one of the helicopter windows. It was time to make his presence known.

Bolan yanked at the door and emerged from the building in plain sight, but as he was aiming for the gunner with the FN FAL .308, another figure jumped out of the Lincoln limousine. Bolan had been spotted. He was forced to reassess his target acquisition and he homed the G3-TG3 on the figure standing in the crook of the limo door, then pulled back sharply as he realized he might not avoid hitting the figure in the rear seat. Bolan wouldn't chance hitting Sheknovi. Even though the man he saw might be another merc, and the window through which an errant bullet would have to travel might very well be bullet-resistant, he wouldn't risk the hit. Instead, he bolted across the front of the car, attempting to outrun the bullets as the figure in the door commenced firing a 9 mm handgun.

The soldier dropped and rolled and found himself under the front end of the mercenaries' school bus. When he rose into a crouch, he spotted the gunner on the move. Just as he'd hoped. When the man was at the front of the Lincoln, standing over the long hood of the car, the Executioner pushed himself into a standing position and strafed his torso from shoulder to hip. A burst of fire from the merc with the FN FAL forced him to cut short the burst, and Bolan retreated around the front of the school bus.

"He's coming around the far side of the limo from you, Sarge," Grimaldi said. The Bell 430 was drifting over them again, and Grimaldi had a bird's-eye view.

"Copy that," Bolan said as he crept to the door of the bus and pushed his way inside. A momentary scan of the interior under the seats told him the bus was empty, unless its occupants were curled up on seats. He watched out the windshield until he spotted the merc with the FN FAL step around the limo, searching for Bolan.

The soldier targeted him through the glass at the moment the gunner realized his mistake. He recoiled behind the protection of the limo, and the burst Bolan fired through the front of the bus accomplished no more than property damage. The glass shattered in one large corner, and a metallic dent winked into existence on the hood of the Lincoln. Seconds later the vehicle squealed its tires and pulled away from the bus, its rear end floating momentarily before it got a solid grip on the pavement. Bolan thrust the H&K through the glass and triggered off the remainder of his magazine, pinking the trunk of the Lincoln and forcing the driver into an evasive swerve. The G3-TG3 chugged dry before a tire was scored. The limousine tore away.

"Watch them, Jack!" Bolan ordered into the radio as he dropped into the driver's seat and twisted the keys that started the big diesel engine with a grind. He yanked the shifter stick into first and popped the clutch, forcing the bus into a bouncing start.

"You want a pickup?" Grimaldi asked from the sky as he swept after the fleeing Lincoln.

"No time for that. You stay on them. Stop them if you can but use no deadly force. I'll be right behind you."

"Got it."

Bolan found himself on the road that led directly out of the hills into the city of São Paulo, and it was sparsely populated with midday traffic. The Lincoln limousine was nowhere in sight, but Bolan knew they had a distinct speed advantage over him. Their vehicle was designed with a muscular engine that would take it comfortably over the rough, sometimes twisting road. The bus was a lumbering dinosaur, forced to slow to a crawl at the corners and without any real capability for quick acceleration.

The soldier had to make the best of it until another opportunity presented itself. Allowing Grimaldi to land and take him aboard the helicopter was out of the question. They'd lose the mercenaries and their prisoner for certain.

"Jack, how am I doing?" he radioed.

"I couldn't even tell you, Sarge. I'm on top of them. We're about five miles away from the company already and moving fast. I can't even see you behind us."

"I'm at least a couple of miles back."

"Keep the pedal to the metal, Sarge. They've reduced to legal speeds. They may think they're home free. They can't see me. I'm way above them."

"Good. Keep them ignorant if you can," Bolan said. He was thinking furiously, scanning the road as he coaxed extra speed out of the lumbering engine and syrup-slow transmission. The bus rattled around him as if every screw was about to come apart. It couldn't have been a worse pursuit vehicle, but for the moment it was all he had. He found himself suddenly at the top of a steep, long decline, and he pushed the accelerator to the floor, allowing gravity to help him bring the bus beyond its typical top speed. The rattle of the windows and body panels and connectors became like the vibration of a box of auto parts. Getting down the two-mile decline took less time that Bolan would have imagined, and by then the steering wheel had taken on a violent shudder. He pushed it hard up the next hill, shorter than its predecessor, then topped the rise and started down again, hanging on to some speed. Bolan felt as if he were barely controlling the rolling contraption as the back end rose at the height of the incline then dipped hard.

Then he spotted a mirrorlike glint at least a thousand feet up.

"Got you, Jack," he radioed.

"Saw you first, Sarge. I'm still right on top of them. They're cruising along at normal speeds."

"Here I come."

Around him the traffic built steadily. Houses, streets and people were appearing in greater density, and Bolan kept an eye out for inattentive drivers. He couldn't slow, but he didn't want to smash some innocent civilians in the process. He was thankful for the lack of traffic lights. So far.

Bolan steered the bus through minor curves in the road without using the brake pedal or reducing his pressure on the accelerator, then found himself with nothing between himself and the limo. A traffic light ahead turned red. The soldier watched the trickle of traffic that crossed the highway as the Lincoln pulled to a stop to wait for green. Bolan had an opportunity, and he might not get another. He had to chance it. He honked his horn and swerved the bus to signal a small, ancient Volkswagen that it shouldn't pull onto the highway. The Volkswagen didn't get the message. It eased onto the road, and Bolan yanked the big steering wheel, pulling the bus into the oncoming lane of traffic. He honked the big horn again as he came beside the Volkswagen at a reckless speed. The older woman at the wheel stared at the hurtling yellow monster dumbfounded before swerving off the road into the grass and braking to a halt. Bolan turned the bus into his lane. Another few hundred yards passed before he caught up with the limo, and the light was still red. Bolan watched the limo's brake lights, saw the vehicle edge up just a little bit. Then the lights went off and it moved suddenly. The bus had been spotted.

The Lincoln pulled into the intersection in a hurry, generating a flurry of furious honks from a tiny Ford that braked and drifted sideways and only just managed to avoid impact. Bolan barreled through the intersection just as the Ford cleared it and was quickly alongside the Lincoln. Despite its quick takeoff it couldn't outrun Bolan's reckless pace. He eased the bus into the rear of the Lincoln until he felt the sickening grind of metal on metal, then pushed the car into the oncoming lane of traffic. The driver of the Lincoln tried to brake hard, but Bolan stood on his brakes to keep himself alongside it. Then the Lincoln driver accelerated in an attempt to slip out of Bolan's grasp, but the soldier wouldn't let it happen. He rammed the bus into the Lincoln and ran it off the road into a field of weeds and small trees.

The Lincoln handled well even on rough roads, but it would have taken a four-wheel-drive vehicle sitting on extra-high wheels to traverse the dips, pits and hillocks that made up the field. It bounced and crashed through several raises in the landscape before coming to an unsteady halt. The front end was crumpled. Bolan spun the bus as he brought it to a squeaky halt in the wrong lane of traffic. The tail end jutted into the oncoming lane, where the wall of the hill had been blasted out to accommodate the road.

Bolan wasn't concerned about maintaining the traffic flow into and out of the São Paulo suburbs at the moment. He had to contend with getting Andrei Sheknovi out of that limousine alive. He wished he had a sniper weapon of some kind. All he had was the big H&K assault weapon. Changing out the empty magazine, he laid the barrel against the lower windowframe in the now empty front windshield frame of the bus and triggered a burst into the rear of the limousine, bursting the right rear tire with a rush of air. The limousine responded with a flash of white reverse lights, and the wheels spun. The tires were run-flats. They wobbled but held up even as the driver forced them to grind against the tough soil and yank the front end of the Lincoln off the pimple of earth that had jacked up its front end. The driver whipped the wheel and dragged the Lincoln to the left, spinning it, then it crunched to a halt. Bolan and the driver of the vehicle were suddenly face-to-face, just a thin pane of glass and a dozen feet of empty air separating them.

The Executioner aimed the weapon directly at the driver. The burst that struck the windshield impacted with high-pitched ricochets that flew away.

Going after the glass was a waste of his time and ammo. Bolan thumbed a 40 mm shrapnel round into the HK79 launcher and deposited the grenade on the ground in front of the limousine before crouching for cover. The bomb detonated with a ringing metallic impact, and when he rose to his feet again he spotted lots of tiny rips and tears in the hood and body panels of the Lincoln. He'd accomplished more than ruining the paint job, though. A wisp of vapor rose from somewhere inside. At least one of the flying pieces of metal shrapnel had wormed its way through a gap in the armor shielding of the engine and found some sort of component inside to damage.

Bolan's satisfaction was fleeting. The limousine powered forward without appearing to have lost any speed or capability, twisting away from the bus and heading toward the highway. The soldier didn't have time to trigger another round before the limo reached the road and was gone.

He climbed through the opening where the windshield had been, crossed the hood of the bus in a stride and landed on the ground on both feet.

"Sarge, you okay?" Grimaldi radioed.

"Jack, they got away. Stay on them. Stay high. I'm going to see about acquiring a quicker set of wheels."

Slinging the H&K on his shoulder, he headed for the road, where a gathering of cars had bottlenecked in one of the tight places between blasted outcroppings. As he approached, the curiosity of the onlookers turned to terror and the people began to shout and maneuver their vehicles for an escape. Confusion reigned, and there were several crashes as cars and trucks slammed into one another.

Bolan held out his hands, low and palm up, to show he meant no harm. If any of the people saw the gesture, they ignored it. The vehicles in the rear were backing away and tearing up the mountain road. Others were honking for passage. None of the drivers gave the others an inch of leeway. Everyone was determined to be the first one out of there. When it became apparent to the drivers at the front of the pack that they weren't going anywhere soon, they abandoned their vehicles and piled onto the rear of a flatbed pickup as it tore between two smaller cars, losing rusty paint on body sides.

At the front of the group, a man on a large motorcycle was revving his engine impotently as he tried to worm his way through the crowd of other vehicles. The soldier knew this was the tool he was in need of. He approached the man, who panicked and jumped off the bike without even turning it off. He joined those fleeing the bottleneck and managed to catch up to the flatbed, where he was hauled on by the others.

That saved Bolan the time and energy of appropriating the bike. He muscled the motorcycle onto its wheels, finding the machine wasn't even stalled. Putting a leg over the seat, he evaluated his new acquisition with an experimental twist of the accelerator.

It turned out to be a Honda Valkyrie Interstate, which had a 1520cc six-cylinder engine that was huge and powerful. It purred with the sound of a well-maintained piece of machinery. Bolan gave a mental nod of thanks to the departed owner and shifted the vehicle into gear, standing to ease the bumps as he manipulated the motorcycle through the weed-filled field and around the school bus. Then he was on the asphalt again, feeling the potholes in the road turn to a well-cushioned vibration as he dragged the bike effortlessly through its gears and up to highway speeds. His confidence in the bike grew as he zigzagged it experimentally, feeling its tires adhering tightly to the surface. He pushed it harder, relaxing into the state of constant alertness that would be required to carry him along this dangerous mountain road at something like double the posted speed limit.

"Sarge, you still with me?"

"Jack, I've found a new set of wheels. Two instead of four this time. I'm coming up fast on our friends."

"They're still on the main highway, but I can see it splits about a quarter mile in front of us. Hang on—looks like they're taking the right-hand fork in the road."

"Affirmative. Got me on visual yet?"

"That's a negative. Wait a second. There you are.

At least I think that's you," Grimaldi said. "Give me a sign."

Bolan veered the Valkyrie in a wide weaving pattern that would be visible even to a helicopter watching from a few thousand feet up.

"Yeah, I got that," Grimaldi said. "You're just a couple klicks back. You'll see the fork in the road coming up quick."

The soldier didn't answer as he veered into the oncoming lane and back again in a lightning-fast move that took him around a puttering Chevrolet sedan, then leaned into the long, slow curve as the road split. A glance at the wheel told him he was closing in on a hundred miles per hour. Soon he'd see the Lincoln, and he'd have to be ready to act. The vehicle was cruising along at just half Bolan's speed and even that was pushing the practical limits of the punctured run-flat tires.

He needed to disable the vehicle without killing its occupants, and he extracted the tools for such a job from his combat harness. He spotted the Lincoln. Maintaining his speed, he came up hard and fast on its rear end, then swerved around it as one of the rear windows slid open. Bolan slowed and turned back, meeting the limo driver's gaze again. The driver's jaw dropped. There was no question that he recognized Bolan. The soldier sped up and lobbed the high-explosive grenade underhanded behind him. He heard the explosion and felt the sudden rush of flying air and debris against his back.

The Lincoln never had a chance. It was a quarter of a second behind the blast, and it drove directly into the cloud of debris, its front end slamming into a newly created pit in the pavement. The front wheels dropped into the hole and crashed. The tires burst apart when the enormous inertia slammed them into the pavement lip and forced the mangled front end out of the hole, tearing up more of the street surface with it. Then the back end collapsed into the pit, blowing the good tire, ripping the deflated tire to shreds and removing the exhaust system. The protective steel shell moved upward into the body of the car, crushing the drive shaft and dislodging the transmission housing. The pile of mangled metal that continued pushing its way out of the pit was far different from the Lincoln Town Car that had entered it.

Bolan braked the big motorcycle and took it into a sideways skid that brought him to a quick halt, then rolled at a cautious pace toward the Lincoln as it shuddered to a noisy stop. The red smear that opaqued the fragmented windshield told him the driver was out of commission.

A side door burst open with the sound of screeching metal. The barrel of the FN FAL landed in the crook of the door and targeted Bolan, who skirted across the pavement and approached from the other side of the vehicle, out of its range. The Lincoln was dead in the water, but how was he going to get Sheknovi out safely?

"Striker, new arrivals coming up fast behind you," Grimaldi called. "I'd say it's reinforcements on their way."

Bolan swore silently when a pair of Land Rover sport utility vehicles appeared on the highway, approaching at high speed. The figure in the door of the Lincoln used the distraction to his advantage, exposing himself over the top of the car long enough to fire the FN FAL, and Bolan dropped to the ground to avoid it, then bounded upright again, triggering the G3-TG3. The rounds skipped off the roof of the Lincoln like flat stones on the surface of a calm pond, but the shooter was out of sight. The twin Land Rovers braked hard and laid streaks of black rubber on the pavement before stopping in a nose-to-nose formation on the road. Their side windows opened simultaneously and a gunner appeared in each with a weapon.

If Bolan hadn't known better, he would have sworn they'd rehearsed the attack. But these were just well-trained, skillful mercenaries. They unleashed twin volleys of automatic fire from their Brazilian IMBEL MD-1 submachine guns. Bolan put the Lincoln between himself and the harsh fire, then found himself stuck. The gunfire peppered the road just an arm's length away on either side of him. He couldn't budge without being cut down.

Bolan thumbed a high-explosive round into the grenade launcher mounted beneath the H&K and aimed it at the clouds. It took off like a child's toy rocket, went almost straight into the afternoon sky, then arced slightly and dropped. It was a tough shot, but Bolan had achieved it almost perfectly. When the round hit the roof of the green Land Rover, it erupted into a ball of flame, quickly reached the gas tank, and burst with another huge blast of fire. The black Land Rover had been moving before the grenade went off. Maybe the driver heard the firing of the grenade launcher and knew it for what it was. The tongues of flame from the Land Rover's twin followed it, reaching out as if seeking an embrace. A blast of flame like a giant hand slapped into the rear of the fleeing vehicle, engulfed it momentarily, then dissipated.

The Land Rover swung around the Lincoln and homed in on Bolan, who unleashed a 40 mm buckshot round at the front end of the SUV from less than thirty feet. The blast scraped paint off the body panels and bounced off the windows, but the damage was negligible—the Land Rover was armored. Bolan dropped to the ground and rolled when the SUV roared over his previous position. He came to a crashing stop when he hit the front tire of the Lincoln and twisted hard and fast, feeling the skin of his torso and arms tear against the rough road surface. Leveling the H&K at the vehicle, he drilled a long, low line of shots along its lower body and undercarriage. The Land Rover whipped around in a hard circle, halting briefly, then sped toward him again. Bolan unleathered his .44 Magnum Desert Eagle handgun as he inched closer to the Lincoln, tucking part of his body underneath it.

The Land Rover driver was determined to take out the soldier, and he wasn't afraid of damaging the equipment in the process. He drove directly into the side of the Lincoln, muscling alongside it, body panels grinding together with a loud sound of distressed, tearing armor plates.

Bolan reached under the Lincoln with his free hand, grabbed the rim of an overheated piece of metal and dragged himself farther underneath the limo as the wide, off-road tires rolled over his previous position. Bolan ignored the sudden eruption of burning pain in his hand, firing into the underside of the Land Rover as it passed within inches of him. Then a piece of metal ripped off by the onslaught of the Land Rover tore through Bolan's sleeve and sliced into his forearm.

The wall of noise ceased and the Land Rover was gone. Bolan knew it would be back soon, and he knew he was in a very bad place.

A noise close by the soldier drew his attention as he tried to free himself from underneath the Lincoln. One of the limo's occupants was on his knees, dropping to the ground. He reached under the vehicle and triggered a handgun blindly. The close-proximity blasts came one after the other, and Bolan knew the shooter would score soon enough. He fought for a response from his injured hand, pushed it between himself and the undercarriage of the Lincoln with an explosion of pain and triggered once. There was a shout from the shooter, who collapsed to the ground, then jumped up and scrambled into the interior of the Lincoln.

The time to leave was now. Bolan crawled out from under the Town Car and struggled to his feet, grabbing the fallen G3-TG3 and searching for the Land Rover. It had been waiting for him, and the tires smoked when it accelerated at him again. The soldier threw himself backward onto the hood of the Lincoln in the split second prior to the impact of the Land Rover, then crashed to the ground on the opposite side as the SUV careened away.

Bolan glanced at the H&K, which was all it took to ascertain the weapon was junked. It had to have been run over, and there was a noticeable bend to its barrel. He dropped it, adopted a two-handed shooter's stance and fired the Desert Eagle again and again into the oncoming SUV. When it was just a couple of paces away from him he jumped out of its

way and heard the sickening impact of machine-gun
fire coming from the rear of the vehicle and crunching off the asphalt around him. He hit the ground in
a judo fall and rolled hard into the weeds and undergrowth on the shoulder. Behind him the Land
Rover screeched to a halt and the machine-gun fire
chopped into the vegetation, shredding it and filling
the air with green confetti. Bolan lay where he had
landed, waiting to feel the rounds find him and chew
into his flesh.

But he had wormed his way deep into the undergrowth. The shooter couldn't see him. That saved
him for the moment. When he heard the shooting
grind to a halt and judged the shooter was changing
his magazine, he made a break for it, jumping to his
feet and charging into the deep weeds and low trees.
More gunfire followed him—this time from the gunner in the limo with the FN FAL. Bolan slipped into
cover behind the biggest tree trunk he could find.

And then he was stuck. He heard the sounds of
urgent voices, the slamming of doors, and all the
while 5.56 mm rounds from the limo popped against
the trunk of the soldier's tree. He was outgunned and
trapped.

The Land Rover roared to life and sped away
down the mountain.

CHAPTER THIRTEEN

Santos, Brazil

The Bell 430 helicopter sat in the sky over the Brazilian shore almost forty miles southeast of São Paulo. Below it the shore was rocky and forbidding at the point where an arm of the mountain range, running parallel with the shore, had veered off course, heading directly into the South Atlantic Ocean. The cliff edge was shattered and broken. The rocks and debris of its destruction littered the waters at the shore, and the sea thrashed and churned angrily among them.

The house had been constructed directly in the midst of the rocky destruction. Big concrete pylons among the boulders supported the sterile lines of the steel-and-glass home. Around the house was a balcony made of steel mesh that would have been more appropriate inside a large industrial warehouse. Several big potted plants had been arranged on the balcony in an attempt to soften the look, but they had quickly died in the harsh, salty air. Now they were brown, decaying vegetation left to rot.

Jack Grimaldi was chewing gum and getting a crick in his neck from looking down on the shoreline mansion, said to belong to a South American mercenary named Henrique Goncalves. This was no freedom fighter. He had no political sensitivities. He took the jobs that paid well—those demanding a high level of military expertise. He had prospered in his line of work, as his extravagant base of operations attested.

Stony Man Farm had identified Goncalves as the mastermind behind the capture of Andrei Sheknovi. When digital images of the dead mercenaries left behind at Oak Development were transmitted to the Farm, they were quickly identified. All of them were known to be employees of Goncalves. It didn't take long for Goncalves's associates to likewise be matched up to the abandoned Lincoln Town Car.

Grimaldi had kept the gunners at bay and picked up Bolan from the battle scene soon after the departure of the Land Rover, which disappeared overland. The soldier had refused medical treatment and quickly took care of the gash on his wrist himself, sewing it with needle and surgical thread from his first-aid kit and disinfecting his numerous abrasions and minor cuts with alcohol and adhesive bandages. As far as he was concerned, the battle wasn't yet over. He wasn't going to surrender himself to a doctor's care until the fighting was done. Performing his own first aid meant he could be sure to apply bandages and gauze where they wouldn't interfere with his range of movement.

The Stony Man pilot winced when he thought of it. He'd rarely seen Mack Bolan as angry as he had been that afternoon. The Executioner didn't take kindly to his own personal failures—and he considered the kidnapping of Andrei Sheknovi a failure.

The intelligence provided by Aaron Kurtzman at Stony Man Farm was less than one-hundred-percent reliable. There was no guarantee that Sheknovi—and his missing wife and son—were being held at the Goncalves oceanfront home south of the city of Santos, Brazil, but it was all they had to go on. Stony Man had been tracking any and all activity undertaken by every suspected and verified Kabat associate and business entity. The *Wamphyr,* a Cayman-based yacht belonging to a Kabat shipping company suspected of fronting arms smuggling, was on its way south into Brazilian waters at full throttle.

"It's a circumstantial connection," Kurtzman had warned them.

"But it's all we've got to go on," Bolan said quickly. "And it makes sense that they'll need a way to smuggle Sheknovi out of Brazil. They can't walk him on board a commercial flight."

Three hours later, Bolan was on the ground while Grimaldi kept an eye on the goings-on from the air. It was nearly dusk. The *Wamphyr* had come to anchor less than ninety miles offshore, due east of the Goncalves base of operations. Lights began to go on, but Grimaldi spotted no movement outside.

"Come in, Sarge," Grimaldi said into the radio.

"Go ahead, Jack," Bolan answered.

"Sorry to tell you this, but I'm running out of fuel. I can stay in this position for maybe another twenty minutes, then I'll have to call it quits."

"Understood. Do what you can."

Grimaldi didn't like this at all. Why were they sitting on their thumbs down there? His hands were getting tired and tense from the constant strain of holding the helicopter in a hovering position.

He really didn't have a choice, and he knew that. He needed a certain amount of fuel to get himself to the nearest landing strip where he could refuel. That was eight miles off.

Maybe the mercenaries were planning on making their move after dark, which meant Grimaldi should go refuel right now. He could get to the Santos airfield, gas up and get back here in under half an hour, right about the time it was really getting dark.

Then he saw a strip of light appear on the surface of the ocean at the shoreline. He raised the binoculars to his eyes and examined it closely. The boathouse doors were opening.

The boathouse was a garagelike structure built right on the water at a point where the sand had been dredged for depth, allowing Goncalves to bring in his boats.

The watercraft that emerged from the boathouse was narrow and close to the water, with the profile of a Mayan ceremonial dagger. The forty-nine-foot Wellcraft Scarab Meteor 5000 was navy blue from Grimaldi's overhead perspective, with black trim and upholstery. It drifted out of the boathouse and bobbed in the water as if lifeless, a small turbulence emitting from its rear end. Grimaldi saw two figures above deck. One of them waved through the closing doors of the boathouse, then the vessel motored away from shore, carefully sticking to the middle of the dredged-out waterway until it was fifty feet from the rocks. Then it powered up, aiming directly into the eastern horizon.

Grimaldi reported the activity to Bolan. "They're moving fast, Sarge," the pilot said as he followed the powerboat from a few thousand feet up and back.

"They've got nice flat seas offshore, and I'll bet they're pushing fifty land miles per hour. I'll bet they've got a couple of 502 horsepower engines under the hood."

"Not a problem, Jack. I'm after them," Bolan said.

"I'll stay with them until you join us."

BOLAN FED GAS to the Yamaha water jet engines and maneuvered his watercraft in a slow, tight circle that pointed it away from the rented wooden dock a few miles north of the Goncalves oceanfront house. The strange delta-wing craft hardly seemed to move at first. The Yamaha power plant—designed for personal watercraft—whined at high revs, overburdened by the large weight of the craft and the incoming tide it was fighting against. Bolan was patient at the controls. As far as he was concerned, he had a large time cushion. No need to push his watercraft. Not yet.

The news from Stony Man had indicated that Goncalves supplemented his mercenary work with some illegal import-export operations out of his oceanfront home. He also had some reputation as an owner of high-end seacraft, usually outfitted to travel faster than the Brazilian coastal law-enforcement agencies' coastal transports.

Which meant Bolan had to have something even faster than that if he wanted to catch up with them. His request to Barbara Price for equipment meeting those needs had stumped her for all of an hour.

Finally, she had called in a few favors in the Brazilian defense ministry. She made a lightning-fast long-distance agreement with a yacht dealer in Santos, who had rushed the watercraft to the pickup location an hour later. Bolan had found it waiting for him at an abandoned private dock outside the city.

Close to shore it was a slow-moving, sluggish boat. Its hull flopped on top of the water like a big dead bird. That all changed as Bolan moved it away from shore and powered up the main engine, a Subaru V4 225-horsepower aircraft engine. The single propeller pushed the craft forward at speeds that lifted it out of the water gradually. Then the Flarecraft left the ocean entirely, shedding seawater as it increased speed and altitude.

The Flarecraft was a modified version of the L-325 commercial ground-effect craft. The ground-effect phenomenon, in which a high-pressure air cushion developed under the wings of a low-flying body, like seagulls flying effortlessly close to the surface of the ocean, gave the hybrid watercraft its unusual capabilities. Bolan quickly brought the Flarecraft up to a steady seventy-five miles per hour, riding at the optimal altitude of about four yards above the ocean's surface. At just three-quarters of its maximum speed, he conserved fuel while still gaining on his prey quickly. Soon he heard from Grimaldi again.

"Got you spotted on infrared, Sarge," he radioed. "You're about three and a half miles behind Goncalves's boat and closing fast. They're running with a yellow taillight."

The dusk had become night, and Bolan found himself looking into a dark gray world. The stars were visible, clear and bright this far away from any metropolitan center, but the sea was an inky slate gray. Bolan had disabled the running lights on the Flarecraft, and he flew through the night like some silent flying reptile prowling the shore of a prehistoric ocean.

Then he saw it—the faint yellow pinprick of light far out into the sea and coming closer rapidly. He reduced power to the Subaru V4 until he guessed he had matched the speed of the Scarab.

"Stony Base, what's their ETA at Kabat's yacht?" Bolan asked.

A moment later Barbara Price spoke over the headphones through the Flarecraft's satellite uplink. "They'll rendezvous with the *Wamphyr* in another twenty-two minutes, Striker. What's the plan?"

"They won't even know I'm there," Bolan said. "I'll let them think that for a while. When their guard is down I'll board the yacht and find Sheknovi."

"Fuel?"

"This craft has extra tanks, at the expense of passenger space," Bolan explained. "I can probably go four hundred miles or more."

"That big boat has got to have radar," Grimaldi said.

"This boat's delta-wing shape has a natural stealthlike radar signature," Bolan said. "Even defense radar has a hard time picking it up. Kabat's crew might spot something on the screen if their hardware's very up-to-date, but it sure won't look like a boat. They'll think they've got a defect or ghosting in their system."

"Maybe they'll think there's a UFO on their ass," Grimaldi said, clearly delighted with the prospect.

"I'll make them wish it was just aliens," Bolan replied.

"Unlike you, I'm on a very limited fuel supply, Sarge. Sorry, but I've got to abandon you."

"Understood, Jack," Bolan answered. "Thanks for keeping an eye on things."

"No problem. I'll be listening in."

Grimaldi signed off and Bolan knew the Bell 430 was heading inland to the landing field in Santos. The plan was for Grimaldi to fuel up there, then stand by. Stony Man Farm would keep him apprised of Bolan's progress at sea. When and if the time came, he would be ready to fly out and extract the soldier and, with luck, Sheknovi.

Until he got the word, he would have to sit there with his thumb up his ass, as he had described it to Bolan. He wasn't happy about it, but it was part of his job.

Bolan would have to go in alone, and, when the time was right for the kill, he would know it, and he would be ready.

GONCALVES REDUCED the tremendous speed of the Wellcraft Scarab's 575-horsepower engines when the lights of the *Wamphyr* loomed in the deepening darkness. The craft was a custom-built, 115-foot motor yacht, ostensibly used by Roger Kabat for entertaining corporate clients. The boat had three large suites and six cabins and could sleep as many as twenty people. There were two large lounges, a meeting room, a dining room and other facilities designed for giving guests all the amenities of a world-class luxury cruise ship. A small landing craft rode at a custom docking facility near the rear of the vessel, and a four-passenger Hughes helicopter resided on the topside landing pad.

Goncalves had been a guest aboard the *Wamphyr* years before when he had purchased an extensive supply of military hardware from Kabat. The man had been clearly impressed with Goncalves's organization. Still, neither had expected to have an opportunity to work together. But when Kabat required assistance in Goncalves's part of the world, he had been quick to strike a deal with the Brazilian mercenary. Goncalves expected to outfit much of his small army on the credit Kabat was extending him.

But the grim reality was that both of them had underestimated the response to Andrei Sheknovi's kidnapping. As a result, Goncalves's army was much reduced from its former size, a fact he intended to discuss at length with Kabat.

Goncalves handed the wheel of the craft to José Oliveira, his second in command. As Oliveira pulled the Scarab against the rear of the parked motor yacht, Goncalves crossed the front deck and stepped onto the dive deck. He ignored the yacht crew, who had been expecting the Scarab to tie up. "Where's Kabat?" he demanded loudly.

The crew looked at one another in a sort of silent dismay, then toward the sliding glass doors opening from the rear lounge, where a towering, lanky, dark-skinned man was emerging in a silk robe, of all things, tied around his waist, over a pair of what might be satin pants. The pants were a solid burgundy, but the robe was a hideous paisley mishmash of colors.

Goncalves thought the man looked like a playboy from the 1970s. As if on cue, the robed man produced a long, curved ebony pipe and clenched it in his teeth. If he hadn't been so thoroughly enraged, Goncalves would have laughed out loud.

"I'm Nuala Leeke, Mr. Goncalves," the man said

in an accent that came from one of the Caribbean islands. "We met here in 1997."

"I remember you," Goncalves said, biting off the words and ignoring the hand Leeke was offering him. "Where's Kabat?"

Leeke was clearly offended by Goncalves's lack of civility. "Mr. Kabat is not aboard—"

"What? Where the hell is he?"

"He's been involved in projects elsewhere," Leeke retorted, his voice getting frostier every moment.

"I was told I'd be dealing with him."

"I'm sorry—"

"I'll bet you are." Goncalves turned and waved to Oliveira, aboard the Scarab.

"What are you doing?" Leeke was losing his cool, and the edge was plain in his voice.

"Leaving."

"What about the business you have to conduct with Mr. Kabat?"

"When Mr. Kabat is here, I'll open the negotiations."

"There is nothing to negotiate, Mr. Goncalves. You made an agreement with Mr. Kabat, and he'll expect you to stand by the agreement."

"Mr. Kabat and I came to an agreement based on specific information he provided me, Mr. Leeke," Goncalves said, turning to face the tall man as the Scarab approached the landing deck. "That information was bad. Kabat either doesn't know his ass from a hole in the ground or he outright lied. Which one is it, Leeke? Stupidity or outright deception?"

Mr. Leeke was clearly aghast. He never got the chance to express his indignation.

"When Mr. Kabat is prepared to renegotiate our agreement based on the reality of the situation—which includes the loss of several of my men—then I'll be prepared to hand over Andrei Sheknovi. Tell him that. And tell him I refuse to deal with his Jamaican faggots in the future."

It wasn't until Goncalves was aboard and the Scarab was pulling away from the rear of the huge motor yacht that Leeke managed to reclaim his self-control enough to put together a coherent sentence.

"Mr. Goncalves!" he exclaimed. "Please wait here and I will try to raise a video uplink with Mr. Kabat. You'll be able to negotiate with him one-on-one."

Goncalves paused as if considering this for a few seconds. Let orgy boy stew. He was pissed off and he held the cards. He was going to get some groveling done for his benefit before he decided to cooperate. "I'll wait here. When Kabat is on the line and waiting I'll reboard."

When he reboarded the *Wamphyr* five minutes later, Goncalves was taken through the lounge, decorated with a trio of young women in revealing evening wear, to a small parlor with a video screen mounted in the wall. A tuxedoed steward entered to present Goncalves with a rum collins with lime—which had been his drink of choice when he had visited the boat years ago. He waved it away. He wasn't going to dull his senses tonight.

The screen was blank. "I told you I would come aboard when Kabat was ready to talk," Goncalves said.

"He's standing by, sir," Leeke replied.

"It doesn't look like it."

"Sir—"

"I'm not waiting for him, do you understand? He's gonna wait for me! I've got what he wants, not the other way around. I want him on this screen in the next fifteen seconds with an apology for keeping me waiting, or I walk and I do not come back."

Leeke nodded and grabbed the phone receiver placed next to the video monitor, speaking into it in a low, pleading voice for a few seconds. Then the screen came to life with Roger Kabat's face, plainly agitated yet attempting to keep a polite and cool demeanor.

"Mr. Goncalves. I'm sorry I've kept you waiting."

"You really screwed me over, you son of a bitch. I hope you're ready to pay for your stupidity."

Kabat said nothing for a moment. His teeth were grinding together. Goncalves liked that.

"I was under the impression that we had already agreed on terms, Mr. Goncalves," Kabat stated.

"The terms we agreed on were voided when I found out how bad your information was. You sent me and my men in on a fool's errand. Now a third of my men are dead."

"And you blame me?"

"If you'd given me adequate information at the outset, I would have been prepared for an aggressive armed response. You said this would be easy in and easy out. You lied."

"I did not lie, Mr.—"

"Then you were too ignorant to know what the real situation was."

Kabat was fighting for control.

"One or the other, Kabat," Goncalves said.

"Maybe there was a stronger military reaction than the facts indicated."

"Wrong."

"What do you want me to say, Mr. Goncalves?"

"I want you to tell me how sorry you are for not having the intelligence to anticipate the nature of this venture."

"All right, Mr. Goncalves," Kabat said through his clenched jaw as he stewed on the double meaning of the words. "I admit it. The blame for this disaster rests entirely with me."

"Good," Goncalves stated with a self-satisfied smirk that he made sure Kabat could see. He finally sat and crossed his legs, looking relaxed. "Then we have a starting point for our new negotiations."

CHAPTER FOURTEEN

Bolan's rebreather hid the bubbles from his underwater breathing apparatus as he crept along eight feet below the surface of the ocean, watching the glow of the *Wamphyr* become brighter above him. The Flarecraft was anchored many hundreds of yards outside the reach of the well-illuminated yacht, and Bolan had made a long, stealthy submerged approach. As far as he could tell, no one knew he was in the area. The lack of response from the yacht told him the radar had failed to detect the delta-wing craft.

He had been toying with the idea of bringing the Scarab to a halt en route to the giant pleasure yacht, but he'd been unable to conceive of a plan that would accomplish it without killing all on board, including Andrei Sheknovi. The lives of an innocent man and probably his wife and child, as well, weren't sacrifices he was prepared to make.

Stealth was the tool that would allow him to achieve his goal. Like the victims of some deranged serial killer, the people aboard the *Wamphyr* were about to find themselves cast into an immensely dangerous situation—locked in a closed environment with a determined Executioner.

He rose to the surface when the black mass of the

yacht was lurking above him, outlined in the glow of her lights. He broke the surface of the calm sea with only his mask, determining where he was along the 115-foot length of the motor yacht. He found himself a quarter of the length from the rear, which put him less than twenty feet away from his goal, a boarding ladder set near the master suite balcony, a private entrance and egress point. Bolan had studied the photos and plans for the yacht in detail. Kurtzman had made easy work of accessing them from the shipyard that had been commissioned to construct the vessel.

Theoretically, Roger Kabat used the suite when aboard the yacht. Bolan doubted he was there now. He would be keeping himself in a more secure hiding place while he engineered his operation. He wouldn't be anywhere so obvious as this floating palace.

But if he was on board, Bolan would see that as a happy bonus.

He pulled himself out of the ocean and hung on the aluminum ladder, inching his way up to the private balcony. The master suite was dark, the sliding glass doors locked.

Bolan stripped off his wet suit and unpacked his waterproof pack. He dried his face and hands, then quickly applied combat cosmetics designed to hide him in the darkness. He donned a vest of webbing and quickly checked out his lead weapon for the probe: a Heckler & Koch MP-5 K-PDW submachine gun, a shorter version of the MP-5, with a detachable sound suppressor and a side-folding stock.

Bolan was no stranger to the MP-5, the SMG used around the world by special operations groups and antiterrorist forces, including U.S. Navy SEALs. The

MP-5 fired a 9 mm round from a thirty-round magazine. In its tactical sling, the MP-5 K-PDW could be dropped for hands-free capability but was immediately accessible should he need it. And Bolan intended to need it.

He outfitted the combat webbing with spare magazines, as well as an extensive selection of incendiaries, bladed weapons and his handguns. Then he was prepared to make his incursion.

His first stop would be belowdecks. His entrance point had been chosen in part for its easy access to one of the utility entrances into the engine level of the ship. He picked his way through the door into the master suite without effort—the lock was designed to keep the door closed in rolling seas more than to keep out intruders—and crossed the master suite to the hallway. The peephole showed an empty hallway. Bolan opened the door and crossed to the door to the utility companionway in three long strides. He saw no one.

Fifteen seconds later he was standing in the engine room, an expansive, low-ceilinged utility level so crowded with machinery and tanks it would have terrorized a claustrophobe. The room was empty of activity. The engines were silent. Only the generator ran, a more economical way of providing energy for the yacht when at anchor than running the engines. And the generator didn't require supervision. The mechanical staff wasn't present.

Bolan planted his explosive charges carefully, where they wouldn't be found. It took him less than a minute to place each of the preconfigured packages. After that, he simply reached over and yanked a cable out of its generator socket.

The generator continued to run, but every light on board the *Wamphyr* faded and died.

KABAT'S IMAGE COLLAPSED and disappeared like a dissipating spirit. The lights in the meeting room followed momentarily.

"What's going on?" Goncalves demanded.

Leeke was as surprised as the Brazilian mercenary. He turned his head from side to side, unable to believe he was suddenly immersed in total blackness. Then he spotted a strip of light from under the door. He stumbled out of his chair and pulled the door open. The lounge, unlike the meeting room, was equipped with a battery-powered emergency light, which cast a harsh white glare on the room. Kabat's on-staff whores were standing in the middle of the room, looking worried.

"Relax," Leeke said over his shoulder to the Brazilian mercenary leader. "We've just had a power outage."

"This happen often?" Goncalves sneered.

"Occasionally," Leeke lied. "When we're at anchor we depend on the generator for power. Sometimes it fails. It's no big deal."

Goncalves emerged into the lounge. The worried look on the faces of the women concerned him.

"I'm going to go wait in my boat," he stated. "Let me know when you have Kabat back on the line."

"Hold on," Leeke said. "Your business with Mr. Kabat was more or less concluded, was it not?"

"Except for the matter of the delivery of the cash."

Leeke nodded. "I understand. I have the authority

to tell you Mr. Kabat will deliver the cash to any account you desire. Including a Cayman Island or Swiss account, which I think you would find far safer than a Brazilian bank account."

"I don't have accounts in either the Caymans or Switzerland," Goncalves said.

Leeke shrugged and raised his palms, wearing an ingratiating smile. "Mr. Kabat will be pleased to open one for you and send you all the documentation you need to access it."

Goncalves nodded after a moment. "I'm going to trust Kabat on this," he said. "He wouldn't try to rip me off."

"No, sir." Leeke's smile faded. "Mr. Kabat would never try to rip you off."

"I'd spread the word if he did. Globally. Nobody would trust him. He wouldn't be able to sell handguns to street punks anywhere in the world."

Leeke looked overserious. "Mr. Goncalves, I *promise* you...."

"Fine. Whatever." Goncalves headed out of the lounge.

WITH THE ACTUATION of the charging handle, Bolan pushed the bolt home and chambered a round into the MP-5 K-PDW. Then he headed topside in the cold glow of the emergency lighting system.

The man who came through the door wore an engineer's uniform and the shoulder holster of a killer. He was both. As a member of the staff aboard Kabat's vessel, he was experienced in dual roles. Bolan knew this fact well. The Stony Man report on Kabat's staff read like a murderer's *Who's Who*.

Therefore, when the time came, Bolan didn't hesitate. He brought the man to a sudden stop on the companionway with the end of the suppressor pressed against his chest. The man glared at him in the strange light, his eyeballs in the shadow of his brow. Then he moved, lithe and quick, brushing the barrel of the H&K away and grabbing for his holster. Only then did the killer realize what kind of man he was up against. Bolan slipped the Beretta 93-R into view like a cartoon character pulling a giant hammer out of nowhere. The 93-R triggered a suppressed tri-burst that crashed through the engineer's chest cavity and dropped him before his hand reached the holster.

Bolan stepped over the corpse as it slithered down the steps, slipping into the hallway and making his way to the front of the vessel, looking for the bridge. He found it, pushing through the doors without hesitation.

Two officers were on staff, looking bored. One was stretched out in a chair holding a silent radio to his ears. The other was staring idly into the open sea. He turned to look at the intruder, then jumped to his feet, grabbing for the weapon holstered on his belt. Bolan aimed the Beretta. The first mate froze, his fingers inches from his weapon. Bolan moved the muzzle of the 93-R a fraction of an inch, but it was enough to tell the mate what to do. He dropped his hands to his sides.

"Captain?" the mate croaked.

The captain glanced up, wrinkled his brow at his mate's strange behavior, then sat up and turned in his seat. Bolan had deliberately stood directly in front of the emergency light that illuminated the bridge so that he couldn't be recognized. The captain knew by the weapon that the man was an intruder. He snapped the button on his radio. "Hines! We've got—"

The Beretta coughed a single round that crashed through the radio, chopped the captain's hand and slammed into the wide bridge window. The captain collapsed into his chair, moaning and writhing, holding his wounded hand. Bolan pulled out a pair of plastic handcuffs and tossed them to the first mate.

"Secure him," the soldier ordered. "There." He indicated a wooden hand railing that ran across the back wall of the room, well out of reach of the bridge electronics.

The first mate's face wrinkled into a furrow of confusion. "I don't know how to work these!"

"You'd better figure it out fast."

The first mate regarded the Beretta 93-R for all of two seconds. Then he quickly figured out the plastic handcuffs and managed to secure his captain's hands around the rail.

"Now the feet. His and yours."

The first mate secured the captain's feet, then his own. Bolan secured the mate's hands, then checked the captain's for tightness. He pulled a detonator and a chunk of plastique out of his pack and molded it to a contour of the primary control panel. He turned on the receiver. The tiny red light glowed.

"I'm staying on the ship for the foreseeable future," Bolan told them. "If at any time I hear the engines of this vessel start, I press the button here." He showed them the tiny remote control in his hands. "That plastique will take out the control panel as well as the rest of the bridge. Understand?"

"Wait a second!" the mate objected frantically. "Anybody can start the engines! They don't even have to be started from this bridge! We can't stop them.''

''You'd better hope not.''

Bolan spotted a flash of light and watched out the rear window of the bridge, which offered an impressive 360-degree view of the *Wamphyr*, as Goncalves's Scarab came to life, its running lights glowing from end to end. The light showed him the activity going on there: a trio of prisoners was being marched from belowdecks on the Scarab and onto the rear of the *Wamphyr*. One of them was clearly a woman, another a child, a man in the rear. This was the Sheknovi family.

There was a flurry of movement as one of the men grabbed Sheknovi by the collar and dragged him up the steps onto the rear landing deck of the motor yacht. Sheknovi tripped and collapsed onto the deck. Bolan could see the figures on the deck laughing, although through the glass and from a distance he heard none of their voices—just the labored breathing of the wounded captain.

Bolan spotted a figure dressed differently from the others: a tall, gaunt man who seemed to be wearing some sort of flowing garment hanging down past his waist. That would be Nuala Leeke, one of Kabat's top-level lieutenants. He was standing in front of the young wife of the Russian researcher. Even in the erratic boat lights, Bolan could see that she was a beautiful woman, half Sheknovi's age, with flowing dark hair. The man in the robe suddenly grabbed her by the throat with one hand and yanked her blouse down to her waist with the other, exposing her breasts, her skin gleaming in the night. The woman tried to back away. Blindfolded, she ran into the gun-

ners gathered around her, screaming and crying. Her
husband was shouting indignantly. The mouths of the
killers were open in laughter. All of it was weird and
distant, like a hideous silent movie.

The woman collapsed onto the deck, sobbing.

Behind her, blindfolded and shackled and motion-
less in the shadows, the child stood listening to his
mother crying.

Bolan had seen enough.

THE SCARAB DRIFTED AWAY from the yacht and
came to life with a roar of its massive twin power
plants. The seas churned beneath it as if suddenly
coming to a boil, then the vessel shot away into the
night.

Leeke wasn't watching it go. He pointed to his
feet. "Cotte, go see what the hell is the problem
down there. I want the damn lights on!"

The man named Cotte jumped to obey. Jim Nivvo,
the unofficial head of security on the *Wamphyr,* gave
Deolinda Sheknovi a shove. She stumbled a few feet
and then stood still again, her entire body shivering.
"What should I do with them?"

"Put them in room three. They'll be staying
aboard," Leeke said. "Get the video system set up
in there."

"Got it." Nivvo put his hand on the woman's
back, lingering there just long enough to feel the soft
suppleness of her bare skin, then pushed her toward
the door. Reetz followed, holding the boy by the collar and half-carrying him to the door.

"Please don't hurt them," Andrei Sheknovi
begged.

"That's up to you," Leeke said. "Their fate is in

your hands one hundred percent, Andrei. They'll be treated humanely while you cooperate. As soon as you stop producing what we want, your woman becomes fair game to everyone on this boat. Understand? And the boy gets to watch it all.''

Sheknovi seemed frozen, then he nodded. "I'll do it. Whatever you want. Just keep them safe.''

Leeke barked a laugh. "Good! Then let's be off.''

He turned to the gathering of gunners milling on the landing deck. "Take him to the platform and keep him there.''

Three men marched up the companionway. Another pair followed Sheknovi, prodding him as he went with the muzzles of their weapons. When they reached the third landing there was a coughing noise, sustained and mechanical. The two figures in the lead went down on their faces, dying without knowing what hit them. The third man in the line recognized the sound and knew he was trapped. The gunner was in front of them. He couldn't go to the right or left, so he threw himself backward down the companionway, colliding with the prisoner and bowling over the guards behind him. They all tumbled down the steps to the second-level landing.

Bolan crossed the helicopter landing pad in two long strides, ignoring the pair he had just killed. Standing at the top of the stairs, he directed the MP-5 K-PDW into the mass of writhing bodies, but didn't fire. One of those men was Sheknovi, and in the darkness he couldn't distinguish the man from the others.

In his current position, the Executioner knew he was silhouetted against the comparative brightness of the night sky, and he pulled back just before a burst of autofire from the rear boarding deck slammed into the lip of the helicopter pad, slashing through the air where he had been standing and flying into the night sky.

"Get him down here!" Leeke shouted.

Bolan flopped onto the rough surface of the landing pad and sought targets on the boarding deck two stories down. Leeke appeared briefly, but Bolan couldn't get off a shot before the man disappeared. A pair of gunners stood in his view just long enough to trigger their pistols, but the soldier wasn't where they expected him to be and the rounds sailed far over his head. Bolan made good use of their moment of disorientation and took them out with a sustained burst from the MP-5 K-PDW.

The survivors guarding Sheknovi huddled close to him as they maneuvered down the steps. They were in full view of the assassin above them and had figured out that the Russian worked as a shield. Bolan pulled back as they commenced firing again. When the shooting stopped, they were gone.

LEEKE PUSHED HIS WAY into the lounge first, dragging Sheknovi by his shackled wrists. The whores huddled in a corner, crying and shouting. Leeke ignored them. He grabbed one of his men. "You! Go find Nivvo! He was taking the other prisoners to room three. Tell him to get the bitch and boy to the *Lupine* and move away from here. Get them out of gunshot range and open a video feed to the closed-circuit system. And tell him to move fast!"

The man exited the lounge and disappeared.

Something landed on the boarding deck outside the lounge with a controlled impact, heavy enough to be sensed. Leeke swore suddenly, realizing he had put himself in a highly dangerous situation. He was inside a room with an emergency light, fully exposed through the wide windows by the light, which also served to mirror the room's image and distort any shadow that might have otherwise been visible outside. A dangerous tactical error. Before he could warn the others the window shattered under the onslaught of machine-fired 9 mm rounds, which chopped into the man standing at Leeke's elbow. The Jamaican dived to the floor as his gunners returned fire. But they were carrying nothing more deadly than their handguns. There had never been a need for heavier weaponry on board the yacht.

A second man grunted when a vicious burst of fire cut into his stomach at the belt line and walked a bloody line up his torso. He dropped hard. Another man followed Leeke to the floor, leaving Andrei Sheknovi standing alone in the room, staring into his blindfold and saying nothing.

The gunfire came to an abrupt halt, the silence interrupted only by the tinkling of glass as pieces of the sliding door continued to drop. Then there was a snick of metal pieces interlocking. Leeke knew the sound. A magazine was being changed out.

"Get that asshole!" he ordered the surviving gunner and gave him a shove. Leeke got to his feet, carefully keeping Sheknovi between himself and the door, then pulled the scientist after him into the bowels of the vessel.

The gunner's first act was to flip onto his back and target the emergency light, putting it out with a single 9 mm round.

Now he was as hidden as the man on the boarding

deck. Neither could see the other. But the guard knew he had an advantage. He knew the *Wamphyr* stem to stern, every inch of her. The man outside didn't. The gunner knew where to hide, where to attack and even where to stage an ambush. He grinned in the darkness, his confidence high. He'd get this bastard with the machine gun. He knew it.

Crawling into a pitch-black corner, he got slowly to his feet, then moved through the blackness with utter calm.

There was a shift of movement on the boarding platform, then it was gone. He squinted into the darkness.

The attacker on the outside was trying to play the same hide-and-seek game the gunner was playing. The man grinned. He could play it so much better. His adversary didn't stand a chance.

His eyes were adjusting to the absence of light. He sought the gunner, peering into the blackness of the shadows. Soon the man on the outside would become impatient. He would move again, and that would be enough for the mercenary gunner to target him and fire.

The mercenary spotted his prey. The man on the boarding deck just stood there in the blackness, but he was watching the mercenary through a pair of strange lenses set into a strap-on type of headgear. The mercenary realized in that instant that he had been outsmarted after all. The soldier moved fast, triggering a series of rounds that cut through the glass and took the mercenary down hard.

WHEN BOLAN ENTERED the lounge, the women in the corner were sobbing, convinced he was about to shoot them down as coldly as he had struck down the mercenaries. He ignored them—they would have little to tell him in the way of useful information—and entered the rear doorway through which Sheknovi had been taken.

There was movement up ahead, another guard detail in his path. Bolan waited for the man to show himself. The gunner fired his weapon before he was fully in the open, hoping to catch his enemy with blind gunfire. Bolan triggered the MP-5 K-PDW submachine gun and chopped into his adversary's exposed forearm, eliciting a scream from his victim. The gunner, in pain, stepped into the open, providing Bolan with a clear shot, which he took. The man tumbled to the floor, out of commission, but still alive.

More guards rushed toward Bolan when he tried to go through the rear door that led to the cabins. He pulled away as bullets slammed into the doorframe. His glimpse inside had showed him an opulent parlor of some sort, with a dressing table, bar, lounge and even a fireplace. He guessed it was the front room of a master suite. Maybe Sheknovi was in the bedroom beyond. Or maybe he was being set up.

He pulled a grenade from his combat webbing, nudged the door open with his foot and lobbed the bomb underhanded. More gunfire slashed into the woodwork and the wallboard before suddenly coming to a halt. There was a gasp that might have been the start of a word, but it never finished.

Bolan didn't hear it, anyway. He had covered his head and ears with his arms and squeezed his eyes shut.

A flash of blinding light and a screech of unbelievable noise filled the parlor. The gunners grabbed their eyes and collapsed screaming onto the floor. Bolan found them on the floor shouting wordlessly like newborns. Within seconds, though, one man was able to raise his handgun and target the Executioner. The soldier calmly raked a burst of machine-gun fire across the men, ending two careers in murder.

He kicked through the door to the bedroom of the master suite. The huge, round bed was fully nine feet wide, but there was still plenty of space around it for the dressing tables and chests that hugged the walls. In the far corner, Andrei Sheknovi sat, handcuffed, in a narrow dressing chair, regarding Bolan with a kind of awed surprise.

The gunner crouching behind the Russian pressed a pistol against the back of the researcher's skull. It was the gaunt robed man.

"Nuala Leeke," Bolan said.

Leeke peered over Sheknovi's head with squinting eyes. "Who the hell are you?"

Bolan raised the MP-5 K-PDW to his shoulder, aiming it like a sniper's rifle. "Let Sheknovi go."

"You're American."

The soldier said nothing, regarding the gunner with supreme patience and uncanny calm.

Leeke had stared down the muzzle of a gun more than once in his life. It had never frightened him before, but this time was different. He saw the look of a killer in the eyes of the black-haired American. He shouted for his men.

"Forget it. They're dead," Bolan announced. "You're next unless you put down the gun."

The lights went on. So all Leeke's men weren't dead, after all. One of them had been assigned to restore power, and he had succeeded. Leeke grabbed the Russian by the back of his collar and dragged him sideways, the pistol jammed firmly into the base of his skull.

Bolan tracked them until they reached one of the dressing tables, where Leeke sat in a chair. The soldier could barely see the mercenary with the Russian standing in the way. Sheknovi would have to drop to the floor or flee before Bolan could risk firing.

Leeke pressed the pistol into his prisoner's spine as he yanked out the table phone with his free hand, speed-dialing with his thumb. He mumbled into the phone, then spoke up.

"Watch the screen, American."

Leeke touched a button on the table, and Bolan saw an ornate lacquered jewelry box with a Japanese design slide down into the tabletop. Behind it was a flat PC screen. The monitor opened to a strangely off-kilter image that refused to focus.

Bolan realized Sheknovi's expression had changed to one of expectant horror as his eyes locked on the screen. The image jerked and became upright, showing a window ledge inside a boat. The glass was awash with glare, then the camera moved to the left and stopped. The man that entered the middle of the screen dragged a thrashing, blurry image that coalesced into a small human figure when the man lifted it by one of its limbs. A young boy hung by one arm, wearing a red T-shirt. His face was terrified, and he looked utterly exhausted.

Sheknovi made a sound deep in his throat. Coming out of the speakers on the monitor were small, tinny squeals from the boy.

"José, do you hear me?" Leeke asked loudly into the phone.

The man on the screen looked directly at the occupants of the room and nodded, a wide smile spread across his face.

"You will kill the boy in sixty seconds unless I tell you otherwise. Do you understand?"

"Understood!" shouted the man on the screen. But his voice was small and ratlike.

The mercenary in the corner gave Sheknovi a shove into the middle of the room, then made a show of putting his weapon into the holster under his left arm and looking at his watch.

"Your son is going to die," Leeke announced.

"No!" Sheknovi gasped.

"If you want me to stop it, you had better start agreeing to my terms pretty damn fast, old man."

"Hundreds will die if you cooperate with him, Sheknovi," Bolan said.

"You can shut the hell up unless you want the boy's blood on your hands," Leeke erupted.

"You'll kill the boy anyway," Bolan asserted.

"I won't kill anybody," Leeke declared. "My job is to deliver Mr. Sheknovi and his family to my employer. In fact, I was specifically instructed to keep them all alive and well. Especially Mr. Sheknovi."

"Then Roger Kabat will kill the boy himself," Bolan stated.

"That's out of my hands," Leeke declared.

"Please!" Sheknovi cried out. "Stop him before he shoots Sergei!"

Leeke glanced at his watch and nodded, a self-assured smirk on his drawn face. "Give me your answer, Russian."

"I'll do it. I'll do whatever you want. Just stop him!"

Leeke pulled the phone back to his face. "Hold up, José."

On the screen, the man holding the struggling child nodded.

"Let's go. Tell your friend to stay back."

Bolan's mind whirled as his soul filled with a rising fury.

"Please," Sheknovi said. "Whoever you are. Stay back. Don't endanger my family."

Leeke nodded and gestured grandly toward the front of the room.

Bolan stood where he was, impotent. All he could do was watch them leave.

CHAPTER FIFTEEN

Mack Bolan had no philosophical argument with the concept of revenge.

In fact, he was about to take some himself.

He planned it in the ten seconds it took for the small landing craft, the *Lupine,* to motor out of its launching platform and disappear from sight into the vast South Atlantic Ocean. On board were the people he had come to save: Andrei Sheknovi, his young wife and his little boy. Bolan had failed them. Now they were almost certainly doomed to torture and death at the hands of the arms merchant, Roger Kabat.

Kabat was outside Bolan's reach, but it occurred to the Executioner that he still might catch up with Henrique Goncalves.

The soldier jogged across the deck and yanked open one of the steel cabinets mounted into the deck of the motor yacht. In seconds he had ejected the inflatable raft and tossed it over the side. He threw out one of the life preservers, its line tied to the deck railing, and quickly descended the side of the ship. The *Lupine*'s lights were still a speck on the surface of the ocean when Bolan started the tiny electric motor on the life raft and whirred away from the yacht.

Silently, he cursed the ineffectual little motor. It propelled the raft at a speed scarcely faster than he could have swum.

When he was a hundred feet from the motor yacht he took the transmitters out of his pocket and stabbed each of the red buttons, one after another.

Behind him, deep in the bowels of the *Wamphyr,* Bolan's shaped plastique charges erupted. The yacht wasn't going anywhere unless it was towed. It wouldn't be used again without a major mechanical refitting.

Bolan would call in authorities to extract Kabat's wounded men, left behind in Leeke's flight. Maybe they would have intelligence to offer. Even the prostitutes might have something of use to offer.

But he seriously doubted it.

He grabbed the oars and dug into the calm Atlantic waters, helping the little motor along. It still took him ten precious minutes to reach the Flarecraft. He clambered aboard and started the engine with a sudden surge of power. He tore away over the water, reached ground-effect speed quickly and became airborne. Reaching an altitude of four meters Bolan banked the craft into a 180-degree turn and pointed it at the shore, roughly eighty miles away.

Between him and the shore was the Goncalves Wellcraft Scarab, heading for home.

The race was on.

Bolan knew the Flarecraft had a published maximum speed of 160 kilometers per hour, or about 100 miles per hour. He dumped the fuel in the spare tank and urged the engines to higher revolutions. The only wind was a light breeze heading south-southwest, which helped nudge him along. The tachometer told him the Subaru engine was approaching the redline when he hit 180 kilometers per hour.

He cursed and played with the wind, maneuvering the craft up and down inch by inch, searching for the sweet spot that would allow him to coax a couple of extra klicks an hour out of the craft without overheating the engines and warping them into a mass of scrap metal.

"Jack!"

"Go ahead, Sarge."

"I'm heading to shore."

"Alone?"

"Yeah. I screwed it up. Sheknovi and his family are on their way to Kabat."

Grimaldi said nothing for a long moment. Then, "You on your way back in?"

"Yeah. One little detail to attend to before I meet up with you. Call Stony and have the Brazilians get to the *Wamphyr*."

"It's still there?"

"It's not going anywhere. I disabled all its drive systems. There's a handful of wounded mercenaries on board, along with some pleasure staff."

"What are these details you're attending to, Sarge? I want in on it."

Bolan smiled grimly. The Flarecraft tachometer was hovering at the bottom of the red. The speedometer registered 186.6 kilometers per hour. "Sorry, Jack. No time for you to get here. This is going to go down in the next few minutes or it is not going to go down at all."

Even as he spoke, Bolan spotted lights ahead and he adjusted his heading minutely to follow them. Within seconds he began to pick up froth under his flying lights. The Scarab was moving fast, ripping up a huge wake. But no vehicle that had to fight its way through water could outrace the airborne Flarecraft. Bolan rode up hard on the rear of the Scarab, running lights blazing. This time he wanted them to know he was coming.

The Scarab increased its speed, noticeable to Bolan mostly in the sudden increase in wake size relative to his distance from them. He opened the window at his side and felt the hurricane-force rush of wind coming in. As he overtook the Scarab he veered to the right, straightened, then banked quickly to the left. The Scarab flashed underneath him, and Bolan dropped the high-explosive grenade out the window.

He had guessed for speed and distance, and the HE bomb detonated precisely where he had wanted it, blowing up a spray of water just ten feet off the front of the Scarab. The Brazilian deftly nudged the boat away from the geyser spouting off his bow. Bolan had hoped for an oversteer that would have flopped the craft onto its side, spilling its occupants into the ocean.

He banked the Flarecraft hard away from the Scarab, slowed to highway speeds and watched the long, slim boat pass underneath him again. There were brief flashes from the Scarab's cockpit, and he heard thumps against the Kevlar underside of the composite Flarecraft hull. The craft had no frame, so gunfire into the carbon-fiber hull was only a problem if it punctured a fuel tank or damaged the drive system. Bolan swung the Flarecraft back and forth like a toy on the end of a pendulum, avoiding more fire until he was positioned for another attack. He increased speed and dived at the Scarab, veering over the front end. He laid the Heckler & Koch machine gun on the window and fired a steady stream across the Scarab, satisfied to see the gunners scatter in a frenzy. The vessel turned to the side to escape the punishing 9 mm gunfire, and one of the cockpit occupants lost it. He flew out of the fast-moving boat almost gracefully, then hit the water like a rag doll dropped out of a car on the highway, flopping and breaking on the pounding ocean surface before disappearing into the night.

Bolan increased his speed momentarily, turning the Flarecraft to the west, then dropped his speed suddenly, falling quickly behind the Scarab. Then he began to push the driver again, creeping up on the rear of the big boat.

On board, Goncalves was shouting for his men to fire at the bizarre aircraft. He was pushing the huge, 575-horsepower engines to their maximum speed, concentrating all his efforts on riding it safely over the ocean. As he reached a speed of seventy-five land miles per hour, the calm waves of the peaceful Atlantic began to seem like hull-pounding rocks in his path. The damn thing was right over his shoulder and closing in hard. Goncalves forced more fuel into the engines, and the Scarab moved upward to seventy-seven, seventy-eight, then eighty land miles per hour. Goncalves was sweating and biting his lip as he steered the monstrous craft toward shore. He could no longer concern himself with the activity of his men. Every fragment of his concentration had to stay with keeping the boat from disintegrating on the pounding waves.

The taunting whine of the Flarecraft props increased in pitch, and the delta wing swooped over the Scarab just a few feet off the port side, accelerating to just a few miles per hour faster than the Scarab. Goncalves grimaced, strategizing. He would allow the aircraft to get just ahead of him, then he would decelerate rapidly, turn off all running lights, and maybe manage to elude it in the darkness.

Then, out of the corner of his eye, he saw the Flarecraft dive from four meters down to just one meter over the surface of the water, eject a small object and swoop up again as the round exploded. Goncalves's heart stopped in his chest. He was dead and he knew it.

The grenade exploded at the surface of the ocean within an arm's length of the hull of the rocketing Scarab, pushing the nose of the vessel into the air. A change of a single degree of incline was enough to transform the boat into a spear point, which sliced through the air to a wing, which caught the air. The same cushion of air that gave the delta-wing craft its ability to fly took the Scarab and flipped it violently backward, slamming it into the water again upside down. Still traveling too fast, it disintegrated upon impact. The wreckage splashed and skipped across the surface of the ocean for an endless two seconds.

Bolan slowed the Flarecraft and began to circle the wreck site slowly.

Composite material pieces floated on the surface. The remains of the big engines were on their way to the ocean bottom. The remains of the crew couldn't even be recognized among the rest of the flotsam.

CHAPTER SIXTEEN

Somewhere over the Caribbean Sea

"How fast can they have units working?" Bolan asked.

Stephanie McCord didn't answer right away. "They'd need emitter components that they surely don't have already. Once they get them, they'll be ready to roll in less than a day, assuming Sheknovi's cooperative."

"We'll assume he will be. Not many men could stand there and watch their wife and children be tortured if it was in their power to stop it, no matter what the cost to others," Bolan mused. "What will it take for them to get fully equipped?"

"We were buying emitter head materials from a scientific firm in Florida," McCord said. "I think we can assume Kabat's people will know all about the place from the data they extract from Sheknovi."

Barbara Price came on the line. "From Sheknovi?"

"Yes. When Mr. Dinitzin brought Sheknovi up to date on the current state of their development of the technology, one of the things Sheknovi would want to know would be the source for the emitter materials. The emitters that they had tested had to be made out of a pretty high grade of custom-formulated, steel-impregnated ceramic. One of Sheknovi's biggest problems when he was building the science town of Lipetsk Nov was getting an on-site frit-smelting facility. So I'm sure Sheknovi wanted to know where he was getting the material in the U.S.''

"Frit is the raw material of processed porcelain," Bolan said for Price's benefit.

"Yes," McCord said. "Back in Russia, Dinitzin and Sheknovi tested hundreds of formulations of special-grade porcelain materials combined with ferrous metals before they came up with a stable emitter material. It has to be able to withstand extreme levels of heat and vibration.''

"Can we be reasonably confident Kabat will use the same source the company used?" Price asked.

"He will if he wants to get a unit up and running anytime soon," McCord said with confidence. "This is not toilet-grade ceramic we're talking about here. It's high-end stuff. Similar to what they use for space shuttle tiles to protect from the heat of reentry. Not many places have the capability to blend it properly. Another problem—I'll guess Sheknovi isn't sitting around with the formula in his head. It was too complex to commit to memory. So the only two places on earth where the tested, perfected formula is still available are in the Lipetsk Enterprises database and in the company in Florida where the ceramic was supplied from.''

"So we go there," Bolan said definitively. "Jack, you getting this?"

Bolan was sitting at a small meeting table in the

center of the aircraft. Jack Grimaldi, with his Stony Man-supplied copilot, was in the cockpit of the corporate aircraft that had carried them on their disastrous trip to South America. "I heard every word. Where in Florida?"

"Senegal's the name of the town," McCord said from her telephone in her apartment in Arlington, Virginia. She had committed herself to consulting with the Farm until Kabat's operation was neutralized. "You'd probably land at Fort Myers. The firm is Senegal Scientific Ceramic Incorporated."

"Got that," Grimaldi said. "ETA two hours and twelve minutes, Sarge."

"I'm not convinced this will be a productive course of action," Price said. "What do you hope to accomplish in Florida?"

"If I can slow down Kabat temporarily that will be good enough," Bolan replied.

"Our friend in the Justice Department can call in somebody else to lock up Senegal Scientific."

"Do it. We're still a couple of hours out. But I have a feeling Kabat wants his new toy to be in working order ASAP, and he'll expedite the formation of his supply chain. I think the people at Senegal Scientific are in a great deal of danger."

"He wouldn't have time to even stage people in Florida yet," Price said.

"Neither did he in São Paulo," Bolan told her. "This is a man with plenty of contacts. He hired mercenaries in Brazil. I'll bet he'll have a group he can hire in Florida. Mafia, street gangs, whatever. There'll be somebody willing to do his dirty work and they're just a phone call away."

There was a moment of silence while Price digested this. "You're right."

"And so what if I'm wrong?" Bolan added. "I'm at a dead end otherwise. Unless you've got a lead on Kabat's location."

"We don't," Price admitted. "But Bear's got everybody on the cybernetics team scanning for him electronically around the world. We'll find him eventually."

"In the meantime I need something to do. I'm not going to sit at the base waiting for one of the computers to beep." Knowing McCord was still on the line, Bolan didn't even use the term *Farm*. As far as she was concerned, the base of operations these code-named men and women were working out of was called Steamroller.

There was a moment of silence. It was Grimaldi who pushed the issue. "Am I changing course for Fort Myers?"

"Yeah," Bolan growled.

"Hold up," Price said suddenly. "We're too late."

"What?" McCord asked, sounding suddenly very worried. "Did they attack them?"

"No. I'm just getting the information now. Bear's accessed the records from their shipper. Senegal Scientific works with a Tampa-based shipping company. They got a call this morning for delivery of fifty barrels of the frit to Lipetsk Enterprises. The truck's already left the mixing facility."

"What?" McCord cried. "How can that be?"

"Easy," Bolan acknowledged. "Somebody called up, claiming to be from Lipetsk. No reason for the people at Senegal to think differently."

"Wired them the payment in advance out of D.C. Claimed they needed it right away," Price said.

"How long ago did the truck leave the facility?"

"Five hours," she said.

"That's not good," McCord stated.

"No," Bolan admitted. "If Kabat's as smart as he's proved himself to be so far, then by this time he's hijacked the original truck and transferred his supplies to another."

Price agreed. "We could easily recruit the eyes of the state police and have the original truck stopped in no time," she explained. "But we can't go setting up roadblocks to stop every truck moving around Florida or in the neighboring states."

Bolan said nothing, his mind whirling as the engines thrummed steadily underneath him. It was looking more and more like he was too late on this one. Kabat was well-organized, with a reach that extended across the hemisphere.

"Stevie, what's their next step?" he said.

"Molding the emitter and firing it."

"Any reason to think they'd require special equipment for that?"

"None," she answered. "I don't know the theories behind the emitter, but I do know the uniqueness of it is in the materials, not the firing of it. Any commercial porcelain contractor could do it. Even the tolerances of the shape aren't all that crucial."

"How many porcelain contractors can there be?" Grimaldi asked.

"Hundreds. There are job shops all over the U.S."

"I'll have the Florida state police start searching for the truck anyway, just in case," Price said. "Still going to Senegal?"

"I see no need," Bolan told her. "We'll just head home and hope Bear's team has a lead for me to follow by then. What's next after the firing of the emitter, Stevie?"

"They wire it up to a set of very specific but common electronics, and then they're done," McCord said. "Then they've got a weapon on their hands. A very inaccurate and very potent piece of hardware."

Bolan said, "I guess we'll have to wait for them to use it."

Boston, Massachusetts

THE RUIN OF THE WOODEN dock had been left where it stood, rotting and collapsing into Boston Harbor. It wasn't ancient. It had no real history. But it gave an added atmosphere of age to the Beacon Hill area of downtown Boston. The tourists took pictures of it. The conventioneers in town for seminars cruised past the half-submerged wooden dock before disembarking and found it interesting. It was a nice addition for a town with a thriving tourist economy, and besides, nobody had come up with an economically compelling reason for tearing down the old dock. Not yet.

The twenty-nine-foot Sunrunner approached cautiously at no-wake speeds, pausing five yards from the sections of the dock that still emerged from the water during high tide. Tied by a long yellow nylon rope to its aft end was a small rowboat that looked as if it had ridden out a hurricane on a rocky shore. It was so battered and corroded, Denny Myers was surprised the thing would still float at all, especially burdened with its cargo.

The big steel case sat squarely in the middle of the rowboat, roped in with a spiderweb of chains. The steel chest was itself old and battered, and a ragged hole had been punched out of one end. A strange beige knob protruded from the hole. The mass of machinery inside had to have been substantial. The rowboat was riding far lower than was safe in the harbor waters. One good wave would swamp the thing for sure. As a last-second safety measure, Myers and Eddie Erwin had secured a flexible hose in the bottom of the rowboat, hooking it up to the Sunrunner's pump. It was busily extracting the water that was washing into the rowboat. So far it was just a trickle.

And they were almost done with the damn thing.

"Hey!"

Myers looked to the shore. The voice was almost nonexistent over the sound from the nearby traffic and the perpetual voice of the ocean. A cop was standing on the shore, waving his arms to get their attention.

"You can't be there!" the cop shouted.

Myers shook his head.

"You can't be there! Move your boat" This time the cop cupped his hands.

Myers shouted back, gesturing with a shrug at the deck of his boat. "Engine trouble!" he shouted back.

Erwin emerged from belowdecks. "What's going on?" he demanded.

"Local cop wants us to leave."

"Fuck him."

Myers spread his hand to the cop and shouted again. "Five minutes!"

The cop was angry. He stomped to his police car,

parked ten paces up the street at the curb. Probably
was on his way to radio for a patrol boat. Myers
couldn't care less. By the time the patrol arrived, it
would be far too late. Myers carefully eased the Sunrunner alongside the protruding dock. Here the
wooden walkway was out of the water, but so slime-
covered and pockmarked with rot that it looked like
anybody who stood on it would sink through the
wood.

"Okay! Hold it!" Erwin shouted from the rear of
the Sunrunner. He was standing on the water deck,
pulling the rowboat up close. Gingerly, he stepped
into the rowboat, causing it to sink an inch closer to
submersion in the water. He maneuvered awkwardly
around the steel case to the rear, uncoiling another
length of rope from the floor. He reached out and
pulled the rear of the rowboat to one of the rotted
wooden pilings that emerged from the shallow floor
of Boston Harbor. It was loose, waggling as he
wrapped the rope around it, but it would hold onto
the rowboat for the next few minutes. After a few
minutes it didn't matter what happened to it.

Next he moved to the front, untied the rope from
the Sunrunner and wrapped it around a stump of
wood that was still, somehow, holding up the algaed
walkway.

"How's it look?" he shouted to Myers.

Myers craned his neck to look critically at the rowboat. "Can you adjust it a little to your right?"

"Yeah."

Erwin pulled the rowboat forward enough to
achieve some slack on the front rope, then looped
rope around the wooden post. The rowboat was held
more tightly. Its prow pointed directly into the heart

of the city of Boston, as did the strange beige knob that protruded from the steel case over his shoulder.

"That's right on!" Myers shouted.

Erwin nodded. As Myers backed the Sunrunner to the rowboat again, Erwin found the small power switch on the front end of the steel case and flipped it on. Then he strode quickly off the rowboat onto the rear of the Sunrunner.

"It's on! We've got two minutes! Let's go!"

The cop on the shore was shouting at them again. He didn't know what they were up to, but he didn't like the look of it. Myers and Erwin ignored him as they quickly spun the Sunrunner in a tight circle and pointed it into the harbor. They increased their speed. The Sunrunner's twin 271-horsepower Volvo engines didn't make it a race craft, but it was probably fast enough to save itself. Myers hoped so. He brought it to its top speed as soon as the depth finder told him he was in safe water.

"Check it out," Erwin said, nodding to indicate the distant flash of lights on the prow of a harbor patrol boat that was coming after them. It was at least a couple of miles back.

"How long?" Myers asked.

"Forty-five seconds."

They said nothing more. Myers concentrated on coaxing speed out of the Sunrunner, riding into the troughs in the waves when he could so the craft wouldn't have to struggle against the waves. The Volvo engines were clearly straining. The tach showed them in the red. Myers was taking a chance pushing them so hard, but they had to survive for a few more seconds....

The police patrol boat was passing the tied-up rowboat.

"Fifteen seconds!" Erwin shouted over the roar of the engines.

"Will it get the police boat?" Myers asked.

"I doubt it. It's pointing away from them."

"Oh, great!"

"Not to worry. The patrol boat'll get called back when the trouble starts. Just watch. Five seconds. Four. Three."

Myers pulled down the throttle, bringing the engines to an idle hum. If they weren't far enough by now, it was too late anyway. As the Sunrunner raised a white wash of deceleration and slowed to a bob on the surface, he twisted. They said nothing, both watching the nearby city of Boston.

"Now," Erwin said.

The first thing they noticed was the cars, suddenly twisting and turning, out of control, slamming into one another and flying off the road into buildings as their electronically controlled braking and power-assist mechanisms ceased functioning. The sound of the crashes and cries of alarm from the people reached them over the water like distant thumps and mewls.

Then they realized the patrol boat had died in the water. Its lights were gone. It floated and twisted in the water as if it were also out of control.

"Oh, shit!" Myers exclaimed. "It got us!"

"What?" Erwin suddenly realized that the Sunrunner had ceased to rumble. The twin Volvos were off.

"It wasn't supposed to get us!" he protested.

"Well, it did."

"It wasn't pointed this way!"

Myers shrugged. "So we paddle. Get the raft."

Both stopped when they heard the strange thump. They looked to the shore, where they saw a column of fire and thick, black smoke rising from one of the vehicles.

One of the crashed cars, Erwin thought.

Then, as they watched, the squad car belonging to the police officer who had been trying to hassle them burst into flame, sending up an orange burst of fire that turned yellow and violent when the gas tank ignited seconds later.

"What's happening?" Erwin said.

The road was a ruin, with stalled and crashed vehicles spread in all directions. There wasn't a car moving and, one after another, they began to smoke, then exploded as their fuel ignited. The occupants were running crazily from place to place in a panicky attempt to escape the explosions. Others were trying to pull victims to safety. Blast after blast echoed over the harbor to the stalled Sunrunner.

Then the water began to boil from underneath the little steel rowboat. Steam trickles emerged from the water, pencil thin at first, then roiling columns of thick steam that hazed their view of the shore.

Soon smoke began to appear out of the bobbing patrol boat, and the officers on board were thrashing at a bright plume of orange that appeared from belowdecks. A moment later they were flying off the sides, heading for the water, and the patrol boat exploded underneath them in a bright burst of orange and a crack of noise that came across the water to the Sunrunner.

"What's it doing?" Erwin demanded.

"I don't know, but I think we should get the hell out of here right now!"

They headed for the life raft, bundled up at the rear of the vessel, and then Myers stopped, pointing at the shore.

He could clearly see the water from underneath the hull of the small steel rowboat sputtering and boiling at a magnificent rate, flopping the craft back and forth on an elevated layer of superheated steam. What he couldn't see was the sudden flare of fire as the nylon rope swung low enough to touch the steel lip of the boat and melt through it in a heartbeat. Then the rowboat slewed wildly on its one remaining rope, swinging to the side, pointing out to sea.

That was when the Sunrunner burst into flame. Erwin screamed and ran for the rail but Myers was too fascinated to move for a second. He saw the control panel start to smoke, the gray smoke of heated plastic. He saw the deck chair cushions melt where they were touching the metal surface. Hearing a rush of flame above him, he looked up to see the plastic material of the sun shade melt in a transparent wave of fire. Then there was a burst of noise from the engine compartment, and he knew his time was short. He ran into space at the rear of the Sunrunner, only to hear and feel the sudden crack of the exploding engines behind him. The boat disintegrated when the fuel burst, and Myers bore the brunt of the impact in his back, legs and head. He was chopped and burned by the flying shrapnel.

Erwin had surfaced and was looking back when he watched the flame engulf the flying body of his companion. He tried to turn away fast but the flame reached him, slashing into his vision and burning his eyes out of his head. He screamed and thrashed at the water.

He died panicking, drowning when he ran out of the frantic energy that was keeping him afloat.

While the city burned.

CHAPTER SEVENTEEN

Stony Man Farm, Virginia

They watched in horror.

"Why do you think this has something to do with Kabat?" Hal Brognola asked. He was on the line from his office in Washington, D.C. Also on the line was Stephanie McCord. Around the War Room table, watching the burning of Boston on the forty-two-inch-wide wall-mounted high-definition screen, were Bolan, Price and Kurtzman.

"The first reports that came in weren't even reporting fire," Kurtzman said. "They were reporting a catastrophic breakdown in Boston's downtown communications network. Then the power grid went. That was twenty-three minutes ago. The reports of spontaneous fires erupting throughout the affected zone started almost immediately afterward."

"I think I can explain it," McCord said into the speakerphone. "Almost all the fire response systems are computerized, especially in downtown areas. They were made inoperative when the pulse was set off."

Bolan shook his head, leaning back in his chair with his arms folded on his wide chest and looking contemplative. "I don't buy it. The fire's too extensive."

"Striker's correct," Kurtzman said. "Even without fire response systems in place, a single accidental fire wouldn't have spread like this one." He nodded at the CNN report on the screen. "They're saying it covers three full blocks of downtown Boston."

"Right. But there is a chance Kabat knew that there would be no good response from the fire department or the building's own fire containment systems, so he set off incendiaries to go with the pulse. A one-two punch."

Bolan frowned as the helicopter cameraman from the news network pulled back to get a landscape view of the conflagration. Orange fire and black smoke poured out of what looked like a single catastrophic flameout that had engulfed a huge part of downtown. Outside that area, however, the city appeared untouched.

"That might explain the damage," Bolan said doubtfully, "but something about it doesn't seem right. Maybe I don't know Kabat's profile as well as I would like, but he doesn't seem like the type to go for gaudy excess. Not when he could let a single gesture make his point. Knocking out a three-square-block area of downtown Boston would have been a significant gesture. Setting off a bunch of fires is overkill."

"Unless the fires are a direct result of the pulse."

Almost to a man they turned their attention away from the screen to the newcomer who spoke. He entered the room casually, but with an earnest look on his face. He wasn't a huge man—about six feet tall, roughly two hundred pounds. He had the complexion of an outdoorsman, weathered. The high cheekbones that might have given him a delicate look were offset by a strong, square jaw and chin and by heavy eyebrows.

Gary Manning was a near-genius and a highly competent warrior. As a member of Stony Man Farm's Phoenix Force, he had fought in more battles than he cared to remember. Just now that action team was standing down. He happened to be at the Farm when the reports started to come in about the Boston fires less than a half hour earlier.

Following him through the door was a large black man with graying temples, dressed in an almost stodgy-looking sweater vest. Huntington Wethers and Gary Manning took seats at the War Room conference table.

"I was confused when I saw these reports coming through on the news. It didn't make any more sense to me than it does to you," Manning said. "There was something not right about the way the fires ignited and spread. Something outside the ordinary. So I found Hunt and asked for his help going through data from Lipetsk Enterprises, the reports on their prototype testing, and I have a feeling we may have figured out the mystery of the fires."

"Our friend Gary has explosives expertise," Price said for the benefit of McCord, careful to use first names only. "Both causing and defusing."

"Are you saying that the magnetic pulse produces heat?" McCord asked over the conference line, clearly skeptical.

"No, we're not," Manning replied. "We're saying the pulse has demonstrated a tendency to excite electrons in ferrous metals. I've been going over the test results conducted by Lipetsk over the past six months, and I've found eighteen noted incidences of overheating in the localized region of the pulse.'' Manning began to fan out printouts of test reports on the table. ''Time after time, Dinitzin and his testing staff had troubles with fires.''

''I know they kept burning up emitters,'' McCord said.

''That was just the start of their problem,'' Manning stated. ''They eventually solved the emitter problem by imbedding stainless-steel powder inside aeronautical-grade fiber ceramic. That would allow them to get at least one good shot out of an emitter before it burned itself out. But once they did get good pulses, they found themselves burning up laboratory furniture. Floors and such. So they moved the test outside.''

''I knew they had some small fires. I didn't think anything of it,'' McCord said. ''There were no more fires once they moved the test into the shed.''

''That's because they were aiming their pulses directly into the earth—after all, the Lipetsk Enterprises goal was to create a mineral mapping device, not a weapon,'' Wethers commented in the deep, authoritative voice that had served him well when he had been a university professor of cybernetics. ''There was nothing to burn. The only time they tried a pulse test with the thing aimed anywhere but at the ground, they made one of their tables smoke. They shut down the power immediately.'' Wethers lifted a sheet of paper off the table and glanced at it briefly. ''Dinitzin reports that when they examined the table after the test, they found scorch marks around the steel screws that held it together. Dinitzin notes as an aside that he is just assuming the pulse has caused the screws to heat up until they started burning the plastic composite of the table.''

''What it does, simply put, is cause excitation of molecules in ferrous metals,'' Manning explained. ''The practical upshot of this is that anything containing steel, iron or whatever becomes red hot. Hot enough to burn whatever it is in contact with. Spontaneous fires erupt. Without communications or automatic fire-containment systems, the blaze spreads with virtually nothing to stop it.''

Bolan looked grim. ''What's this thing look like?''

''It's as big as a boom box,'' McCord answered. ''Maybe bigger. They slapped the electronics together in a big hurry and didn't have time to finesse the design. The emitter head itself could be anywhere from eight to twelve inches in diameter. I doubt they put a lot of effort into emitter head design like the Lipetsk research team was doing. It could be round, square, oblong, whatever.''

''The designs I've looked at seem to require a power source,'' Manning prompted.

''Right,'' McCord said.

''The power grid was out almost instantly, and the evidence points to continued operation by the emitter for as long as a few minutes, which indicates they had a generator or high-output batteries at work,'' Manning said.

''The kind of battery pack you're talking about would be expensive,'' Kurtzman stated. ''Not hard to come by but rare enough that it would be traceable.''

''Right. A generator, then,'' Bolan said. ''We're

still not talking about a large batch of equipment. It would fit in a van, easily.''

McCord was silent, as was the rest of the table. The scene from Boston switched to a street-shot video. The announcer was saying they had just managed to get a camera crew on the scene.

Smoke filled the streets, drifting among the people and the ruin of buildings and vehicles. Blackened cars and heaps of garbage littered the scene. A twisted mass of human remains passed briefly before the camera lens before the cameraman moved beyond it. The on-the-scene reporter was trying to keep her cool, but she was plainly fighting for self-control as she described the mayhem. The camera turned to a section of a street where a makeshift triage had been established. A handful of men and women were scrambling among rows of bodies, most of whom were blackened with burns and reddened with blood. Several of the bodies, clearly, had gone beyond the point where these good Samaritans could offer service. A pair of ambulances was arriving in a wail of noise that drowned out the news report, coming to a halt next to a trio of ambulances already loading in victims.

The camera turned as a distant scream reached it, and it was just in time to see a large section of a burning, eighteen-story hotel collapse. As it did so, the tongues of burning residue splattered across the street, engulfing more people in flames. One paramedic became wrapped in a large plastic sheet of what might have been an awning, burning with a sickly orange flame. He thrashed for a moment until he was tackled by a man in a business suit, who rolled him on the concrete until the flames were extinguished. A second victim, a woman, panicked when a tongue of flame caught her outfit on fire and she ran, screaming. The reporter, her cameraman and a group of others pursued her, shouting for her to drop and roll. She was heading for the water, and just five paces in front of the cameraman she suddenly tumbled off the concrete-reinforced shore and plummeted into the harbor. By the time the cameraman reached her, she was floating facedown in the gentle movement of the water, steam rising from her twitching body. The scene cut as someone plunged in the water to get her.

"Jesus," Hal Brognola whispered distantly, uncharacteristically subdued. "You people seeing this?"

Bolan was. And in his gut writhed a burning worm of anger. If he had managed to hold on to Andrei Sheknovi, this horror wouldn't have happened. If he had acted more aggressively to track down Kabat...

Self-recrimination was a waste of his time and mental energy.

"Bear," Bolan said, "do we have anything to go on, here?"

Kurtzman shrugged, looking frustrated and a little ashamed. "Sorry, Striker. There's nothing. We don't know where Kabat is. We've found no electronic trace of him anywhere in the world. I can give you a list of his properties, but it would take us weeks to check them all. And he might not be at any of them."

"Let's get on those properties anyway. We'll divide them up. Able, Phoenix and me. Hal?"

"You'll have the go-ahead for it," Brognola said. "The Man's going to want to have plenty of activity going on this. We're sharing what we know with the

FBI. They'll have their own investigation running, of course.''

"We going to give them our suspicion of a link with the Kabat pulse equipment?"

"I don't see why not. We'll share in any further intelligence they get, as well."

"Barbara?" Bolan asked.

"The teams can be on it in just a few hours," she said.

"Okay. Let's see if we can do any good at all."

"You know what I'm wondering?" Gary Manning commented. "How's Kabat reacting to this? He's got to be about as surprised as we are about the effects of the pulse."

Bolan's eyes were hard as polished steel. "To him it's icing on the cake."

BOLAN DIDN'T EVEN manage to get out of the building before their plans changed. He was summoned to the War Room and saw the message posted on Kurtzman's monitor.

"This came to you?"

"Yeah. And to about twenty thousand other e-mail addresses inside government domains."

"It's from Kabat," Bolan said. "'Unless fifty million dollars is deposited into my account in the Cayman Islands, I intend to burn the Kenilworth neighborhood of Chicago at 2:00 a.m. tomorrow morning. Those who visited my house in Hatteras know I have the capability.'"

Bolan shook his head. "So much for selling arms. Kabat's found a more lucrative means of capitalizing on his investment."

"Yeah. High-level extortion," Kurtzman said. "So what do we do about it?"

"Trace the e-mail?" Bolan suggested.

"Already working on it, but I'm not optimistic. It's been shuttled and reshuttled all over the planet. Akira's trying to rig our automatic tracking software to source it. Maybe we will, maybe we won't."

"Until then," Bolan said, "I plan on being in Kenilworth tomorrow morning."

CHAPTER EIGHTEEN

Kenilworth, Illinois

It was the kind of town that skewed all the counts when census takers tried to come up with averages. Income per capita was among the highest in the nation, and it was probably the richest community in the state of Illinois. Almost every adult was a college graduate. Almost every adult owned more than one car. Number of new housing starts per year inside town limits: zero. Kenilworth was happy with its population in terms of size and demographics. It didn't want anybody else. It didn't allow restaurants or retailers to come into its town—any establishment that brought in the general public was unwanted. Strict zoning ordinances kept them out. The houses were large and expensive, but for the most part not so ostentatious as to invite tourists.

What the people of Kenilworth most wanted was to be left alone inside their town. They would go to the nearby city of Chicago or to other local communities for their shopping or dining.

What they really didn't want was attention.

And yet, by early evening they were the focus of the nation. Network news trucks descended on the community, filming the homes and streets and attempting to get interviews with residents. When these efforts failed in most cases, the news crews went to the homes of the people who worked in the homes of Kenilworth, interviewing maids and drivers. They went to the schools, accosting the children of the people of Kenilworth and interviewing them. Curious onlookers from throughout the Chicago area came to photograph and to videotape the houses and streets.

On the networks, the scenes of the wealthy, tidy town juxtaposed with the horror of the conflagration in downtown Boston were too striking, too alluring to ignore. The footage was played together over and over throughout the night. The message, restated repeatedly by announcers, was that this tranquil community might share Boston's fate in just a few short hours.

An emergency meeting of city officials resulted in calls for extra police protection and a complete lockdown of the city. The large degree of political clout wielded by certain citizens succeeded in getting the streets closed to all but residents and their employees.

By midnight, Kenilworth was locked up as tight as a Gulag.

"Seems somehow criminal to keep U.S. citizens off their own streets," Gary Manning said over the noise of the patrol boat he was steering across the calm, greenish waters of Lake Michigan, many miles north of the city of Chicago. The large homes of the city of Kenilworth faced the water.

"Can't blame them for calling in every favor they've got for keeping their people safe," Bolan said from behind the Tasco field glasses he was using to monitor activity onshore. Nearly every home was alive with activity. Hired security guards, Kenilworth local police and extra law enforcement borrowed and hired from nearby communities patroled the streets. Fire engines from throughout the northern suburbs were strategically positioned.

The boat driven by Manning, who had been borrowed from Phoenix Force at Bolan's special request, was only one of several roaming the shore, which included the Chicago police and the FBI. Bolan and Manning had needed to present federal identification three times in the past two hours. Now they were beginning to recognize their comrades in the late-night patrol.

They had taken to the water after Kurtzman's analysis of the damage in Boston, based on the frantic account of survivors and eyewitnesses to the initial destruction, pointed to placement of the emitter at the water's edge, or even in the water. Bolan knew the harborfront. It would have been extremely simple and risk-free for someone to park a boat big enough for the emitter and its generator on the shore, then flee before the device activated.

Bolan lowered the glasses and sat back in the chair next to Manning, who was steering the boat at near walking speeds. He and Bolan shared a look, one of frustration.

"Something's not right, is it?" the big Canadian asked.

Bolan shook his head.

"So, what is it?"

"All this had to have been expected. Kabat knew that. These are his class of people," Bolan said, waving toward the shore. They were passing a ten-thousand-square-foot lakeshore home of red brick. "He'd know exactly what kind of people he was dealing with. He'd know they'd pull out all the stops to protect themselves."

"Sure. So maybe this isn't his target at all," Manning suggested.

"That's what I've been thinking. He's successfully marshaled nationwide attention—"

"Diverted from where?" Manning finished.

"I've been trying to figure that out," Bolan said. "All this attention wasn't on any one place. It's not really diverted from anything. On the other hand, if he manages to do the same type of damage to this neighborhood he did in Boston, despite the best efforts of these people to protect themselves, the effect would be devastating."

Manning frowned. "I'm not following."

"Look at it this way. Kabat picks one of the wealthiest, most influential communities in the nation. They do their very best to keep him from getting at them. They call in all their favors. They make all the threats the rich and influential can make. They demand and they get the very highest level of cooperation from state, local and federal officials. Kabat comes in and successfully strikes at them anyway. If this town isn't safe, then what place in the U.S. *is* safe?"

Manning nodded, catching the drift. "No damn place."

The soldier nodded. "So Kabat comes up with a very carefully considered amount of money. Fifty million dollars would be almost impossible for even these people to come up with in less than twenty-four hours. Even if they were willing to be extorted, and they aren't. Kabat designed this ransom to not be paid. He wants to burn this place to the ground. The next time he'll ask for real money, and the next time, maybe, he'll get it."

Manning wasn't a man who was easily amazed. He'd seen his share of the good and bad in men. He was silent, almost taken aback, allowing their patrol boat to drift in the calm lake.

"So we've gone in a big circle and we're back to the beginning," Manning said, frustrated. "We think he'll strike this town. These people. Right under the noses of more law-enforcement personnel than probably live in the place, and in—" he glared at the glowing hands of his watch "—in one hour and forty-eight minutes. How will he do it and how will we stop it?"

Bolan glared across the lake at the well-lit homes and grounds of the movers and shakers of Chicago's upper crust. "This is Kabat's class of people. Maybe one of these homes is owned by Kabat."

Manning nodded. "If he owns a home here, he could have had the emitter and its generator in place before the announcement was e-mailed."

The Executioner gave him a wry look. "What do you think are the chances of getting cooperation from the good people of this burg for a door-to-door search of every building until the emitter is found?"

"None," Manning said.

Bolan already had his phone in his hand. The number was scrambled and dialed through the security protocol in seconds, then Aaron Kurtzman picked it up on the first ring.

"Bear," Bolan said, "we think the emitter is already on-site in Kenilworth. We need to know if Kabat's got a house here."

"If he does, he won't make it easy to figure out. It'll be under a false name or hidden behind corporate ownership."

"Get on it. If we can figure out which house, we can put a stop to this thing. And you know we don't have a lot of time."

Manning was already steering them to the shore.

THE COP IN THE PATROL CAR met Bolan's gaze, nodded almost imperceptibly and drove past the house without slowing. His partner didn't even appear to see the soldier crouched in the bushes.

"Steamroller One here," Bolan said into the radio. "Check in, teams."

"Steamroller Two, ready," Manning replied. Bolan spotted him pressed up against an old heavy maple across the lawn.

"Red Team leader, ready."

"Blue Team leader, ready."

"Red Team, be ready to move in on my say-so."

"Copy that, Steamroller One," Red Team leader answered, allowing Bolan to hear the displeasure in his voice.

Bolan didn't care that the leader of the FBI team was angered at being relegated to the third rung in the new chain of command. But he was less than confident that the Red Leader would perform at one hundred percent. Right now there was little he could do to remedy the situation. The rapidly assembled confederation of FBI and Chicago SWAT teams had been put definitively under the command of Bolan and Manning. The FBI agent had been told to yield his authority or tender his resignation on the spot. The instruction had come by executive order. Apparently the White House was also very aware of the time constraints on the operation.

The time cushion was now under an hour and a half. They had to get past an armed guard that might be in place, find the emitter, bypass its safeguards and shut it down. All within that ninety minutes.

And they weren't even sure they had the right house.

Kurtzman and his cybernetics team had culled through the official files of every resident who owned a home within the city limits of Kenilworth. Many of the homes were second or third residences. Some were owned by rich foreign nationals. Some were owned by corporations. Only one house couldn't be traced.

It was clearly some sort of corporate sanctuary, but tracking down the identity of the people behind the corporate structure that held the deed hadn't been accomplished. Multiple layers of bureaucracy had been put in place specifically for the purpose of disguising ownership. Somebody was without doubt trying to hide something in the house at 481 Clument Avenue in Kenilworth.

But was that someone Roger Kabat? Was this where the emitter had been placed? The only way they would know was by searching it.

Bolan and Manning had been struck immediately by its ideal positioning for just such a strike. It was almost dead center in the middle of the town. A perfect spot for doing a hell of a lot of damage.

Another cop rolled by, right on schedule. It was important to keep up appearances. Briefed on the probe about to take place, the local police patrol, which had been composed of cops from several local communities since dusk, continued unabated.

The Blue Team of City of Chicago SWAT personnel had surrounded the house at 481 Clument. The Red Team, all Feds, was ready to follow the Bolan-Manning probe inside.

The FBI leader had argued for a sudden barrage that would take Kabat by surprise. Bolan insisted on a clandestine strike. He didn't want to give anyone time to sound an alarm that would almost surely trigger an early power-up of the emitter. Once it started functioning, the entire town was just minutes away from destruction.

The trick was to not let it start to function.

Bolan signaled Manning and the two men slipped through the yard, staying in the shadows as they proceeded to the front of the house.

The soldier found a well-hidden spot in the shrubbery and peered through the front window. The white sheers hid the room from view, but not the tiny electric feeds that indicated a vibration-sensing alarm system.

"Steamroller One, this is Two," Manning radioed. "I've got laser perimeters set up on the side windows."

"Not in front," Bolan said. "Just electric sensors."

"I'll take care of that." Manning appeared at his side moments later, examining the pane of glass.

"The curtains make using a laser here impractical," Manning said. They didn't bother to consider the implications of that seemingly mundane fact. If this was Kabat's house, why would he allow an aesthetic feature like front-window sheers to compromise the superiority of laser-sensing equipment, which he'd used elsewhere? That seemed to tell them they were on the wrong track. If this was Kabat's house, the lack of a laser sensor on the picture window might mean there was a more insidious sensing device inside.

Manning used a tiny, gun-shaped instrument to drill into the window frame. Then he used a tiny, surgical-grade scope to fish around inside the frame until he grabbed one of the leads to the window. He grabbed it in a tiny clamp that cut through the electric insulation and connected with the live wire and cut it, gripping either end so as not to interrupt the circuit. Next he plugged a tiny wire from the clamp into a tiny, handheld computer on his belt. He looked at the display, nodding. "It's not an intelligent sensor. This will be a piece of cake."

It took him less than sixty seconds to drill a second time, grab the second wire and complete the circuit with the first by connecting the two clamps.

"Okay," Manning said. "This window's no longer protected. We can let ourselves in."

Bolan quickly applied high-strength adhesive to a pair of suction cups and stuck them to the glass of the window by their plastic hands. The rubberized plastic helped muffle the sound as he started to cut a large triangle out of the glass. The heavy-grade cutting tool, however, was still no match for the thick glass of the picture window. Bolan had no illusions about the level of sound he was creating. If there was anybody inside within a room or two, they couldn't help but hear him.

When the cutting was done, he carefully tapped

the glass with a rubber hammer, breaking it in two pieces that came out with the suction cups. When it was done, there was enough of an opening to allow them entrance.

"Steamroller One here," Bolan radioed. "We've made a way in. Any sign of activity?"

"Red Team leader here, Steamroller One. No sign of activity."

"Blue Team?"

"Not a thing, Steamroller One."

Manning grinned in the darkness. "You first, Striker."

Bolan stepped inside and crossed the room in silence, searching the doorways to other rooms with his lead weapon. Again he was making use of the Heckler & Koch MP-5 K-PDW submachine gun. Short and maneuverable with its side-folding stock, the personal defense weapon, as it was called, was ideal for room-to-room combat. The suppressor on the unit was detachable. Bolan could remove it easily enough for enhanced maneuverability when the need for silence was ended. And Bolan had no illusions. Even suppressed, the machine gun was anything but silent.

Manning was inside just seconds after him. He followed Bolan to an archway that led from the living room through a library, then to a dining area.

"Musty," Manning said quietly.

Bolan had noticed it, too. The air wasn't circulating much. The air conditioner might not be working. The heat of the long-gone afternoon was still trapped inside. Kurtzman's electronic probe of utility use by the house showed low levels of electricity use, zero gas use and only enough water use to account for the automatic lawn sprinkler system.

All this added up to nothing definitive in Bolan's book. He wasn't about to let his guard down until he knew for certain there was no one in the place.

It took them just three minutes to completely probe the 2,500-square-foot lower level. There was no evidence of habitation, no whisper of sound from the upper level. Manning found the alarm control box in a pantry off the cold, bare kitchen. While he disabled it, Bolan looked around. The clock on the wall was stopped, its battery dead. The clock on the range was five hours off. The refrigerator contained beer, soda and an open box of baking soda with a sell-by date more than a year old.

"System's disabled," the Phoenix Force commando whispered to Bolan.

Bolan got on the radio, speaking quietly. "Red Leader, this is Steamroller One. The alarms are disabled. Proceed inside with caution. The ground floor is clear and we're heading up."

"Understood. Red Team is moving in."

Bolan and Manning had already determined the house had a single stairway accessing the upper floors, and they quickly made their way to the second level.

It took them another five minutes to tour the second floor, finding no one and nothing except an empty house. The Red Team leader, FBI Agent Frank Denis, rendezvoused with them at the stairs, and they headed together to the third floor. Red Team fanned throughout the first and second floors, they, too, finding nothing.

Bolan was feeling a growing sense of frustration.

If this house turned up empty, he had nothing to go on. No way to stop the conflagration before it could start.

Then he spotted movement as his eyes became level with the third floor of the house. Bolan and Manning drew back as rounds from a submachine gun slammed into the wooden railings, sending a rain of splinters over them. The FBI agent, a few steps behind them, had his back pressed against the wall with his eyes wide, a Glock 22 pressed against his cheek and pointing at the ceiling. Manning and Bolan waited in silence, their eyes locked on the open space at the top of the stairs. Then they moved.

Bolan climbed the steps suddenly and spotted a black shadow flying across the outlines of a shaded window. He targeted the movement, anticipating the gunner's position, and fired a brief burst. A figure fell heavily to the floor. Then Manning fired a burst. A person stumbled into view and fell prone on his face.

"At least now we know we've got the right place," Manning stated.

"Give me some lights, Red Leader," Bolan growled.

The FBI agent found the switch on the stairs and fiddled with it. "Nothing."

Manning stepped out of the stairway and crossed to the wall switch there, finding it to also be non-functional.

"Glasses," Bolan said, and he and Manning dragged on the Tasco night-vision lenses strapped around their headgear. The darkness of the third floor became a sea of sickly green, accented by the warm but cooling bodies of the two gunners.

"Time?" Manning requested.

"T-minus twenty-six minutes," the FBI man whispered.

Bolan had guessed they were under the half-hour mark. The probe was going slower than he would have liked, but it was a complicated house, probably three times the size of the average American suburban home. And, just when they knew the danger was at its worst, they needed to be the most careful. But Bolan felt a sense of relief. The presence of machine-gunner guards told them this had to be the right house.

"Steamroller One to all teams—be advised we've engaged the enemy on the third floor of the house. Two suspects are down. Be prepared for more gunfire and possible escape attempts."

"Blue Leader here, Steamroller One. We're all eyes."

Bolan and Manning began a leapfrog probe of the top-level rooms, followed closely by the FBI agent and a trail of agents who took up positions in the cleaned-out rooms.

But room after room came up empty. Within ten minutes Bolan and Manning had cleared the entire third floor. Every bedroom was empty of both men and machinery.

When Bolan and Manning met again at the head of the stairs, the big Canadian pointed his weapon at the attic pull-down ladder mounted in the ceiling.

Bolan radioed their intention to proceed into the attic of the house. "Blue Leader, are there windows of any kind into the attic?"

"One second, Steamroller One," the SWAT leader answered, then Bolan heard a lightning-fast exchange among the various SWAT members posted around the house. Within twenty seconds the Blue Leader was on the radio to Bolan. "Steamroller One, you've got a single exhaust fan at the rear and an adjustable attic vent window on the front. Nobody's getting in or out either one without kicking out the vents first. No other openings visible on the exterior."

"Let's proceed with caution," Bolan said. "This is a blind approach in every sense."

When Manning grabbed and dragged down on the handle, the ceiling panel swung down and the ladder descended to the floor. The attic was black and silent.

A small item the size and shape of a fist bounced down the ladder and landed at Manning's feet.

CHAPTER NINETEEN

Bolan and Manning were almost instantly airborne. Manning retreated down the hall, turning his back and landing in a crouch that exposed only his Kevlar-protected back to the coming blast. Bolan moved himself at the FBI agent, who stood staring at the grenade with a kind of numbed horror. The soldier tackled the agent to the floor, shielding the man with his body, and heard the blast as they both impacted the hardwood floor. Bolan recognized the sound and squeezed his eyes shut, shouting to Manning.

"Masks!"

Bolan grabbed the gas mask hanging on his belt and dragged it over his face by feel, knowing that to open his eyes would be to blind himself with the stinging gas from the CS grenade. He heard the Red Leader and the FBI agents on the third floor beginning to cough and hack.

The soldier inhaled and exhaled hard and fast, tasting the gas inside his mask and hoping to clean it out with his breath before opening his eyes, knowing that a few precious seconds were passing. Then he forced his eyes open. The gas inside the mask was only sufficient to make his eyes water. He could see through it. As he propelled himself to his feet, he spotted a pair of feet coming down the attic steps and he reacted with instinct and speed, spinning and kicking savagely at the steps. The wooden steps were flimsy and supported only at the ceiling, so the kick jarred them from under the feet of the man coming down. He cried out as he lost his balance, collapsing down the steps, then slamming face-first into the floor, smashing the glass of his gas mask. He managed to keep a grip on the .44 Magnum pistol in his hand until Manning materialized out of the thick cloud of gas and slammed his foot into the man's side. The pistol flew away and the man grunted, his breath knocked out of him.

Bolan stepped to the bottom of the stairs and triggered the MP-5 K-PDW into the blackness, then he rushed up the steep stairs, diving across the blackness as a burst of .32-caliber gunfire cut through the space. Bolan's night-vision goggles turned to white under the bright onslaught, and he dragged them onto his forehead under the gas mask.

The Executioner knew he was acting rashly. He also knew time was getting very short. He twisted onto his back, sat up halfway and let loose a 9 mm burst at the point where the gunfire originated. There was a sudden intake of breath followed by a heavy thump. Bolan was already moving, knowing his gunfire could be targeted just as easily as anyone else's, and he intended to stay one step ahead of the competition. He rolled to the side, got to his feet, then lunged forward as he heard the stutter of .308-caliber automatic weapon fire. Several rounds slammed into the slanted ceiling and the wall behind him, but he felt the distinct impact of a bruising round punching into his chest. He ignored it, pushing away the pain and loosing a volley of his own. He cut through the place, knowing his opponent was moving, as well.

He released the subgun's trigger and tried to listen past the sudden cessation of suppressed gunfire. There was a rustle of movement far to the right, and Bolan instantly had it targeted. He swept the submachine gun in a sideways figure eight, then dropped and attempted to roll. His body stopped hard against something solid. He waited.

Someone was still breathing. Breathing hard, breathing raggedly, but alive. Then he heard a sharp intake of breath.

Movement below. In the blackness of the attic the only visibility came from the dim opening in the floor. Someone was coming up the steps. Bolan spotted the top of a head and knew it was Manning. The big Canadian wasn't going to let the soldier fight this battle alone.

Bolan heard the rustle of movement, recognized it as the readying of a weapon and pinpointed it. He triggered one burst that chopped into that nebulous point in the blackness.

Panting breath came from the other side of the attic. Someone had been hiding in the blackness. He launched himself into a run, determined to make a break for it. Bolan saw him in a quick silhouette as he crossed to the stairs, going straight for Manning. The runner fired a burst of rounds on the run, intending to shoot his way directly through the Phoenix Force commando. Bolan twisted and directed a volley into the running man at the same instant Manning unleashed a horrendous burst of fire from his chattering Calico. The running man was cut in two by the combined machine-gun fire.

Then the attic was filled with silence.

BOLAN SCANNED THE INTERIOR of the attic with his flashlight. "Clear!" he called. "Get some light up here."

Red Team had fled to find clear air. Replacements were arriving with gas masks, and one of them staggered up the attic steps holding a pair of flood lamps on power lines feeding from an equipment truck in the street. He flipped them on. The light flooded the attic with noontime brightness, clearly illuminating the riveted aluminum cabinet that dominated one corner of the room.

Red Leader came up the steps in a gas mask, still coughing from his exposure to the CS grenade.

"What are you guys doing?" he demanded.

"Evaluation," Manning answered from a prone position. He was examining the cabinet closely, using a penlight for better illumination of the underside.

"You guys have had your share of the fun. Now this is my baby."

Bolan gave the FBI agent a look that could have frozen water. "What do you know about the emitter?"

"I know I'm in charge of it. My orders were to let you guys lead the probe. I did so, and now that part of the operation is over. I don't know who you guys are, but you're no longer welcome at this crime scene." The agent yelled down to the third floor. "I want Faisel and Lomieir up here now! We've got less than ten minutes to shut this thing down!"

Manning was too engrossed in his examination of the seemingly featureless aluminum cabinet to pay attention to the blustering agent. Bolan was standing still, arms folded, eyes icy. For the first time the FBI leader took a look around the attic.

The exposed beams of the floor and walls of the attic had been nailed over with plywood, but the finishing had stopped there. The attic was littered with bodies. The corpse nearest to the stairs was in especially bad shape, blood pooling around him for several feet and his abdomen nearly ripped in two as if with a dull saw.

"Jesus," the agent muttered. "You guys are brutal."

A pair of men trotted up the steps and came face-to-face with the dead man. They blanched noticeably under their masks and stopped to look.

"Time is running out, agents," the Red Leader reminded them.

"What's that guy doing?" one of them asked when he saw Manning.

"Leaving," Red Leader announced. "You and you. Out."

"We're staying," Bolan said.

"Like hell. We have work to do, and you're only going to get in our way."

"You don't even know what you're dealing with."

"You have insight we don't?" asked one of the newly arrived engineers.

"I know the emitter isn't here," Manning announced.

That got everyone's attention.

"What do you mean?"

"Not enough mass," Manning said, showing the

handheld sonar device he had in his hand. "This box is mostly air."

"I don't believe it," the agent replied. "You two. Check it out."

"Don't touch it," Bolan said.

"What?"

"It's there for a reason. If it's a decoy, it may be booby-trapped to set off the real emitter, wherever that is. A simple radio transmitter would do it."

"We'll be careful."

"Don't." His voice was so low and full of menace that the engineers froze.

"Look, pal, this isn't your command any longer, got it?" Red Leader said. "The bad guys are dead. That means this is my game now."

Bolan had turned away from the FBI agent as if the man didn't exist. He was shining his flashlight at the sharply slanted ceiling, and he rubbed his finger along a bare plywood seam.

"It's here," he said, "under the floor. Maybe even in the ceiling. This is all freshly laid wood. They're hiding it right under our feet."

"Bullshit," Red Leader protested.

"Let's start ripping it up," Manning said.

Bolan opened a tool chest that had been dragged up with the engineers. He found a pry bar and a small hatchet, and he handed the pry bar to Manning.

"Now just a damn minute!" Red Leader said. "I'm not authorizing you guys to come in here and start ripping up this place while we—"

"And I'm not going to stand around and argue with you when we've got less than ten minutes to shut this thing down," Bolan growled. "Get more men with pry bars up here."

"I think that guy is right," one of the engineers said. "If there's a low sonar mass reading inside the box, then the machinery has to be elsewhere. It could be hidden under the floors easily enough."

"So why not look through them using the sonar?" Red Leader demanded.

"That might take hours," Manning declared. "We don't have hours."

Bolan didn't bother to listen to the argument that erupted between the engineer and the FBI agent. He started in the middle, guessing that the gaps in the rafters would need to be at their widest to allow the emitter to be staged, and slammed the hatchet into the wood sheeting. It ripped through a large portion of the board. Bolan grabbed the tear in the wood with both hands and hoisted it up. The wood bent, then cracked, then shattered into several big pieces that he tore off by their stringy connections and tossed away.

Underneath was old, grayish-pink insulation.

As he started working on the next plywood sheet, he noticed the engineers had found hammers and had started prying boards up with the nail grips. Manning was feverishly attacking floorboards at the other end, putting his back into the effort. Red Leader was staring bitterly at his engineers, trying to determine a face-saving course of action.

The attic, Bolan realized, covered the entire square footage of the house. That had to be upward of two thousand square feet. With a sinking feeling he realized that they would need a full half an hour to check beneath each and every plywood piece that had been nailed into the floor. If the emitter was behind the ceiling wood panels, another hour would be needed.

They were going to have to get lucky.

And Mack Bolan believed in making his own luck.

"Get your men out of the house," he ordered the Red Leader.

"What? Why?"

"I can shoot through the floors and listen for a metallic impact," Bolan explained quickly.

"With that?" the Red Leader asked, nodding at the Beretta 93-R Bolan had drawn. "You're not going to get through the floors and ceilings with a 9 mm."

"The danger to your men isn't from the gunshots. The danger is from the booby trap that may have been placed on the emitter. It might blow itself up, and us with it."

At long last the Red Leader decided to get cooperative. "Okay. We're getting out." He hurried down the steep stairs, yelling for his men to clear out. The pair of engineers didn't follow him.

"We'll stay and help you out."

"No need. We'll manage. And it's too dangerous," Manning said. "I'll be able to put a stop to the emitter if it can be stopped. If I can't do it, nobody can." He wasn't boasting. He was stating the facts.

The engineers looked at each other, then hurried out.

Bolan pointed the silenced weapon at the floor and fired it into the middle of a plywood panel. The cough of the weapon was loud and masked the sound of the impact, but Bolan and Manning both were sure they had heard only the crack of punctured wood.

He marched quickly along the length of the big empty attic, firing the weapon four times into each plywood sheet. When he reached the end he started back again on another row.

Manning glanced at his watch while Bolan changed his third magazine.

"In three, two, one. Time's up," Manning declared.

Bolan stood still. "I don't hear a generator."

Manning seemed to pale. "You think we were led on a wild-goose chase after all, Mack?"

Bolan triggered another round into the plywood beneath his feet, and they both heard the clunk of the 9 mm round slamming into something metal.

"Let's go," Bolan growled. He slashed at the wood as if it were soggy cardboard, ripping it away in big, ragged pieces that tore at his hands. Underneath the board was a strange collection of components wired together. All of it was covered by a clear, Plexiglas shield imbedded with a small glass device.

A single power indicator showed that the unit was on.

"Mercury switch," Manning said, pointing to the glass device. "I'd bet my back teeth it's wired to blow the thing if there's any movement. We're lucky the shot didn't disrupt it enough to blow it."

"It's packed in dynamite," Bolan said. "Designed to blow itself up when the fire reaches the unit." A plan materialized in his head in a second, and he spoke quickly. "We wrap a loop of nylon rope around the power feed, toss it out the window and get the hell out. On the ground floor we yank the cord and disrupt the mercury switch and blow the thing up before it has a chance to do its damage."

"Let's do it," Manning said. He grabbed a long strand of nylon cord that had come as part of the engineer's kit.

Bolan slipped the nylon cord under the cable that led away from the emitter unit, careful not to nudge it even slightly, compressing the old insulation underneath the cable so that it wouldn't make contact with the cable before he wanted it to. As he finished, his eyes fell on his watch. Zero plus one minute, fourteen seconds. What was happening out there?

He heard the sounds of shouting and a scream, strangely muffled by the walls.

Manning had finished knotting a second nylon rope to the first for added length, and they flung the loose end through the moveable vent at the far end of the attic. "Go!" Bolan ordered as he held the end so the rope around the power cable to the emitter wouldn't be disturbed when the slack tightened.

Then he bolted down the steps, chasing Manning to the third floor then following close on his heels down the stairs and out the front door. He tore across the front yard, heading for the side of the house where the rope dangled. He ignored the clouds of smoke that were already drifting through the streets, the flashes of yellow flame from the nearby buildings, the shouts and the strange darkness that came from the absence of electric power. There was no sound of machinery or vehicles. They were all dead. There was only the rush and crackle of growing fires.

Bolan heard Manning on his heels.

"Get out of here!" he shouted.

"Let me do it—"

"Gary, get the hell out of here now!"

Manning was suddenly gone, obeying his orders,

as Bolan tore around the far side of the building. He found the dangling piece of fluorescent yellow rope, grabbed it high in the air and pulled it down to the ground with all his strength.

Something on the other end of the rope caught, held for a heartbeat, then gave.

The big house seemed to shudder, then the top half was obliterated by a blast that filled the night with unreal white brilliance. It blinded Bolan, even with his eyes squeezed shut, until he felt the rush of fire and the hammer of debris slam into him with the force of a speeding train.

Then all the brightness turned black.

CHAPTER TWENTY

Kenilworth, Illinois

"Mack!"

"I'm okay," Bolan said even before he realized he'd regained consciousness. Manning was trying to pull him up and drag him away from the burning house. As the soldier balanced on his feet, he felt the unsteadiness in his limbs that came from the shock. The exposed flesh on his nape was alive with heat and felt abraded. He propelled himself into a jog, feeling the speed of the movement and the impact of his legs on the ground pounding his senses into clarity. He could see the odd darkness around him. The streetlights, the house lights and every vehicle were black. The only lights in evidence were the flashlights in the hands of the law-enforcement officers who were milling about, confused and without purpose.

Then, as Bolan reached the street, just as he was thinking he was coming back to a state of complete awareness, he wondered for a moment if he was turned around, looking somehow in the wrong direction. In front of him, a house was bursting into flame.

"Gary," he said, gesturing at the mansion across

the street, a big colonial style mansion, "we've been had."

Manning stared at the blaze that was erupting from the exterior walls of the house. First there was a small constellation of tiny, glowing spots where the nails and metal connectors under the siding became red hot, then they began igniting the wooden frame supports and siding. Inside, the heat quickly ignited the carpeting and drapes.

"Kabat took no chances. He had more than one emitter in place."

"At least we cut the damage by half," Manning said hollowly.

"Tell that to them," Bolan said, as a wail of terror came out of the big colonial mansion.

Bolan jogged across the street, dropping his useless electronics and unneeded hardware onto the grass. In seconds the tiny pinpoints of overheated metal pieces had turned the house into a wall-to-wall conflagration. The windows on either side of the front door were already dancing with orange flame. Bolan pulled back just before he grabbed the knob. He had no idea if it was ferrous metal or not, but the lock mechanism inside would almost surely be steel, meaning it would fry his flesh the second he touched it. Instead he turned and solidly back-kicked the door just under the knob. The wood broke, and a second kick swung the door open.

The soldier ran inside and found himself surrounded by fire on all sides. He heard the screams again and followed them to the second floor. The walls were covered in flame, which clung to the plaster like a blanket and collected on the ceiling like blowing snow drifting in an alley. The heat was intense, and the hot wind that flowed over Bolan from down the hall fried his burned skin. He gritted his teeth against the pain and ran into the inferno, crashing through another door that had been made invisible by the fire.

A woman was in the room, standing over a man whose clothes were burning him alive. Bolan grabbed the man and rolled him across the rug, extinguishing the flames partially. He breathed the smoke and the smell of roasted flesh and felt the heat closing in on him.

The walls had been burning. The floor was heating up and starting to smoke. The supports underneath the floor were starting to ignite. A black spot appeared in the carpet and quickly grew.

"Come on!" Bolan ordered.

The woman's terrified eyes seemed to focus slightly. "We can't move him. He's burned."

"We can't stay here," he said and gave her a shove into the hall. Bolan knew that the safest place to grab a burn victim was under the arms, where the victim was least likely to have been burned. He dragged the man out the door in a run, listening to the grunts of pain coming from the half-conscious victim. He watched as a large sheet of blackened skin was scraped off onto the floor, but there was little he could do about it. There was no time for merciful treatment.

He stumbled into the woman at the top of the stairs as she stamped and slapped at the fire that had ignited her blouse. Bolan felt the fire jump to his hair. He was in the middle of an inferno, and standing still was enabling the flames to take their hold of him. He grabbed the woman's wrist in one hand and the man's collar in another, and made a run for it. He heard the woman's screams and the grunts of the man as he yanked them like half-filled potato sacks down the stairs. The entryway was a wall of flame, and Bolan couldn't see the door through the blaze. He made a guess, charging into the fire blindly.

All of a sudden the heat dissipated and he was in the darkness again. There was a rush of liquid noise, and he felt himself being drenched with water.

"We've got more over here!" someone shouted. "I need three stretchers right now!"

"No, I'm okay," Bolan said, wiping the muddy ash off his face and breathing deeply of the cool, clean night air. "These two people need help."

The man was still. The woman was moaning and trying to make her way to him when she was engulfed by emergency teams. Bolan looked around for Manning. The Phoenix Force commando hadn't followed him into the house and was nowhere in sight.

The next house was burning, too, as was the house beyond it, Bolan saw, as he jogged into the street. And the house beyond that.

He realized that the streets were no longer dark. Despite the entire lack of electrical power, the town was suffused with a bloody orange glow that came from all around him. Every building within his range of vision was being consumed in flame. Bolan's intention of following the blazes in search of the second emitter wasn't do-able. Every house was completely engulfed, and there was no way to tell which had been burning longest.

Bolan glanced at his watch. To his shock, he realized the conflagration had started only fourteen minutes ago.

People were dying around him, and there was nothing he could do. He didn't know where the victims were, and he couldn't have reached them if he did. He didn't know where the enemy was.

He had rarely felt so impotent in all his life.

He spotted a figure waving to him, and he approached a knot of emergency crews standing around a makeshift triage in a court, with five burning houses surrounding them. Manning was there.

"You burned?" he asked.

"Just a little singed around the edges," Bolan said.

"I tried to track down the progress of the fires to the source," Manning said. "I got distracted along the way." He gestured with a blackened hand to what appeared to be a family of victims, two adults and two children, huddled together on the grass looking dazed. "But the source of the fires seemed to be in this court. In that house."

Manning nodded to the house at the end of the street, withdrawn from the others in a bank of trees. It was fully engulfed in flame, like all the others. "If I was trying to do the most damage, that would be a good starting point," he said. "An emitter directed out of the top floor would fan out that way and get maximum exposure to property. If our first emitter had worked, it would have started a fresh line of fires at what may have been the outside range of this emitter. Maximum carnage."

Bolan nodded. "We'll know soon enough."

"Yeah."

There was a change in the light. The orange glow around them became whiter, and Bolan turned, realizing he was seeing headlights. A car approached the triage and came to a quick stop with a brief squeak of tires. It was an antique, gleaming, perfectly restored Mercedes, at least forty years old. A flat-bed two-wheeled trailer was chained on the rear bumper. It was a landscaper's trailer, but all the equipment had been dumped.

Manning nodded, understanding. "Too old to have electronics."

"Yeah, but all steel," Bolan said, jogging up to the stopped car. He placed his hand on the body panels and handles.

"I think it stopped!" The driver who jumped out was in his late fifties with thin silvery hair and a gray goatee. "I took the chance. We need to get some of these people out of here."

"I think you're right," Bolan said. The steel parts weren't getting any warmer to the touch.

Then the night turned to daylight as Manning's house exploded with a burst of thunder. Bolan put an arm over his face and listened to the rattling of debris as it tumbled to the ground around him, but they were too far away to get hit by anything large.

"That's it," Bolan said. "The second emitter is out of commission. Driver, let me take your car."

"I got wounded people I need to transport out of here, mack," the goateed gentleman protested.

"The emitters are destroyed. We can get emergency equipment in here," Bolan explained. "Ambulances and emergency helicopters can do a lot more good than pulling them out in a trailer. I can be back before you can get these people on the trailer, anyway."

The goateed man nodded and tossed his keys to Bolan.

CHAPTER TWENTY-ONE

Major Antoine Delagones was called in to work at six o'clock in the morning, Eastern time.

Delagones hadn't known what to expect when he took the position of medical doctor on call for the mysterious and highly secretive federal operation. He had never heard of the operation prior to his recruitment by a high-placed Fed in the Justice Department, Hal Brognola. Brognola was acquainted with a general who had been impressed by Delagones's work with field injuries during Desert Storm a decade ago, and who had followed the doctor's career since. Brognola had apparently been networking for a military, combat-experienced physician to take a tour of duty with the operation.

The general hadn't recommended that Delagones take the position. "Truth is, son, I don't know a damn thing about the operation. It's not Army. At least I think it ain't. They sure the hell haven't cleared me to have knowledge of it."

That had given Delagones second thoughts. An operation so secret an Army general hadn't been briefed on it—wasn't even supposed to officially know it existed?

"The only reason I even know about it is because

I happen to have known Hal for a long stretch, son,'' the general had confided to Delagones. "He uses me to recruit good people. I find them for him every once in a while. Those people go in, do their job and come out again and rejoin the regular military. They don't talk about what happens, so I don't even know."

Delagones joined the operation out of curiosity more than anything else. Only after he'd gone through more secret swearing and confidentially agreement signing than he'd ever thought a bureaucracy could dream up was he told anything about the place.

It was called Stony Man Farm.

The call for his services came from Barbara Price, his Stony Man boss—she wasn't military so he didn't call her his CO. It had conveyed a sense of urgency but not emergency. He was flown in immediately.

"Hey, Doc," Aaron Kurtzman said. The wheelchair-bound computer expert was the first person Delagones ran into upon entering the facility. The man they called Bear was always unfailingly friendly to Delagones, but today there was a grimness in his demeanor.

In his compact but state-of-the-art medical facility, Delagones found the man they called Striker.

Delagones didn't know who this guy was, but he scared the hell out of him. He came and went, obviously a highly respected and important personage at Stony Man Farm and just as clearly not one of the nine-to-five staffers. Some sort of an agent, he had more freedom than any of the others. He would be gone for weeks and months at a time.

He wasn't the tallest agent Delagones had treated

in his office, nor the most muscle-bound. But his piercing blue eyes, sharply contoured face and simmering personality made him somehow distinctly menacing and powerful. Delagones had no doubt the man was a trained and expert killer. Striker saw all, with eyes that absorbed information and detail like a dry sponge absorbed water. He moved with the grace of a cat, perfectly comfortable with his body, like some sort of intensely cross-trained martial artist. Like the martial artist, Delagones was sure this man could move like death-dealing lightning when the time came.

"Good morning. What did you do to yourself this time?"

Striker was on the exam table. His eyes had been closed, but he hadn't been sleeping. When the man sat up his eyes were deep and ringed in black. He hadn't slept in a long time. "Got burned."

"Take your shirt off," Delagones said without probing further. He washed his hands, thinking about the reports that had been on the news about the horrible fires that had taken place in a wealthy community near Chicago the previous night and in Boston two days ago. Some sort of super arsonist at work. Somehow, this Striker may have been involved.

He turned and frowned. "Aren't you in pain? Do you want something?"

"No narcotics."

Delagones sat on his wheeled stool and peered with a physician's fascination at the long burn wound on the man's abdomen and lower rib cage. The flesh was blistered and hardened, scabbing in some places, inflamed in others.

The doctor kicked against the table and rolled across to one of his pharmaceutical cabinets. "We've got to get you on antibiotics, anyway, first thing." He found what he wanted among the hundreds of tiny bottles in the pull-down shelves and prepped a syringe. He put a large dose of antibiotics into the man's flank.

Then he got to work cleaning the wounds.

AKIRA TOKAIDO SLIPPED a new CD into the minidisk player strapped to his leg, dragged on the lightweight headphones and cranked it. He'd slept just a few hours in a bunk at the Farm, and now he was relieving his boss, Aaron Kurtzman. The big man in the wheelchair hadn't slept a wink in more than twenty-four hours.

The minidisk was his custom mix of decades-old epics by one of the dinosaur heavy-metal bands and some faster-moving industrial dance metal. Tokaido liked it all. And it helped keep him awake. He found it gave him the perfect level of mental distraction when he was programming.

Or when he was watching his programming function.

The highly complicated piece of software he and Kurtzman had customized in the past few days was one of their most ambitious cybernetic projects. They had conceived it a while back, knowing that there were going to be instances when they would absolutely have to trace the location of an e-mail message. Kurtzman performed the top-level design. Tokaido did most of the more insidious and invasive application programming. Carmen Delahunt, Hunt Wethers, even Gadgets Schwarz and Gary Manning had thrown in their two cents' worth during its development.

The software used a master application that roamed the Internet servers and watched their e-mail activity. For every server type, a piece of slave software was used to automatically bypass security protocols and firewalls to get information.

It was notoriously hard to maintain all these applications, since server protection systems constantly evolved, but they had found that they were often— not always—able to break into a system if they did so nondestructively. In other words, they could watch all the private activity they wanted. It wasn't until they started damaging data that they were attacked more aggressively and kicked off.

The software had been used by the Farm several times during the past few years. The latest version of it was being used now, to watch the Internet around the world for another batch of e-mails from Roger Kabat. Dozens of slave routines were operating, searching, reading private e-mail messages, analyzing their contents, shuttling suspect messages to more sophisticated software for further analyzing. Hundreds of thousands of messages were being read.

It was all flagrantly illegal. Clear-cut invasion of privacy.

But much of what Stony Man Farm did in the name of true justice was against the law. And if Kurtzman's software was violating the privacy rights of the people, he was doing it for the one-and-only purpose of protecting them from their murderer. Messages that had nothing to do with Kabat and his grand extortion-or-arson scheme were ignored and purged from the Stony Man system.

So far, not one message had been kept.

As sophisticated as it was, Tokaido almost constantly needed to maintain the various slave applications and the reports generating from hundreds of servers. He was bored with it all, his mind turning over potential software upgrades to the current system. Any pattern a human could see on a computer screen the computer itself should be able to recognize and deal with. The trick was describing the pattern to the computer in terms clear enough for the computer to understand it perfectly.

Tokaido read an e-mail message from a man to his former girlfriend. The man was clearly emotionally disturbed. The vernacular and vocabulary he used were such that the Stony Man software had flagged it and tracked it as a possible Kabat message.

Tokaido purged it.

The screen was empty for a moment.

The minidisk changed tracks and sent the opening power chord of a new song through Tokaido's head.

He didn't hear it, because at that moment three windows popped up on his PC, then a half dozen more, each showing exactly the same e-mail message. Each window covered up the previous window. Ten more popped into view, then suddenly new windows started coming up so fast Tokaido watched them move on his screen as if he were watching high-end computer animation.

Tokaido did three things at once. He slammed his leg against the leg of the desk and hit the Off button on the minidisk player, he stabbed a button on a keyboard to start a labyrinthine search operation that would expand worldwide in a matter of seconds, and he tapped the Send button on the phone system.

"He's doing it," Tokaido announced into Kurtzman's bedroom.

Five minutes later, Aaron Kurtzman was at Tokaido's side.

BOLAN STRODE into the Computer Room still buttoning his shirt over the mass of bandages covering his torso. "How's it going?"

"Not yet!" Kurtzman said, staring at his screen and shuttling between one window and another. "The e-mails started coming just a few minutes ago. Akira started the search at once, but no results yet."

"How are you tracking it?"

"By planning ahead," Kurtzman replied without taking his eyes from the screen. "Our burglar spider has already analyzed hundreds of servers and firewalls and security systems, figured out how to get in and take control of them and stored the information for this moment. Right now we're breaking into thousands of on-line computers around the world, finding the Kabat e-mails as they come through and allowing our search software to track down the source. Since the source is almost always another server, we get in and repeat the process, databasing all the results. Eventually we'll find the origin of all these messages. We hope."

As the cybernetics staff worked, Bolan moved to a spare monitor and looked at the latest Kabat message. It was short and sweet.

The U.S. government is hereby served notice: my price has doubled to $100,000,000. Announce in the media your intentions to pay this sum in full upon demand, or the next target is your nation's capital. You have twenty-four hours.

Bolan considered the implications.

The body count from the burning of Kenilworth was at fifty and climbing.

The death toll from the Boston attack was almost as high, but the number of people in the hospital was over one hundred. Burn victims, car crash victims, victims of panic.

But when Kabat set off his emitter in Boston he hadn't realized its potential as an arson tool. Imagine the mayhem he could perpetrate in a big city with a couple of well-placed emitters if he knew what he was doing.

Bolan tried to estimate in his head the damage from an emitter pointed at a steel-beamed skyscraper in downtown Washington, D.C. The deaths would be in the thousands.

"Bear, tell me you've got something."

Kurtzman held up his left hand for a moment's reprieve while his right hand flew on the keyboard, then stopped suddenly. A tiny green icon appeared on his screen.

"Striker," Kurtzman said with a grim smile, "I've got something."

CHAPTER TWENTY-TWO

Stony Man Farm, Virginia

Stony Man Farm was expert at fielding small, highly effective antiterrorist special operations groups. Rarely could the organization be accused of using too many forces to accomplish the task at hand. Overkill was almost never the most effective way of getting the job done. Barbara Price knew the lesson well.

But sometimes it was ideal to simply throw everything you had at the enemy.

Like right now. Two teams—eight men, plus the Executioner, with support staff on alert at the Farm, Yakov Katzenelenbogen and Cowboy Kissinger at the wheel of waiting ground transport nearby and Jack Grimaldi hovering out of earshot in a military transport chopper big enough for all of them.

All to stake out a one-room fishing shack.

Mack Bolan was commanding the two Stony Man teams. He was wired to both groups via the digital satellite and cellular communication system rigged for seamless field communications between all parties. He would serve as field commander until such time as the two teams needed to split up and work independently.

Bolan was determined to stop this strike before it occurred. He wouldn't let any more innocent people die at the hands of Roger Kabat.

They were on the south shore of the wide mouth of Virginia's Rappahannock River, eight or ten miles from where the waters mixed with the water of Chesapeake Bay. The nearest town was a village called Saluda. The nearest city of any size was Richmond, Virginia, forty-five miles due west.

The shack was a wooden square on a foundation of concrete blocks. It had been painted green once, years ago, but the paint was so old it had mostly worn off or faded to gray. By contrast, the leased Chevrolet utility van was a rich sky blue, shining new.

Bolan stood on the roof of the Grand Cherokee with a pair of tripod-mounted field glasses, hidden from the fishing shack by acres of wooded ground. After watching the building for more than two hours, he was calm and only mildly expectant. It was too early for the activity to begin. And he had the patience of a professional soldier, trained in the jungles and honed to a high level of skill over years of fieldwork.

Things would commence in their own good time.

Besides, it was too early for Kabat's strike force to move. They didn't even know if they had a target.

Brognola had alerted the team that morning to the official word that was going to come out of the White House.

"The Man's standing firm," the big Fed told them from his Washington, D.C., office on a predawn conference call. "He'll make the announcement this afternoon at 1:00 p.m. That's when Kabat's deadline is up. The Man will go live to tell the American people that the U.S. will not negotiate with terrorists."

Brognola said nothing for a moment, letting his people come to terms with that fact.

"Bear, how good is your lead?"

"Very good."

"Explain it to me. Without the technical vocabulary, if possible."

"We used our e-mail tracking software to trace yesterday's message back to its source in real time," Kurtzman explained. "We had to burglarize the security systems on a few Internet service providers along the way, and they're going to be very pissed off about it, I'm sure, but they'll never know who got in. We found the e-mails originating from a dial-up on the East Coast. From there we tracked back the call that was commanding the mass e-mail. It was coming in via a digitally coded cellular model connection. We homed in on that and triangulated a geographical source for the call. That gave us our source.

"Then we put an electronics truck on the scene to intercept all future phone calls coming in or going out of the vicinity. Kabat's people made the mistake of using the same digital coding protocol on future calls as they used for their e-mail message. The e-mail message served as a Rosetta stone. By the time our truck was on the scene, we'd broken their coding enough to get audible signals out of their calls."

"And those calls were traced to this building?" Brognola asked.

"Actually to the phone used in the shack. At least one of those calls was made from the vehicle last night when it drove into town. But they seem to be staying at the shack, and their calls have said that one of the pickups will be made at the shack."

"Pickups?" Brognola said.

"They're going to take delivery of one of the emitters, we believe," Barbara Price said. "Their location on the water would make it very easy for them to have it delivered by water, but that's not a given."

"The problem," Bolan said, "is that the calls we've eavesdropped on indicate they'll get delivery of just one emitter at this location. And there'll be more than one."

"You got some sort of indication of that from their message?" the Fed asked.

"Yes. But I would assume so anyway," Bolan stated. "The features that make the emitters so attractive to Kabat as an arms trader also make it easy for him to plant backup redundant units for extortionary purposes. If he did so in Kenilworth, he'll do it in D.C."

"Agreed. But how many?"

"Two or three." The speaker this time was Yakov Katzenelenbogen. An older man with an ageless face, he had silver-gray hair and blue eyes that shone with a teenager's vitality. His missing arm had been replaced with a prosthetic device covered with rubberized plastic. The hand and fingers were flesh-colored—very natural looking. During his days as a warrior, commanding the Phoenix Force special operations group, Katzenelenbogen had fitted the fake hand with a number of mechanical killing devices that had turned the impairment into a unique field advantage. He had retired from field duty and served as Stony Man tactical adviser. The former Israeli army intelligence chief had an innate feel for behavior and motivations of the enemy—whomever that enemy might be.

"Why so few, Katz?" Bolan asked. The Executioner had known and fought side by side with Katzenelenbogen on more occasions than he could remember. This was one of the few warriors on the planet who might still teach him a thing or two. He had a deep respect for the man's insight.

"In my opinion this is just another step in Kabat's grand scheme," Katzenelenbogen said. "Boston was his first demonstration. Kenilworth was another. Washington, D.C., is just one more. A demonstration."

"I'm not following. Are you saying he doesn't intend to use the emitters on D.C.?" Kurtzman asked.

"No, he most definitely does intend to use the emitters, because he most definitely does not intend for his extortionary scheme to work. Not this time," Katzenelenbogen explained. "Mack, you said you realized that the Kenilworth attack was one such demonstration. He asked for too much money. He demanded it with too little lead time. He didn't give the people of that town time to get scared enough for their resolve to crumble."

Bolan nodded. He saw where the man was going with his thinking.

"Kabat is doing the same thing with his Washington, D.C., strike. He's asked for just a little too much money. He's given the U.S. too little time to respond. The U.S. government will respond, naturally, with its longtime standard response to terrorism and extortion—we will not negotiate. One day is not enough time for people to get scared, to start to voice dissenting opinions.''

"Yes," Bolan agreed. "If he'd given the country a few days to think it over, there might actually have been some movement to give in in the name of sparing lives."

"That makes sense," Brognola said from the speaker on the table in the Stony Man Farm War Room. "But, Katz, you still haven't explained why you think there will be just two or three emitters deployed in D.C."

"Because right now Kabat has a limited supply," Katzenelenbogen said. "By our count of the specialized porcelain inventory he ripped off from Senegal Scientific, he's only got enough frit for five units left."

"So he'll use two of them on D.C.," Bolan said. "The world will know he still has three units left, so when he goes to make his last play—his real play, when he asks for some real money—the world will be very aware he has the capability to carry out his threat."

"That seems to make good sense."

"But it's still just guesswork," Bolan stated. "We can't be absolutely sure of anything. There are no guarantees when you're trying to predict the behavior of a madman."

Katzenelenbogen nodded grimly, then said aloud, for the benefit of Brognola, "Agreed."

"We can't ever guarantee anything in this line of work," the big Fed said. "We'll try to stop the emitters from being activated in Washington, D.C. But all we can do is the best we can do.''

Bolan was staring at the table when he suddenly realized Brognola had been addressing him directly. But he said nothing. The words were meaningless when the parade of the faceless dead was marching through his thoughts. He wondered how many ghosts would make up that parade if he failed to stop the D.C. attacks. The number of dead could be in the thousands.

"STRIKER, THIS IS Stony Base," Barbara Price said in his headset.

"Striker here."

"The President's on the networks. He's making his announcement."

"Affirmative. Check in, teams."

"Able One here," said Carl "Ironman" Lyons, former L.A. cop, former Justice Department investigator, commander of the three member Able Team. "We're ready, Striker."

"Phoenix One here," said the British-accented voice of Phoenix Force commander David McCarter. "We're standing by."

Bolan watched through the glasses as he listened. The shack was still. No one was coming or going.

Then he saw a blur on the dark blue-gray mass of the wide river behind the shack. He spun the electronic focus on the glasses to bring the blur into his depth of field.

The ten-foot pleasure boat was painted a deep burgundy, and it motored toward the shore at a steady, unhurried pace. The woman in the rear was lounging on the seat trailing a fishing pole. The man at the steering wheel was shirtless, drinking a beer. They were a haggard-looking pair in their late forties, and their boat was just as unkempt and almost as old.

The interior of the boat was dominated by a large wooden crate.

Bolan quickly reported what he saw. Ten minutes later he announced that the pleasure craft was tying up on the rickety dock off the fishing shack.

They waited there. Fifteen minutes later a man emerged from the shack. While the fisherwoman kept her pole in the water and kept an eye on their surroundings, the men moved a ramp into the craft and wheeled the crate onto it. It was mounted on low dolly wheels, and they pushed it up the ramp with considerable effort. The intensity of concentration on their faces was clearly visible in Bolan's binoculars. He could almost hear their grunts and profanity.

Once the crate was on the dock the going was much easier. They wheeled it up the ramp and onto the rocky grass, then repositioned the ramp at the rear of the Chevrolet van. Without the rocking of the boat, they found getting the crate into the van a less frustrating undertaking. In seconds they were done.

"We're moving out," the soldier called.

As the small pleasure craft moved away from the shore, the man from the shack drove away in the van.

"Stony Base, I'm sending a digitized image of the pleasure craft," Bolan announced.

"Roger that," Kurtzman said. "I'm getting it, Stony One."

"The Coast Guard has a team standing by for us," Price said. "They're ready to move as soon as I get the word to my contact. We'll have that pair in the pleasure craft watched and picked up."

"Let's wait on that, Stony Base," Bolan said as he jumped into the Jeep, jamming the field glasses and tripod behind his seat. Katzenelenbogen moved the SUV into Drive, and they were rolling before Bolan had his door closed. They pulled onto the highway just a few hundred yards behind the van.

"We're intercepting a call," Kurtzman announced. "The van driver is letting somebody know he's on his way."

"Stony One here. We tracing the destination of that call?" Bolan asked.

"Of course."

"Phoenix, go ahead and make your move on the fishing shack."

"Phoenix One here," McCarter radioed. "We're moving in."

"Stony One, I think we just got a major break," Kurtzman said. "Our friend in the van is going to make a stop somewhere and meet up with someone—it might be our second emitter team."

"Why the meeting?"

"Unknown. Something apparently needs to be exchanged. Can't tell what from their conversation, and I'm not guaranteeing it's who we want it to be."

"Stony One to Able One. You with me, Able?" Bolan radioed.

"We're rolling, Stony One," Lyons radioed. "We'll stay back far enough so the perps in the Chevy van won't see us. Stony Two, keep us informed of our route as it changes."

"Roger that," Katzenelenbogen replied.

"Able One, be prepared to take up the trail of the second team when we rendezvous with them," Bolan said.

"We'll be ready, Stony One."

PHOENIX FORCE HAD spread out through the waist-high grass at the water's edge and through the lightly wooded patches of growth near the shore of the river.

"We'll be ready, Stony One." The words came from Carl Lyons, leader of Able Team, before Phoenix Force changed frequencies.

"Hear that?" T.J. Hawkins muttered over the new frequency dedicated to the Phoenix Force probe. "Able gets all the good jobs."

"All right, mates," David McCarter radioed, his voice brisk. "We've got a job to do and we're going to do it by the numbers, no mistakes. Got that?"

"Got it," came a series of replies.

"Got that, Phoenix Five?" McCarter asked.

"Got it, Phoenix One," Hawkins replied a little sheepishly.

McCarter was satisfied. Hawkins was the youngest and least experienced of Phoenix Force, but he was a first-rate commando with superlative combat skills. He'd get over his disappointment at being left with the grunt work.

Forget that. All indications could be wrong. They might very easily stumble upon major players or important intelligence inside that fishing shack. The job had to be done, and it had to be done right.

"Let's move," McCarter radioed.

The approach to the fishing shack had been timed and planned during the past few hours of surveillance. Further instructions from McCarter would be redundant and distracting. He let the experts do the job they got paid to do.

Rafael Encizo, the Cuban-born Phoenix Force

member, and Gary Manning, the big Canadian, made a leapfrog approach from the southeast along the shore, making effective use of the tall grasses and slogging through the shoreline mud. It took them three minutes to move from their staging plot a hundred yards away to within ten paces of the east side of the shack, which contained a single small window. It was covered with blinds. One of the pair constantly watched the window during the approach. The slightest movement of the blinds would have been noticed instantly. The movement never came, but that didn't mean there couldn't have been gunners standing behind the shades watching their every move.

Calvin James, the black former Navy SEAL, approached from the west, the windowless side of the building. He was charged with watching for movement on the north side of the shack, which faced the dock and the water. He moved with stealth, coming to his stopping point just ten feet from the west wall of the shack, secure behind a pile of old junk and a rotting wooden rowboat.

T. J. Hawkins and David McCarter approached the shack from the front, angling toward the front door until they came together in a low depression offering a little protection just a few yards from the front door.

The shack remained quiet. McCarter paused long enough to get a visual positioning on his team, then gave them a brief wave.

Phoenix Force moved as swiftly and silently as a striking snake. James sprinted to the north side of the shack and flattened himself next to the seaside door. McCarter and Hawkins approached the front in a crouch, eyes peeled for movement in the front windows. Encizo and Manning approached and dropped under the side window, then Encizo slammed the butt of his M-16 into the glass.

As he heard the window shatter, McCarter kicked in the door and Hawkins swept the interior of the shack with his M-16.

He saw no movement in the dim interior.

The back door opened, and James did a closer proximity search.

Hawkins saw his teammate's shoulders sag.

"Nothing."

The others congregated inside the shack. One room, no furnishings except for a bare Army cot that looked as if it dated from the Korean War, and a tiny gas stove.

There was no litter, no discarded papers, no cooking pots, nothing.

"We struck out," Manning muttered.

"Sometimes," Hawkins said, "you wonder why you bother to get up in the morning."

CHAPTER TWENTY-THREE

Virginia

Bolan calmly read off the plates on the Ford pickup. "It's rented," he added.

"We'll run it anyway," Kurtzman said. "You never know. Were you guys able to get good shots of the drivers?"

"Katz is working on it," Bolan replied.

They were parked in the lot beside a chain pizza restaurant. Traffic was whizzing by on the road that separated them from the BP gas station where the Chevrolet van had pulled in to meet with the Ford pickup.

Katzenelenbogen had set up the tripod inside the Grand Cherokee and was fiddling with the electronics on his laptop, zooming in and adjusting the digital camera. He was shooting already, but had yet to procure a good facial shot of either of the drivers, who had entered the gas station convenience store upon arrival.

When they emerged, Katzenelenbogen was ready. He had the camera focused on the door and scored with two high-quality seconds of high-contrast images of both faces.

"Stony Two here," he radioed. "A couple of good shots coming to you, Stony Base."

"Receiving them," Kurtzman said as the images passed through the cellular modem connection on Katzenelenbogen's laptop.

Bolan was busy observing the activity across the street. The pickup driver passed a manila envelope to his companion. The driver of the van was a tall, broad-shouldered, clean-cut black man, who smiled broadly when he peered into the envelope. He nodded and placed the envelope inside the van. The short, stocky white man driving the pickup laughed and climbed into his vehicle.

"Stony One here," Bolan radioed. "Able One, looks like your target's about to take off."

"Copy that, Stony One," Lyons returned. "I see him. We're ready to go."

As the pickup pulled out of the gas station and onto the road, Able Team's Jeep Wrangler Sahara wheeled out of a doctor's office a quarter mile back and took off after it.

"Got it, Jack?"

"I'm on it, Stony One." Bolan glanced up and spotted the big military chopper hovering far above them. It glided away after the pickup. The computer lock Grimaldi and his Farm copilot would establish from the chopper would make losing the truck almost impossible. Between the chopper and Able Team's ground tracking, they'd follow the Ford pickup to its ultimate destination.

But the pickup wasn't yet loaded with its emitter—if it was, in fact, the vehicle that would place the emitter. They still had to get the device. Until they did, Bolan didn't want to chance tipping their hand by nabbing the van.

The black man entered the washroom. He was gone for just a minute, and when he reappeared he was wearing an Air Force uniform. He grabbed the envelope from the front seat and made quick work of applying the special labels to the van that told the world he was a United States Air Force colonel.

That, Bolan knew, would get him into all kinds of secured government parking lots throughout the D.C. area. Lots of good targets.

Which one would it be?

TWELVE MINUTES LATER, as they pulled onto the interstate, Bolan was getting an idea which target Kabat was going for.

Katzenelenbogen was just as intuitive. "I have a feeling we're heading for the Pentagon."

"Yeah," Bolan said. "Stony Base, this is Stony One. Our target is heading into the Pentagon. We need to stop him at the gate if at all possible."

"Right," Price said. "Hold on."

Midday traffic was light on the interstate, and the exit to the enormous government building, home to the world's most powerful national defense infrastructure, was coming up quick.

"If they manage to stop him at the gate, he might just activate the emitter then and there," Katzenelenbogen said, as he steered the Grand Cherokee off the highway, slowing to keep his quarter-mile cushion behind the van.

"That would still inflict a hell of a lot of damage to the cars in the parking lot, but it would be too distant to affect the building itself, if the range of the

Kenilworth and Boston emitters can be used as a guide,'' Bolan observed. "He'd have to get well into the lot, close to the actual structure. We have to stop that from happening.''

"We could stop him ourselves. Right now,'' Katzenelenbogen added.

"Not near the highway,'' Bolan said. He didn't even want to consider the consequences if the emitter was activated, even for a moment, in the vicinity of fifty-five-miles-per-hour traffic. Every one of those vehicles would lose control instantly. No steering, no brakes. The death toll would be horrendous.

"Stony One, here,'' Bolan radioed impatiently. "We getting through to them, Stony Base?''

"Not yet, Stony One,'' Price answered. "It's not as easy as you'd think. Hold on.''

Katzenelenbogen finally closed the gap between himself and the Chevy van as the vehicle headed for one of the Pentagon entrances. There were three cars ahead of it. The military guard on duty was chatting politely with the driver of a big Buick, his hands at his side and his face expressionless.

He waved the Buick through. His partner, watching the exit, was at ease. No one was leaving at the moment.

A Volkswagen Beetle barely paused at the gate before being waved through. There was just one car between the entrance and the van.

"Stony Base, we're out of time.''

"Stony Base here,'' Price said. "I got through to my people. Now it's in their hands.''

"How long?''

"That's a big unknown, Stony One.''

"Be advised we're going in pursuit if the van passes security."

"Careful, Stony One. You don't want to take friendly fire."

"Understood." But Bolan knew there might be no choice.

The driver of the red Saturn SL1 took twenty seconds to produce whatever identification he needed to get through the gate. As the Saturn pulled inside, Bolan spotted the entry guard's partner answering the booth phone. Bolan saw the man stiffen, then nod tersely. The van edged forward to the guard, who glanced at the front bumper stickers and raised his hand, as if about to wave the van through, then, at a word from his partner, he held his hand face up to the van, bringing it to a halt.

The guard's demeanor changed rapidly from professional politeness to formal seriousness. His hand went to his pistol holster as he spoke to the driver of the van.

Then the guard stepped back, drawing his weapon. He never even got the pistol clear of the leather before a burst of gunfire slammed into his chest, driving him backward into the booth and into his partner. The shooting continued, a sustained volley that followed both bloodied men to the floor of the booth and out of sight of Bolan.

Katzenelenbogen stomped on the gas and pushed the Grand Cherokee into the rear of the van, spinning the wheel in an effort to shove the van off the road and over the curb. The van driver reacted too fast, spinning the wheel away from the curb, and hit the gas, rubber screeching. There was an explosion when he slammed into the security spikes that ripped through all four wheels, but he kept going. Katzenelenbogen didn't hesitate before following the van over the spikes, and the Cherokee's tires shredded on the points.

The Cherokee was equipped with rims that would allow it to run at speeds of up to fifty miles per hour with the tires destroyed. The Chevrolet van was equipped with run-flats, which worked fine when punctured, but the damage done by the security spikes had ripped them to shreds, and black rubber flew off as the van's driver swerved and steered the vehicle toward the Pentagon building.

Any moment, Bolan knew, he'd decide he was close enough, then activate the emitter.

Bolan had already primed a high-explosive round into the M-203 grenade launcher mounted under the barrel of the M-16 on his lap.

He was ready to blow that van to oblivion.

Then Katzenelenbogen said, "Company!"

A pair of Pentagon security cars spun into view just four car lengths behind the Cherokee, their emergency lights spinning.

Bolan watched the Chevrolet van swerve into the curb and onto the grass at the edge of the parking lot.

"He's going to park it right next to the wall," Katzenelenbogen shouted.

"Be ready to let me out."

"Shit! We're dead, Mack!"

The Cherokee made a sudden grinding sound and lurched to an unsteady stop. Katzenelenbogen was pushing with both his real and prosthetic limbs against the steering wheel, trying to force it to turn broadside to the huge wall of the Pentagon building.

Bolan shoved the door open and jettisoned himself, hitting the ground and somersaulting over the M-16/M-203 and coming to a stop on one knee.

Only then did he realize he was seeing uniformed troops storming on foot in his direction. They were just a dozen paces away. The Pentagon security force was reacting to the Stony Man warning with speed and skill.

Bolan did his best to ignore them as he aimed the grenade launcher at the Chevrolet van. It stopped just inches from the brick wall.

"Don't shoot!" The driver was out of his vehicle, looking every inch a U.S. Air Force colonel. His hands were raised to shoulder level.

"Put down your weapon now." The very authoritarian voice was from one of the armed guards, and Bolan sensed more than saw out of his peripheral vision that they had targeted him with more than one M-16.

Bolan knew how it looked. A stranger with an automatic weapon was threatening a member of the U.S. military. Bolan knew that if he didn't comply—especially if he fired his weapon—he would be instantly fired upon by the Pentagon security detail.

Bolan also knew that if the emitter wasn't destroyed, and destroyed in seconds, the Pentagon was going to erupt in flame. Innocent people would be dead, maybe by the hundreds.

There was no choice to make, really.

The steel barrel of the M-16 was already hot in his hands.

Bolan fired.

CHAPTER TWENTY-FOUR

The Pentagon, Washington, D.C.

Katzenelenbogen pushed open the door and jumped out. He saw the grenade as it streaked by and heard the rattle of M-16 gunfire that took Bolan to the ground like a tackled quarterback. Katz shouted, but the sound was obliterated in the blast of the high explosive, which turned the Chevrolet van into a ball of flame. The driver of the van disappeared, swallowed by the blast. A huge pillow of black smoke billowed up the wall of the Pentagon until it reached the open sky and expanded into a cloud.

Katzenelenbogen came up short as he rushed around the front of the Cherokee. The security detail was directing four M-16s at his chest from just paces away.

"We're Justice, goddamn it!" he shouted. He wasn't looking at any of them. He was looking at the crumpled figure of a man on the grass, and the darkening stain underneath him.

Somebody rummaged in his jacket and lifted out his weapons and his ID. "If you're Justice, why did your friend just murder an Air Force colonel in cold blood?"

"That colonel was a terrorist in disguise."

"Oh."

There was a strange buzzing sound, which distracted Katzenelenbogen from the hideous sight of his fallen friend. He glanced up at a distant pair of double doors on the side of the building. They were flung open, and the buzzing turned to the screech of a fire alarm and a billow of black smoke.

"ABLE ONE."

"Able One here," Carl Lyons replied.

"Things have just gone to hell for Katz and Striker, and their target is on to them," Price said. "How's your target?"

Lyons wondered what "gone to hell" meant. He would find out later. What was important at the moment was the behavior of the man in the pickup truck. Had he heard about his companion's run-in?

"Nothing to report, Stony Base. We're still parked. Our man isn't in sight."

The pickup had pulled into a low-income residential neighborhood, and the driver seemed to be stalling for time. He had circled a few blocks before coming to a halt in front of an empty lot.

Lyons parked the Jeep around the corner behind him. The Jeep was mostly hidden from the man, therefore he was only barely in sight of the Able Team SUV. The stocky man slumped in his seat, tapping the steering wheel for five minutes.

"Hold on, Stony Base, I may have activity," Lyons reported as a rusty, wobbling panel truck crossed the intersection in front of the Jeep and slowed. It appeared to be circling the pickup, but halted suddenly when the vehicles were side by side. The rear end of the panel truck flew open and a ramp was lowered. A large wooden crate of about the same dimensions as the crate seen going into the van at the fishing shack was dollied down the ramp. The ramp was moved to the rear end of the pickup, and the crate was quickly loaded. Then the dolly and ramp were thrown into the rear of the panel truck, and it pulled away. The pickup driver jumped into his vehicle. The loading had taken just forty-five seconds.

"Looks like he just took delivery, Stony Base."

"Hold on, Able One," Price said. Lyons read a strange note in her voice—impatience or distress, which was utterly foreign to the cool and utterly in-control mission controller they knew. He looked across the front seat at fellow Able Team member Rosario "Politician" Blancanales, who looked worried.

Something had happened.

"Able One, take him down and destroy that emitter now!" Price said suddenly.

"On our way, Stony Base."

Lyons stomped on the gas. He popped the shift knob into Drive and spun the Jeep around the corner as the pickup began to roll forward. The driver spotted the approaching vehicle. Somehow he knew he was in trouble, and he accelerated, pulling away in a hurry.

"We can't let that guy get to the expressway," Hermann Schwarz said from the back seat. "He'll turn on the emitter when he gets near traffic."

"Then he'll stop," Blancanales said. "So will we, and we'll take him down."

"Think about it—that thing starts disabling cars

that are going fifty-five, sixty-five miles per hour. All of a sudden those drivers lose control.''

''I get the picture,'' Blancanales said. ''It wouldn't be pretty.''

Lyons got it, too. ''Be ready. I'm giving you guys a shot.''

As the pickup rounded a corner, Lyons steered the Jeep over the dried-up front yard of a small brick house. Blancanales and Schwarz were ready, and unleashed a barrage of M-16 fire into the rear of the fleeing pickup.

Blancanales peppered the rear end of the pickup, shooting for the tires. The pickup driver heard the shots and swerved to avoid them. As Lyons straightened and Blancanales and Schwarz hurried to change their magazines, they saw that the fleeing vehicle appeared unscathed.

''I know I hit that window,'' Schwarz protested from the back. ''That pickup's shielded.''

''We expected that,'' Lyons said. ''That's Kabat's SOP. He's not afraid to spend money for the best equipment. Gadgets, get ready to use stronger measures.''

''You got it. But I'm not happy about using big guns in residential areas.''

''Neither am I,'' Lyons admitted, ''but stopping our friend fast saves lots of lives.''

Schwarz was already crawling over the seat into the rear of the Jeep, and in seconds he had ripped back the soft top and raised the mounted Browning .50-caliber machine gun into firing position. He strapped himself in behind it, grabbed the gun and shouted above the rush of wind and the engine noise.

''Ironman! Go!''

Lyons stomped on the gas and the four-liter engine thrummed to high revs, bearing down suddenly on the fleeing pickup truck. There was a big diesel engine under the hood of the pickup, but it was built for torque, not speed. It wasn't going to outrace the lightweight Jeep. Schwarz aimed the machine gun forward, waited just long enough for the pickup to come into his sights, then laid down on the trigger. The sudden rattle of large-caliber machine-gun fire rang out, peppering the pickup's side body panels. Then they heard a sudden blast and a ping of a ricocheting bullet. Lyons's foot came quick off the gas, and the Jeep fell behind the pickup. From the passenger seat Blancanales unleashed a burst of M-16 rounds, but the pickup steered away and the driver quickly rolled up the bullet-resistant glass.

"I almost had his wheels!" Schwarz protested.

"But you couldn't have shot at them with a hole in your head!" Lyons retorted over his shoulder. "Here comes your second chance."

He accelerated quickly again, driven by urgency, knowing full well they were less than a mile from the expressway. That was a minute of travel time at current speed. He inserted the Jeep next to the pickup truck, and Blancanales put down a cover fire on the driver's window. He wasn't about to let this guy shoot at his friend again.

Schwarz raised the rear end of the Browning to his forehead to bring the fire down to the pickup's tires, then watched in amazement as the fire cut into the rubber without doing more than take off big black chunks.

"He's got solid rubber tires!"

"Then shoot for the box," Blancanales said.

"Maybe you can put the emitter out of commission."

Schwarz found the big wooden crate a much easier target and began to unload his huge container of .50-caliber rounds into it with a steady rattle of gunfire that vibrated the entire SUV. Lyons kept the Jeep behind and to the left of the pickup, giving his Able Team partner a clear shot. The wood disintegrated and flew in a trail behind the pickup, which began to swerve.

"Highway's coming up!" Lyons shouted.

"Got that, but the thing's well protected. I'm trying to break through." Schwarz's barrage exposed the metal plates under the wood. Suddenly the pickup disappeared as Lyons steered directly behind it—they were on the entrance ramp.

"Did you kill it?" Blancanales asked.

"I doubt it. It's all solid metal plate. I just dented it."

"How will we know?" Lyons demanded loudly.

"You'll know!" Gadgets retorted.

"Somewhere there's an opening in the steel for the emitter," Blancanales said.

"Probably on the front end of the crate," Schwarz shouted. "I'll never get at it—"

Schwarz flew forward as the Jeep decelerated abruptly, slamming his face into a roof support before the straps stopped him. "Steer left! Give me a shot!" he shouted.

Lyons grabbed the wheel with both hands as the Jeep ground to a halt, finding it almost immovable. Then Blancanales pushed himself across the cab and grabbed the wheel with him. The Jeep drifted slowly into a sideways skid at the end of the ramp, then spun backward as it came to a halt on the interstate shoulder.

Around them was sudden chaos as every vehicle in their field of vision lost control simultaneously, flying out of lanes, into one another, into the steep grade of the entrance ramp. Two slammed solidly together and somersaulted in a mass of metal and flame, fusing into a single pile of wreckage.

Then more vehicles sped into the area of influence of the emitter. Unable to bring themselves to a halt as they spotted the pileup, they slammed into the chaos at full speed. Those who did begin to brake to avoid the wreckage suddenly found themselves without power as they came close enough to the pickup truck.

Within seconds the expressway was like the aftermath of battle.

Schwarz saw none of it. He jumped to his feet as the Jeep stopped, shook out the dizziness from his run-in with the roof support and looked for the pickup. It was turned broadside, seventy-five yards away from the Able Team Jeep. The driver's side faced the traffic.

Schwarz saw why the pickup driver had parked as he did: a tiny black opening in the steel plate showed underneath where the wood had been blasted away. It was probably the size of a quarter. Schwarz was amazed that all this mayhem could come out of an opening that small.

He targeted the hole and triggered the Browning.

The first car burst into flame not far from the emitter. Its occupants were alert enough to flee, and seconds later the car's gas tank burst as Schwarz walked the denting impacts of the .50-caliber rounds across

the front of the metal protective plate, finally insert-
ing a half-dozen rounds through the emitter opening.

"How will I know?" he shouted.

"We're still heating up," Lyons shouted, as he
and Blancanales jumped out of the cab. "You didn't
turn it off."

Schwarz steered the machine-gun fire at the rear
of the vehicle. Armored or not, he might find a way
to break through the body panels into the gas tank.

Lyons shouted. "Gadgets! We're heating up!"

"I'm going for the fuel."

In quick succession another pair of nearby cars
reached ignition temperature and burst into flame,
their gas tanks going within seconds.

"That's gonna be us!" Lyons warned.

"There are people in those cars," Schwarz protested. He was laying on the Browning, sending a
steady stream of red hot metal into the rear end of
the vehicle. There had to be a way through. The plat-
ing couldn't possibly stand up to that onslaught.
Could it?

"Gadgets!"

Schwarz spotted a woman backing away from her
blazing, crashed vehicle, limping on a bloody leg and
shouting at the slumped figure she was forced to
leave in the front seat. Then the air exploded and
engulfed her.

"I gotta stop it." Schwarz said it more to himself
than anybody else. He noticed close-proximity
smoke in his peripheral vision and saw it rising off
the surface of the Jeep. The paint was burning.

"Get away now!" Lyons said somewhere behind
him. "That's an order!"

Schwarz squeezed harder on the trigger as if he

could push enough extra power into the rounds to help them break into the shell of the pickup, then felt the truck moving beneath him. It was Lyons and Blancanales, coming up behind him. They were coming to manhandle him off the smoking Jeep.

Schwarz held on tight. He felt their hands on his arms.

The driver of the pickup truck had been trapped by the machine-gun fire. He had to know that, even out of the line of the emitter's sight, the truck would heat up soon enough. He looked as if he were going to exit the passenger side and make a run for it. Schwarz wanted to cut him down with the machine-gun fire, but he didn't dare stop. Lyons was shouting in his ear and another wrecked vehicle burst into flames, then another, then another. He felt his flesh burning, and knew it was the steel in his hands and the metal all around and under him overheating. Lyons and Blancanales were going to pull him away from the firing Browning, and he couldn't let that happen, or more would die.

The pickup truck opened up with a ball of orange fire that pushed it forward and obliterated its contents. The flames knocked the driver to the ground, where he lay still, burning.

"All right let's go!" Schwarz cried. The three of them scrambled ungracefully off the rear end of the Jeep as a whoosh of fire filled the cab. The tires exploded and melted simultaneously. As the trio leapt across the on-ramp and tossed themselves bodily into the depression on the other side, the vehicle detonated.

CHAPTER TWENTY-FIVE

Stony Man Farm, Virginia

Price was waiting on the front porch as the big transport helicopter descended onto the Stony Man Farm grounds. Its doors opened to reveal a collection of bandaged and bruised-looking men. Schwarz's hands had been burned and were wrapped in gauze. Lyons and Blancanales wore small white squares on their arms and faces where they had been burned in the chaos on the highway. Able Team had remained on the scene of the pileup for over an hour, helping stabilize the wounded and assisting paramedic teams.

Bolan emerged. His eyes had the black-circle look of the recently drugged, but they burned with deadly intensity. He walked stiffly, his mouth a hard line.

"Mack, how are you?"

"I'm okay," he said with a slight smile, forced for Price's benefit.

She saw the wreckage of his shirt and she inhaled quickly. It looked like it had been attacked with a blowtorch. Then he had limped inside.

"How is he really, Katz?" Price asked when the Stony Man tactical adviser emerged from the chopper with Jack Grimaldi.

"A few bullets cut across the hip where the Kevlar jacket slipped up when he was shot. He's black and blue. He lost blood and that's the worst thing. He's going to be weak for a while. It could have been a hell of a lot worse."

"How'd he manage it?" she asked.

"He curled up," Katz explained. "He fired the weapon, dropped it and went into a fetal ball when the security detail started firing at him. Those guys were good shots. His profile and their skill meant all the rounds hit him in the torso. The jacket took most of the rounds."

HAL BROGNOLA SAT across the table from his assembled crew and said simply, "A quarter billion dollars."

"The targets?" the Executioner asked.

"London and Moscow."

Bolan nodded. The rest of the assembled staff of Stony Man Farm exchanged looks and whispered comments of amazement.

"Now here's the catch."

Brognola suddenly had everyone's attention again.

"The two hundred and fifty million is to be paid by the United States. And only by the United States. As punishment for U.S. interference with Kabat's former strikes, and most especially for the U.S. neutralization of the Pentagon emitter. Any attempt to include non-American funds in the total will result in activation of both emitters."

"He's punishing the U.S. for defending itself?" Barbara Price protested.

"He punishing us, the Farm," Bolan said. "He's punishing me."

"That's crap," Brognola stated. "We had every right to fight back."

"Still, it makes for a neat package of cause and responsibility," Bolan said. "Think of the psychological impact of what Kabat has done. He targets two of the most high-profile cities among our allies. One a figurehead in international policy making and enforcement, the other a fading superpower whose people have plenty of reason to envy the rich Americans. By broadcasting a motivation for the extortion, he puts the blame on our shoulders. No matter how ridiculous it may be, it'll be enough for the people of Russia and England to latch on to."

"Yeah," Kurtzman muttered. "It makes sense. The pressure that will come to bear on the United States will be enormous."

"It already is," Brognola admitted. "The ransom messages were delivered around the world at the same time. Within minutes the Man had phone calls coming in from the British and Russian governments. Got a call from the British prime minister. The gist of those calls was that this was a U.S.-created problem and it was up to the U.S. to solve it. Naturally, they want it solved without endangering their own people.

"This puts the U.S. between a very big rock and a very hard place," the big man from Justice added. "We either pay the ransom, caving in on a decades-long policy of not negotiating with terrorists, or we chance allowing Moscow and London to burn. And we get vilified by every nation on Earth."

"How long have we got?" Price asked.

"Four days. That's a long time compared to his previous demands for payoffs. Striker, you said the other two attacks went too quickly to be sincere extortion attempts. You said Kabat never intended to collect on those, that he was working himself up to a single major action and a single big payoff. I think this may be it.''

"I think so, too," Bolan said. "How is the President planning on reacting?"

"He'll pay." Brognola shrugged. "There's not much choice."

"I'll shut him down first."

The big Fed glanced at the Executioner, curious. Bolan had spoken with utter conviction.

"How can you be certain?"

"I owe it to him," Bolan said. "How were those messages delivered?"

"Private couriers. No e-mail this time," Brognola said. "Maybe he caught on to how we were tracking him."

"So where is Kabat now?"

The question had been hypothetical. To everyone's surprise, except Bolan himself, Aaron Kurtzman answered it with one word: "Malaysia."

PRICE KNOCKED LIGHTLY, then stepped into the small room. Mack Bolan looked at her as she entered. Standing in nothing but shorts, he held the remains of the shirt in his stitched-up hands.

Price stepped up to him wordlessly, took his wrist and moved him in a half circle.

"Jesus, Mack!"

"Just bruises."

She wanted desperately to run her hands over the massive blotches of black, blue and sickly green that seemed to pigment the man's entire lower torso.

They were angry black in the center, where the bullets had hit him, growing lighter and more colorful near the rims.

Instead she stepped in front of him, putting her hands on his chest, where the skin was a normal shade, and looked into his face. "What good would it do me to say you shouldn't go?"

"None at all."

"Phoenix could handle this."

"Kabat is for me to deal with."

"You know you're not at full capacity, Mack. You're hurt. You need downtime."

"I'll have it. It'll take twenty hours to reach the Malaysian peninsula."

She looked directly into his eyes and said, "Please."

"I'm going."

She put her hand on the back of his head and pulled him down to her face, kissing him long and deep, then held his face in close contact with hers for a moment, her eyes closed.

"Then," she whispered into his ear, "be careful."

CHAPTER TWENTY-SIX

Borneo Peninsula, East Malaysia

The resort complex of Hong Kong underworld millionaire Yiang Che-Xin stood on a slight rise in the ground in the midst of a valley more than five miles long and three miles wide, surrounded by hills covered in rain forest. It was remote, seventy miles by air from the nearest city, but this complex didn't need a city. It was a model of independence, with its own power generation facility, landing strip and water supply. Supplies were transported in by air at great expense. Lesser commodities were trucked in, and although the roads were all bad and the trip was long from the ports, a truck arrived almost every week with more building supplies. Yiang Che-Xin viewed his estate as a work in progress.

He had insisted on locating his estate on the lands of an indigenous people, purchasing their loyalty with outlandish outlays of money and gifts. The small village of two hundred animists had gone from having one satellite dish and five trucks to possessing houses, televisions and cars for every family.

He turned his house into a private resort with a golf course, tennis courts, casino. His guests were the movers and shakers in the Asian—and global—underworld.

One of his guests was one of his best suppliers. Mr. Roger Kabat had sold millions of dollars in weaponry to Yiang, who distributed them throughout Asia through his contacts in Hong Kong, China, Taiwan, South Korea and even Japan. Everybody profited substantially. Kabat and Yiang were the closest of friends.

When Kabat was in need of a place to stay—a protected place, untraceable—Yiang had been more than happy to make him his guest at his resort. Even if taking in Kabat meant taking in the man's entourage.

Especially with Kabat giving him a cut of the profits.

The complex Bolan saw as he hung over the valley in the deep night on the square ram-air parachute was dominated by a central hub—a massive, octagonal megastructure that satellite reconnaissance imaging showed to be in the order of sixty thousand square feet. It was estimated to be forty feet tall, making it four stories aboveground. From each of the eight compass points jutted a wing, which curved and meandered like the tentacles of some massive, land-locked octopus across the valley. Each wing measured from ninety to a hundred fifty feet in length, varying in width from fifteen to fifty-eight feet and terminated by narrowing to just ten feet in width and curling into a loop, almost meeting itself to form a circular, enclosed courtyard. All the wings were a single story in height.

This architectural nightmare dominated the center

of the valley like a medieval castle, flanked by the huts of the fiefdom.

Bolan spun the canopy and aimed himself at the top of the ridgelike hill that towered a thousand feet above the level of the valley. He had watched his package of hardware disappear behind it minutes earlier. He needed to land, find the package and establish a satellite link with Stony Man.

Then he would need to march into the valley, locate Kabat and put a stop to him. And he had less than twenty-four hours in which to do it.

As the ridge rose up to meet him, Bolan searched for a clearing, which he failed to find. The best he could find was a kind of natural aisle that had developed when two rows of trees had grown up side by side. As his dangling body inserted itself into the aisle between the trees, he craned his neck to watch the parachute canopy and steer it through the upper branches of the rain forest. There wasn't room for it. The inevitable happened. A corner of the chute caught on a branch and the billowing mushroom of air collapsed. The soldier found himself falling, lurching to a stop ten feet above the earth, then falling again. He hit hard, rolled to dissipate the impact and got to his feet.

There was a jarring sensation in his leg. The bruised flesh of his hip was screaming. He ignored it.

He had to find that package.

The beacon sent out a signal to his helmet electronics. Twenty minutes later Bolan was dismantling the package. He erected the portable satellite dish at the top of the ridge and powered it up. First he tested out the local radio.

"G-Force, Stony One here, come in."

Grimaldi answered at once from his chopper, on the way back to the airport at the Malaysian city of Miri. "Read you, Stony One. Hope your landing was okay."

"It went okay."

Bolan quickly signed off with Grimaldi and switched to the satellite. It would line up and adjust itself automatically, giving him almost constant communication with the Farm. The batteries with it would last up to thirty-six hours. Which was more than he would need.

"Stony Base, Stony One here."

"Read you loud and clear, Stony One," Price said. "How was the trip down?"

"Bumpy landing."

It took the soldier an hour to creep to the valley and wind his way through the silent villages. Dressed in a blacksuit, his face painted with combat cosmetics, he was as dark as the deep shadows to which he clung. That wasn't going to last. Dawn in this part of the world was less than an hour away. Those in the community who still farmed would be rising soon.

He had a contact to make. It would be a difficult one because the contact didn't know him and wasn't expecting him.

Bolan had spent more than an hour during the flight poring over the schematics for Yiang's estate complex. The schematics had been extracted from the Russian database Kurtzman had recently succeeded in accessing using decryption data supplied during their raid at Kabat's Outer Banks home. The communications made by Mosty Sigulda had been

most helpful in allowing Kurtzman, along with Akira
Tokaido, to roam a secure Russian Intelligence
server. They had made little use of it at the outset
for fear of being identified as an intruder and shut
out. But when the most recent threat had come from
Kabat, Kurtzman took the chance. He broke into the
system and sacked the place, taking anything and everything he thought might be of interest. Among the
data that was downloaded was one vital scrap of Russian Intelligence: Kabat was in hiding in Yiang Che-
Xin's Malaysian estate complex.

The Russians knew because the Russians had been
keeping a low-level intelligence operative in place in
the complex for seven months. She was Chinese, recruited from Taiwan by the Russians in the early
1990s, and had worked her way into Yiang's employ
first as a concubine, then as a secretary. She was
good, if her rapid progress was any indication. She
had quickly made herself an important and trusted
member of the household.

If she could be contacted and convinced to cooperate, Bolan might be able to make this a quick
probe. Get in. Neutralize Kabat. Get out.

"Can we trust this data?" Bolan had asked Kurtzman.

"No," Kurtzman said. "It may all be bad. I may
have been detected and identified during my initial
electronic scan of the Russian server. After which it
would have been a simple exercise for them to fill it
with junk. If it is junk, it has been very carefully
assembled to look good. And doubtless a lot of it is
good—nobody could have faked as much stuff as
was on that server."

"But how do we tell what's fact and what's fiction?" Bolan asked grimly.

"Exactly. For example, the Russians would certainly know we're trying to track down Kabat. They could easily have made up all this intelligence about him being at this Malaysian estate."

"Sending me on a wild-goose chase."

"And buying time for the Russians to locate Kabat themselves and snatch his technology."

"Yeah." Bolan was thoughtful. He looked at Kurtzman and started to speak. "Bear—"

"If I had to make an educated guess, I'd say there's a sixty percent chance that Akira and I were able to roam the Russia system undetected the first time, which means they would have had no reason to fake this data."

Bolan nodded. "That's good enough for me."

He would know soon enough.

The intelligence had told him about the stream that cut between the estate and the village, and he was prepared for it with waterproof packs for his equipment. Taking one of the bridges was out of the question. He emerged on the other side, hid the waterproof packs and surveyed the grounds.

The grounds around the complex had been artificially segmented in sections of a few acres each. Each segment replicated a natural type of terrain or garden. There was a Malaysian rain forest—with the same kinds of trees and ferns Bolan had recently landed in on the hill—a Chinese temperate forest with large deciduous trees and undergrowth, a southwestern American desert with a dozen century-old saguaro cactus, and so on. All these gardens were paved with brick walkways for casual strolling. Bo-

Ian speculated idly that maintaining the grounds had to cost millions annually, but he didn't really care about the follies of the rich. His main concern was the challenge each garden would pose to his probe.

They were an advantage so far. Bolan found it extremely easy to identify his location at a glance by determining which garden he was in. Since Yiang liked contrast, he had tended to put different types of gardens next to each other. He found the garden he wanted easily enough—a replica of very formal European grounds, with shrubbery laid out in squares and other perfectly manicured geometric designs. The garden ran up against a long, narrow extension of the house, and this was where Bolan would find his Russian agent.

He made effective use of the cover, sprinting in a crouch from bush to bush until he came to the window of the room he believed the agent to be. It was shaded. He went up, jumped, got an easy handhold on the exposed wooden support beam of the single-story roof and dragged himself onto the ceramic shingles. He paused, allowing the pain from his bruised back and hip to die down. He couldn't, wouldn't, allow the injuries to interfere with this probe. He opened a steel vault in his mind, deposited the pain inside, closed it and forgot the combination.

There was a series of frosted plastic bubbles set into the roof to allow natural sunlight inside, as the blueprints had said there would be. So far so good. It took the soldier a minute to start the nuts with the stainless-steel wrench in his pack and remove them with his hands. He did so soundlessly—he hoped. It was difficult to judge how much noise his moving and creeping were generating inside the structure.

Maybe none. Or maybe he was so loud there was a security squad en route to apprehend him.

He pulled the panel up a few inches and looked inside. There was darkness, too deep to peer through, even with his eyes adjusted to it. He donned a pair of thermal imaging glasses and looked again.

It was a bedroom, as expected, with a large, low sleeping platform, a sitting area, a television and a bookcase. It was empty, as Bolan hadn't expected. All he could see was a faint brightness indicating dissipating warmth in the messy bedclothes. Someone had been sleeping here. Where were they now? The door to the private washroom was open and inside it was dark, as well.

Had the occupant heard Bolan and fled? He disposed of that possibility. The bed was too cool. The occupant had been gone for longer than he had been on the scene.

Was the Russian agent off performing some nighttime espionage herself?

Bolan needed to get inside, but he couldn't afford to get caught doing so. He lowered the skylight, crept across the roof in a hurry, and within a minute had another skylight removed. It was over the long hallway that ran the length of that arm of the building. It was empty, lit only by tiny hidden lights at ankle level. Bolan lowered himself inside and used the recessed light cavity to install a small, invisible laser alarm unit. The soldier activated it and passed his hand in front of the unseen beam. A loud alarm beeped in his headphones. He raced down the hall ten paces, stuck another such unit in place and tested it. The beep was just as loud and of a slightly altered pitch.

Then he went back to the skylight. He leapt, grabbed the frame and hauled himself up. He'd been inside ninety seconds.

He moved back to the skylight over the bedroom of the Russian agent. He removed it fully and lowered himself inside, speaking in a low voice to Stony Man.

"Stony One, here."

"Stony Base. We read you, Stony One," Price said. She had been monitoring him constantly, although there had been no conversation for a long time. That didn't matter. She let him do what he needed to do without the distraction of her interference.

"I'm sending video."

"We're getting it, Stony One. I don't see much yet."

Bolan had a lot to do, and he assumed he didn't have much time to do it in. He circumnavigated the room, depositing a handful of bugs, then he moved to the small chest of drawers and makeup table, rifling the contents. He found ID and a few innocuous personal papers. He turned on his flashlight with a narrow beam just long enough to read the passport. The passport was Taiwanese and the printing was in Chinese and English characters. Name: Dao Mei. Nationality: Taiwanese. Age: 28. A sultry Chinese face, and even the bad passport photo couldn't disguise the fact that she was beautiful.

"Stony Base, here. That's our girl."

"Affirmative."

"So where is she hiding, Stony One?"

"Unknown, Stony Base. She was gone when I got here."

"Stony One, you've got just thirty-one minutes until dawn in your neck of the woods."

"I'm already pushing it," Bolan agreed. The black sky had been showing the first tinges of gray when he left the roof. He finished with the drawers and began going though the wardrobe. Nothing in the clothing. He withdrew a soft-sided suitcase from the rear of the closet, finding it empty—and finding an odd flap of material dangling from the bottom. He flashed his light on it for a second, long enough to determine it was a hidden tiny compartment in the bottom support panels of the suitcase. Whatever had been inside was gone.

"Looks like our secret agent is out taking pictures, Stony One," Price said.

"Affirmative."

"Stony One, what's your next step?"

Bolan was thinking about that. He could wait for the woman to return. The question was to try to convince her to work with him. His chances of success were slim. She'd be unlikely to cooperate with a strange American agent without orders from her superiors. And any orders from Moscow would tell her very specifically to not work with him. He would have to incapacitate her and hide her somewhere. Her absence would be noticed, a search would begin and a high level of alert imposed on the complex. Bolan's chances of getting in to find Kabat and Andrei Sheknovi would be drastically reduced.

"Stony Base, I'm going to hole up for a while," he said.

"Agreed, Stony One. It's your only real option."

Yeah. His only option.

The alarm in his headphones began to scream.

CHAPTER TWENTY-SEVEN

Malaysia

He paused long enough to adhere the tiny digital monitor to the ceiling on the skylight frame. It was designed to be ceiling-mounted, and the lens was fixed at a twenty-five-degree angle. Bolan strung the wires to the roof, from which the power supply and transmitter could send the signal. It took precious seconds to accomplish all this, which meant he was still lowering the big plastic skylight bubble into place when Dao Mei entered the room.

She was preoccupied with her own stealth, otherwise she might have noticed the movement of her ceiling panel. Bolan didn't bother to replace the nuts on the affixing screws. Unless there was rain or high winds, the skylight would be fine without them, and putting them on might make noise enough for Dao to hear.

Or her companion.

Bolan didn't know about him yet. Price was watching the video feed and saw the man with Dao, recognizing him at once. She wouldn't distract Bolan with the information right now. He had one priority at this minute: get to cover fast.

The soldier knew his danger. The sky was getting lighter. The grounds were becoming more visible. He needed a hiding place, and he would prefer it to be nearby. He didn't want to have to make the arduous trip into the rain forest if he didn't have to.

He had already identified a precious few options when he scanned the blueprints of the complex. One was a roof decoration near the point where this wing of the complex, the west wing, adjoined the main building. The cover was a stylized pagoda, and the schematics showed it had no function other than decoration. It was rectangular, five feet wide and seven feet long, but just four feet high. Bolan moved as rapidly as caution would allow toward the main building, dropping flat against the roof when he heard footsteps in the garden below. The heavy tread told him it was a man. Guard? Maintenance? Just one of Yiang's guests out for a predawn stroll? The man never walked into the soldier's line of vision and strolled away at an unhurried pace. Bolan practically sprinted through the predawn light to the pagoda, knowing full well he might find the pagoda utterly unfit as a day-long hiding place. It could be enclosed and impossible to break into soundlessly. It could be too small. It might not even exist—who knew when the Russian schematics dated from?

There it was. It looked to be as big as Bolan had estimated, and the gap between the slanted open roof of the decorative piece and its walls would be big enough for him to access. Inside, the floor of the pagoda was the apex of the pitched roof, and it was littered with leaves. It was ideal. Bolan pushed in his pack and squeezed himself inside as he heard the approaching sound of conversation in Chinese.

For a moment he crouched in the darkness of the interior, convinced he hadn't moved quickly enough and had been noticed by the men in the garden. But their conversation continued without change, and they were gone.

"Stony One, here."

"Stony Base. Where are you?"

"Hiding place number one turned out to be acceptable. It's a tight squeeze and I don't think there's room service, but I'll make do."

"Check out your video monitor when you can," Price said. "There's a friend of yours on-site. Looks like he's also going to be spending the day in hiding. But he gets to spend it with Dao Mei."

Bolan's monitor was a tiny, low-resolution unit, but when he saw the figure pacing the floor in Dao's room he recognized the battered Russian face immediately.

"Mosty Sigulda."

"None other, Stony One. He and Dao Mei came in as you were leaving."

Bolan scrutinized the face of the woman lounging on the bed. It matched the face from the passport. She spoke to Sigulda in Russian.

"Our translator's feeding us real-time translations," Price said. "So far they're bemoaning their failure to find whatever it is they were out looking for."

"Which is what, Stony Base? Have they specified?"

"No specifics, Stony One, but I suppose you can draw your own conclusions."

"I can," Bolan said. "While I'm sitting here, you might as well brief me on the situation."

"The news isn't good," Price said. "CNN has just reported that the Kremlin issued a statement placing the responsibility for the attack squarely on the shoulders of the U.S. It was a very official declaration. They're trying to say in not so many words that if the U.S. allows the attack, Moscow will consider it an attack by the U.S."

"They're trying to scare the U.S. into paying off Kabat," Bolan said. "Are they sincere? What's the temperature reading at the White House?"

"The Man is scared, too. He spent some private time on the phone with Russia and came away with the impression they're serious. They just might retaliate militarily."

Bolan considered that. If Russia attacked the U.S. in retaliation for Kabat's strike on Moscow, the U.S. would have to be the bigger man, so to speak, and simply take it. That wouldn't go over well with the people. Political careers would topple as a result. Would the politicians risk it?

Because if they acted on the will of the people who demanded counterretaliation, the dominoes would start to fall.

"What's the British prime minister saying?"

"He's a little less accusatory."

"So are we prepared to pay?"

"Yes."

A simple answer, with massive implications. Once the U.S. bowed to international extortion the problem would mushroom. Enemies would start sabotaging foreign friends of the Americans worldwide.

That couldn't be allowed to happen. Bolan would see to it or die trying to prevent it. And he would do or die sooner than even he thought.

"I'm going to shut down my equipment, Stony Base, and wait this day out. I'll keep only my audio link to you open. You let me know if anything happens I should know about."

"Will do, Stony One. Get some sleep."

"I've got nothing better to do."

"Affirmative."

Bolan settled in to wait. He could eat from the rations in his pack, get some rest, and that was about it.

He didn't like it. But he could wait with a warrior's patience.

IN FACT, it was just six hours later when Barbara Price brought him out of an uncomfortable slumber.

"Stony One, here," he answered. He found himself drenched with sweat in the oven-hot enclosed space.

"We've got a situation I think you should know about."

"Tell me, Stony Base."

"Dao Mei has figured out where Deolinda Sheknovi and her boy are being kept in the complex. Sigulda's planning to assassinate them."

Bolan's spine stiffened. "The woman and her son?"

"Yes. He wants the technology for Russia, and he's convinced that he can put a halt to Sheknovi's cooperation with Kabat if Kabat doesn't have his family any more to hold hostage."

"When will he do it?"

There was a moment of silence. "Dao Mei thinks she can sneak him through the complex during the afternoon banquet. Another ten minutes."

Bolan was already crawling out of his self-imposed

isolation. He flattened on the sun-hot tiles of the roof and crept over the long, narrow wing to Dao's room. The gardens were empty, but the soldier knew he was exposed, taking a tremendous chance. But he *would not* allow Sigulda to gun down an innocent woman and child.

Bolan knew what it was like to lose a family. The sense of loss. The sense of waste.

"Stony Base, what are they doing now?"

"Dao's on the bed. Sigulda is pacing."

"Is he about to leave the room?"

"No. Dao's insisting they wait another five minutes before venturing out."

"Are they armed?"

"Not Dao. Sigulda's got a 9 mm in a shoulder holster under a blazer."

"Tell me when Sigulda is facing away from the skylight."

Bolan tuned in to the audio coming out of the room beneath him. He could hear Sigulda pacing. He heard what might be the sounds of a magazine page being turned. Bolan was thinking he was glad he hadn't replaced the screws on the skylight the night before.

"Now, Stony One! Sigulda's in the washroom!"

Bolan didn't hesitate. He grabbed the plastic skylight bubble, pulled it off and went feet-first through the opening with the Beretta 93-R in his hand. He landed and went into a crouch as Dao got to her feet in a hurry and Sigulda stepped out of the washroom with his hands still on his zipper. He gave a loud, Russian exclamation.

"Don't move."

Something in the soldier's voice told Dao the command was deadly serious. Sigulda was locked in a kind of shocked paralysis. When he recognized who it was he faced, he, too, knew he should obey the command. This American could kill in a heartbeat.

"How did you—"

"Shut up. Not one word or I give you the bullet through the forehead you should have received a long time ago, Sigulda."

The Russian shut up, looking distressed.

"Dao Mei." Bolan turned to Dao, but the muzzle never moved off the Russian. The woman started when he said her name. "Remove your weapons slowly and place them on the bed."

Dao cooperated, removing a tiny .22 handgun from a thigh holster that was virtually invisible under her colorful Indonesian skirt. She put it on the bed.

"That's all," she said in English.

Bolan tossed her a pair of disposable handcuffs and pointed to Sigulda. The Russian groaned, remembering the last time the Executioner had put him in the plastic restraints.

"Put them on him and do it correctly," Bolan commanded. "If you try anything out of line I will shoot you. Do you understand?"

Dao nodded, wide-eyed. Bolan knew this young agent was either well beyond her level of best courage or she was a good actor. If she was merely acting frightened, she was very, very good. She secured Sigulda's wrists, then his ankles with another set of cuffs. Bolan instructed her to lie on the floor, face-down, while he checked the cuffs and found them to be secure. Sigulda went to the floor next, on his face, while Dao was cuffed. Then Bolan moved them to the wall. The simple act of standing with feet bound was awkward and would quickly become very uncomfortable.

Bolan opened the conversation. "I won't let you kill the Sheknovi family, Sigulda."

Sigulda was getting hit with one shock after another. "How did you know that was my intent?"

Bolan shrugged. He wasn't about to give away any of his secrets. Sigulda's eyes grew wide and he turned on Dao. "You did this! You brought in the Americans!"

Dao seemed to shrink from the big Russian, and her cowering almost caused her to lose her balance. "I didn't!"

"You didn't want me to shoot the woman and her boy. Was that all it took to turn you traitor, Dao Mei? A weak stomach?"

"No, Mosty, you have me wrong," she protested. "I didn't contact the Americans."

"Actually," Bolan said, "my people broke into your computer system."

"Ha! Not too likely." Sigulda spit.

"Now, Ms. Dao, I need the same information you were providing our friend here—where are Deolinda Sheknovi and the boy being held?"

"What will you do when you reach them?" she asked.

"If possible, get them out of here. Once they're away and safe, I'll try to reach Andrei Sheknovi and get him out, as well. If I run into Roger Kabat along the way, that's all the better."

"You help him and you're dead," Sigulda said to the woman. Dao's eyes locked on his, tight with fear.

And that was when Bolan saw it. Something intangible, something like a mist that came and went in her expression as she looked at her partner. Somehow, Bolan knew her true nature then and there.

Dao Mei wasn't the frightened young woman she pretended to be.

"You want to save that family, Dao?" Bolan asked. "I can help you do it. And the U.S. will protect you if you do."

Dao apparently was having trouble drawing her eyes from the evil intensity of Sigulda, but she did it, as if she were turning from the darkness to face the light. Bolan smiled inwardly. In reality, she was turning from darkness to deeper darkness, and she didn't realize he knew it. "Yes. I want to save them. That little boy is innocent. He can't die because of all this."

"Sorry," Bolan said with a shrug. "You can't win them all, Sigulda."

Sigulda glowered and was silent. Bolan could almost see the satisfaction the man was attempting to keep from showing on his face.

BOLAN DRESSED in Sigulda's spare clothing. The casual shirt, he found, was big enough to put over the blacksuit, and the blazer hid his hardware. He carried his pack with him. It looked like nothing more than a big workout bag. He might be heading to the well-equipped gym that Bolan was sure Yiang had included somewhere on the premises.

"Tell me about this place. Keep your voice casual," Bolan instructed Dao as they strolled the long corridor to the main building.

"Yiang Che-Xin designed the original structure himself, which was built in 1991. It has been under construction continually ever since." Dao took on a tour guide's voice. She had given guest tours in the past. "Today it has ninety-three guest rooms in four wings, with lodging for over two hundred staff in two wings. This is one of the staff wings."

"Number of guests currently on the premises?"

"About thirty. Roger Kabat and his people."

"Which wings are which?"

"The four wings radiating out west and southwest are for guests. The two heading east and southeast are for staff."

"You accounted for six of the eight. I assume one of the remaining wings is Yiang's private residence."

"Yes. The wing heading northwest."

"The last wing? The one pointing north?"

"More guest rooms under construction."

A lie. Bolan had observed the areas of construction during his descent on the parachute. All the construction appeared to be taking place at a large building, maybe a theater, not directly attached to the main complex. The maturity of the gardens had been apparent throughout the complex, except around one of the southwest wings.

So the north wing wasn't under construction. It had been where it was for a long time. That meant Bolan would find one of his targets there—Deolinda Sheknovi and her son, Kabat and/or Andrei Sheknovi and his manufacturing facility.

They entered the main building, and Bolan found himself walking through a re-creation of a city street of the Hong Kong of the 1950s. The floor was cobblestones, the storefronts and homes crowded close together on either side of the street. There was a fish market, multiple vegetable stands, a newsstand racked with Chinese and English language publications and Hong Kong newspapers—all with dates from June, 1959. The street was extremely authentic, down to a glass roof forty feet overhead allowing in natural sunlight, although, like a Disneyland replication, it was too neat and clean to be real.

"No automatons for a human touch?" Bolan asked.

"Yiang Che-Xin uses humans for the human touch," Dao said. "As many as thirty-five people work this street every day. They bring in real produce and meats and fish for the stands. They have an entire four-hour script that they go through, imitating real life on the streets, and they go through it twice nightly. There are musicians, beggars and prostitutes. Chinese guests love it. They can look in the shops and flats, purchase food for their dinner, even buy a whore. I'm told this is modeled after the street where Che-Xin grew up." She waved her hand as if in dismay. "Proof that some people have too much money."

"Where are we going now?"

"To the Sheknovi family."

After they reached the end of the faux Hong Kong street, they crossed a massive atrium with lounge areas, dining areas and a gambling parlor. Unlike the fake street, this section of the complex was open and operational, with impeccably uniformed staff wiping tables, polishing equipment or simply standing in wait. Bolan could imagine that, even when the complex was at maximum capacity, the complex was prepared to provide each guest personalized service at every turn. It reminded Bolan of one of the huge theme hotel casinos in Las Vegas, but done one better.

But his concentration was locked for the most part on Dao Mei. She was going to make a move at some point, and she was so good she wouldn't broadcast it. He had to be prepared.

It came as they entered the wing that jutted directly west out of the main building. Unlike the staff wing, there was a guard on duty, standing inside the door to the corridor. He told them to stop in a firm voice.

Dao looked scared as she approached, and she stammered an explanation in Chinese. The guard didn't understand her. He was European, which meant he was probably one of Kabat's men and not a Yiang enforcer. He held a stubby Bizon-2 machine pistol in his hands.

But he wasn't prepared for Dao Mei. As he stepped within arm's length her arm shot out, slamming a blow into his face that sent him reeling. His senseless fingers couldn't hold onto the machine pistol when she extracted it from his grip, and she brought it to bear on Bolan.

The Executioner was already triggering the Beretta 93-R, and the round drilled through the soft flesh on the underside of her elbow, destroying the bone and tendon. Her hand was suddenly lifeless, and the machine pistol tumbled. Dao gave a sound like a grunt. She was so in control she didn't pause to evaluate the damage before reaching for the weapon with her good hand. The 93-R triggered again. The round smashed her other arm just below the elbow, but the effect was the same. Her tendons were tattered.

She got to her feet, her eyes blazing at the Executioner, her bloody arms dangling at her sides, and then the pain hit her.

The guard freed a handgun from his holster at that moment and aimed past Dao at the soldier, and then the 93-R fired three times. The shots came one after another in such rapid succession it was as if they were a machine-fired triburst. The first round took the enforcer in the groin, the second in the abdomen and the last in the sternum.

Dao dropped at the same moment the dead man crumpled. Unlike him, she still lived. She was panting, her eyes unseeing, and already a thick cold sweat was standing out on her forehead. She was going into shock quickly, and it wouldn't be long before she was incoherent.

Bolan found the first room on the corridor empty, and he dragged in the corpse and Dao Mei one after the other, then moved a rug in the corridor to cover the spilled blood.

The room was occupied, but the occupant was gone for the time being. The corpse went under the big Western-style full-size bed. Dao went on the floor next to it.

"Dao Mei, tell me where to find Deolinda Sheknovi."

Dao rolled her eyes in his direction and began issuing Chinese profanity in a low murmur.

"You have fifteen seconds to comply." He nudged her jaw with the suppressor on the 93-R.

"North wing. In the back."

Bolan made quick work of clamping tourniquets on each arm above the damage. Dao might lose her forearms, but she would live. By the time he bound and gagged her, she had passed out. Bolan replaced the box spring and mattress over them, satisfied that the two bodies were out of sight. If the room's occupant returned, he wouldn't know they were there unless he got on his hands and knees.

But eventually Dao Mei would come to and make her presence heard. How long Bolan had before she was discovered was a big unknown.

He left the room and returned to the octagonal megastructure, walking unhurriedly. None of the staff gave him a second glance. When he was within sight of the north wing, it became apparent he wasn't getting inside this way. A pair of guards flanked the entrance.

He'd have to enter the wing by another route.

Dao Mei might already be missed by her employer, the Hong Kong crime boss Yiang Che-Xin. Bolan could expect a search to commence, escalating into a high-level security alert.

It would be good to leave the complex before that happened.

He would have to act fast to accomplish that.

The time had come to end this nightmare, at whatever cost.

CHAPTER TWENTY-EIGHT

Virginia

Bolan returned to Dao's quarters feeling agitated at the time wasted. He had just come to a difficult decision, and one he might very probably live to regret.

"I'm going to set you free, friend," Bolan said, pressing the cold steel muzzle of the 93-R's suppressor against the temple of the handcuffed Sigulda. "But first you give me your promise. You won't intentionally harm the Sheknovis. You'll help me get them out of here."

The Russian agent nodded. Bolan sliced through the gag with the wire cutters on his multitool.

"Say it."

"I swear."

"You try any slick moves, like your companion Dao Mei, and you'll regret it."

Sigulda opened his mouth, then had second thoughts and closed it.

"I've tried getting into the north wing from the inside, but it can't be done unnoticed. There's a guard on duty." Bolan's wire cutters quickly chewed through the plastic cuffs, revealing bloody red indentations. Sigulda had been struggling, which only tightened the cuffs. "We're going over instead of through."

Bolan knew he had only seconds to get Sigulda on the roof before the agent became temporarily incapacitated again, this time with pain. The sense of urgency building in his gut told him there was no time to waste. This would be the first place they would look for Dao Mei.

"Stand on the bed."

Sigulda did as he was told, waving his hands limply as the blood flowed into them.

Bolan jumped, seized the frame of the open skylight and hauled himself onto the roof. Then he freed himself of his equipment, reached in and grabbed Sigulda by the hands. The Russian tried to grip Bolan's hands with his but wasn't able to make them work. Bolan found himself pulling a deadweight. He hoisted Sigulda's arms through the opening, then allowed his body weight to hang by the arms as he moved into a crouch and pushed against the roof, using his back muscles to haul the man onto the roof. Then he laid him out flat. Sigulda was moaning in pain, wiggling his feet and hands.

"Quiet," Bolan ordered as he replaced the skylight. The soldier's pack was there, and he pulled out the MP-5 K-PDW, slinging it around his neck, then he dragged the Russian to his feet. "Come on."

"Give me a minute. It hurts like hell."

"We don't have a minute. Let's go."

They crept over the roof toward the big octagonal hub, passing the decorative pagoda where Bolan had hidden. An access ladder was bolted to the walls of the hub, which was some ten yards taller than the wings. Sigulda moved slowly on the ladder, full function in his hands and feet not yet restored, while Bolan kept watch. He was thankful that the complex was sparsely populated at the moment. He couldn't see anyone in the surrounding gardens, and he had yet to detect exterior electronic surveillance. So far they were unnoticed.

Once they were on the roof of the main building, they moved out of sight of the ground level. Bolan glanced through one of the skylights and saw no sign of abnormal activity inside.

They descended another access ladder to the roof of the north wing.

"Belasko," Sigulda said, using Bolan's alias. "Give me my gun."

"Use this." Bolan handed him the Bizon-2 machine pistol he'd appropriated from the dead Kabat enforcer.

Sigulda looked at it and checked the cartridge, frowning. "No more promises of loyalty, Belasko?"

"You've already made your promises. You know what I'll do to you if you betray me."

THEY CREPT about fifty paces along the roof before Bolan gestured for a halt. Sigulda dropped to his knees, staying low and out of sight. Bolan crouched, listening.

The Russian didn't know what the man was listening for. There had been no sound, and they hadn't seen anyone.

Sigulda became impatient. "Come on."

Bolan pulled a hand across his throat, commanding silence. The Russian was getting irritated. He would just as soon rid himself of this man right here and right—

There was a cough, and Sigulda froze. Someone was standing under the eaves of the building directly below them. They could probably reach down and tap him on the skullcap if they wanted to.

Now, how had the American known that guy was there?

A moment later came the familiar zip sound of a lighter, then the aroma of cigarette smoke. The shuffling of feet. After four minutes a door opened and closed again. There was no further sound from below.

Bolan and Sigulda moved on.

They reached the end of the wing, where the building curved in a loop and almost met itself, forming a circular courtyard. The opening was gated. The courtyard contained a small swimming pool and a collection of plastic toys scattered on a quarter-acre of grass. Deolinda Sheknovi was sitting on a wooden chair watching her son play. The boy seemed happy enough with a large plastic fire truck he could sit on and pedal. The young woman had the haunted, hollow-eyed look of the prisoner.

Two guards were in the courtyard with her. They were in casual slacks and tropical-weight shirts. There were no jackets to hide the shoulder holsters.

Sigulda listened to the American agent's plan for taking out the pair of guards. It was a good plan, and when it was done Sigulda knew he would be free to follow his own directives.

The Russian crept to the place on the roof above one guard, while the American positioned himself over the other. The American gave the signal, and they both jumped.

Deolinda Sheknovi saw them and started to

scream. But the eruption of violence she witnessed was so sudden and so brutal she gagged, making no sound. She saw the big, dark-haired man land on the ground and flash a huge curved blade into the throat of one of her guards. The strike was so fast, so hard, the knife penetrated the man's throat up to the hilt. Blood cascaded down his chest and the man's eyes went wide, but he never made a sound. Across the courtyard another intruder landed on the walkway and struck the other guard with a flashing dagger. He was slow, and the guard reacted quickly, slamming the knife hand away and reaching for his gun.

Then there was a loud coughing sound. The first man had pulled out a long-barreled handgun and triggered it across the courtyard, cutting down the second guard.

The big, dark man had just killed two guards in under ten seconds.

Deolinda rushed to her son. Thank God he had been facing in the opposite direction. He hadn't witnessed the murders, and as he turned to look at the commotion she had him in her arms and faced him away from the killers.

"Are there other guards here?" the big, dark man demanded in English.

"No. Who are you?"

"We're going to get you out of here."

"Sorry, Belasko. That's not going to happen."

Sigulda aimed the machine pistol squarely at the Executioner. Bolan gazed at the Russian coldly, holding out his gun hand and allowing the 93-R to dangle loosely.

"I have to follow my orders. They can't live."

"I guess I shouldn't have trusted you after all, Sigulda."

"I guess not."

"Even you can't gun down an innocent woman and her child in cold blood."

Sigulda shrugged. "Watch me."

"I'd rather not," Bolan replied, then moved. His left hand flipped the big battle blade across the empty space, and Sigulda watched it coming at him with sudden horror. Then the already bloody knife slammed into his chest, crashing through his ribs and cutting into his heart.

Deolinda squeezed her eyes shut, but her ears couldn't close out the last gurgle of breath and the thump of the collapsing body.

When she opened her eyes again she saw a curious thing. The big American carried the bodies one after another, stacking them like firewood against the wall under one of the big windows into the room that had served as living quarters for herself and her son. She realized he was putting them where they would be out of sight.

"We have to move fast," he said simply. "We're going on the roof."

She nodded. She trusted this murderer, she realized. She certainly had no reason to, but before she knew it, he was pulling her son onto the roof of the structure. She went next. The boy watched the dark man with a mixture of awe and silent fear.

"We move fast and low," he said. "No sound."

"I understand," the woman said.

They practically ran down the length of the north wing, then climbed onto the central building, crossed it in under a minute and paused at the edge. Bolan powered up the radio and donned the headset.

"Stony One, here. Talk to me, G-Force."

"G-Force, here. I've been waiting to hear from you."

"I'm going to ask you to make a run into the valley. The woman and her boy are going to be on the roof of the main building. Come in and get them."

"I'll do it if I can stay in the air long enough."

"I'll be distracting the locals."

"You're not coming with us?"

"No. I still have to pay my respects to Kabat. You get the woman and boy to safety, then come back to your staging position. I'll let you know if and when I can be lifted out."

"Understood. I can be on top of you in five minutes."

"I'll start my distraction in three."

Bolan signed off, then spoke quickly to the woman. "You wait here. A helicopter will come pick you up in just a few minutes. He will take you out of here, to someplace safe."

"What about Andrei?"

"I'm going to get him next."

CHAPTER TWENTY-NINE

Malaysia

Bolan took three steps from the woman and triggered the big Desert Eagle twice. The .44 Magnum rounds punctured a single fist-size hole in the big bubble of Plexiglas that opened up the sky to Yiang's bizarre replication of Hong Kong. Bolan looked down on the streets below. The actors who would come to play their roles as shopkeepers, shoppers, whores and housewives hadn't yet arrived. That was ideal, because Bolan was going to bomb the place. He dropped a single HE through the small opening in the glass and watched it tumble through open space. Then he turned to the Sheknovis and put his fingers in his ears. The boy smiled at him and did the same thing.

The HE detonated under their feet, and downtown Hong Kong began to smoke and burn. The skylight shattered and fell away.

"Stay here. You'll be picked up soon," he told Deolinda Sheknovi.

"What about my husband?" she demanded, still dazed by the blast. "Where are you going?"

"To find him." Bolan offered no further explanation, but stepped to the edge of the roof and descended the utility ladder quickly onto the southeast wing. He could hear shouts and confusion beneath his feet. He had their attention. Now he needed to direct it elsewhere. He jogged along the roof of the wing for twenty paces before launching himself over the edge and landing in one of the gardens, this one patterned after a Japanese rock garden, his feet crunching on the carefully raked gravel. He spotted figures moving swiftly through the corridor behind the wide picture windows. And they noticed him. One man had seen his unlikely arrival and stopped to stare at him. Bolan's instant assessment of the man told him it was a local, unarmed, maybe not even aware he was working for an international crime lord. Bolan triggered the Desert Eagle three times into the glass, avoiding the man but bringing down the picture window. He heard shouts and screams beneath the tumult of collapsing glass.

The sound would reach into the main building and summon all interested parties.

The soldier sped alongside the wing, following its curves and twists until he came to the courtyard. He slipped into the courtyard, finding it empty, and shouldered open a door into the corridor. It was abandoned, but he heard the pounding of approaching footsteps. He pulled the Desert Eagle and triggered random shots into the walls and ceiling. The big Magnum rounds tore out chunks of wood and carpeting and brought the sound of pursuit to a halt.

They knew they were on the right track. Bolan pushed through the door again, reloading on the run, and slammed it noisily behind him. He exited the courtyard and circled it, heading for the half-completed theater along a brick walkway. The excavation of an acre of earth was being prepped for the laying of a foundation. A work crew was busy hammering together forms for the supports that would contain the concrete. The workers were idle, watching the activity in the main building, wondering at the plume of black smoke drifting lazily from it.

As Bolan jogged toward them, they seemed to realize he wasn't one of Yiang's guests. They were builders, not enforcers, and they backed away in a hurry. One of them held up his palms and pleaded loudly in an Asian language Bolan didn't recognize. The soldier headed for the big earthmover parked alongside the excavation, clambered into it and started the diesel engine with a twist of the keys in the ignition. Then he waved the MP-5 K-PDW over the heads of the workers and ordered, "Get out of here."

Whether they understood him or not, they obeyed, fleeing in the direction of the village.

Bolan spun the earthmover 180 degrees and raised the front-end bucket until he could just see over it. People were beginning to gather outside the southeast wing, and a group of non-Asians had come together, marching in his direction—Kabat's men.

He spotted the distant speck of Jack Grimaldi's Huey approaching over the surrounding hills.

It was time to make things interesting. Bolan wrenched the controls that sent the earthmover rumbling toward the southeast wing. The enforcers were spreading out as they approached him. The Executioner waited for them to close in, then saw the first of the men appear on the left of the big blade. The man took his sweet time aiming, and he didn't have the skill to make an effective weapon of the machine pistol at one hundred feet. Most of the rounds punched into the ground. He directed his aim upward and a few more bounced off the heavy steel of the machinery.

By then, Bolan had achieved his target carefully and fired the Desert Eagle twice in rapid succession. The man dropped. The soldier pivoted to the other side of the big blade and triggered three more rounds at the next figure to come into his field of view. When the gunner toppled, Bolan dropped the handgun at his feet, stood in his seat and unleashed a barrage of 9 mm fire from the MP-5 K-PDW, cutting down the two gunners as they were turning to flee.

It had been almost too easy. The first showdown was already over and the rumble of the Huey had to be just becoming audible. Bolan pushed the earthmover to full speed and slammed the big blade into the southeast wing of the complex, tearing out a mouthful of wood, steel and glass. Sparks from ripped conduit flashed off the blade. He cranked the machine away, then advanced along the side of the building another ten feet before slamming into it again, forcing the blade to scoop out more wall and ceiling. The diesel engine protested when the debris started to bog down its progress, and Bolan pulled away fast. He couldn't afford to get hung up. He spotted a figure fighting his way through the ruin of the building from the inside corridor, and the man emerged in front of the soldier with a machine pistol.

It was the dark, effeminate face of Nuala Leeke, the man who had finessed Bolan in South America and escaped with Andrei Sheknovi as his prisoner.

The soldier sank into his seat and spun the earthmover to put the blade between himself and the gunner, but the big diesel moved the machine slowly compared to the quick hands of an experienced gunner. The burst of rounds slammed into the metal frame of the driver's compartment, and Bolan experienced a sting of pain as a round slashed across his scalp. Then he felt a rush of numbness in his left hand. Bolan realized the round had skimmed past his skull and lodged in his shoulder.

He slammed the earthmover forward, rushing directly into the ripped-up section of the wing, directly at Leeke, and he heard the scream distinctly over the rush of the diesel engine. When he backed away the man was pinned against a foot-long splinter of wood—the earthmover had impaled him on it. Bolan clambered from the vehicle.

"Don't kill me, don't kill me," the man begged.

"Tell me where to find your boss and his Russian prisoner if you want to live."

The man nodded. "Maintenance building."

Bolan was perplexed. "Maintenance building? Where is that?" No such building had been visible on the diagrams he'd seen.

"Out there." The dying gunner looked across the grounds of the complex, north of the abandoned construction project. There was a small, low building, which Bolan had barely noticed. It had the look of a shed for storing landscaping equipment.

He left Leeke hanging where he was, jumped into the earthmover and headed away from the building. A growing army of gunners was congregating outside the main building, trying to decide how to get near enough to Bolan to take him out, while another group was becoming increasingly concerned with the Huey descending on top of the main building. Suddenly a group of hardmen ran for the building, bursting through the entrances while the others began to shoot at the helicopter. The aircraft descended onto the roof and out of sight.

"Stony One, here. Come in, G-Force."

"Go ahead, Stony One."

"Company is on its way up to you."

"How much time do I have?"

"Less than a minute."

There was no response, then Grimaldi was back on the line again. "I've got them, Sarge! Alive and well!" Bolan watched the Huey ascend from the roof with a rush of blades, curving in a big arc that took it up and away.

"I'm home free unless they've got antiaircraft weapons," Grimaldi radioed.

"Get them to safety, G-Force. Then get back here ASAP."

"Understood."

Bolan found the group of gunners turning their attention to him, and he knew the usefulness of the earthmover was just about done. He laid down a row of machine-gun fire over the blade before clambering out of the seat and leaving a live HE in the driver's compartment. Then he climbed to the rear and jumped to the ground, sprinting away from the earthmover, keeping the rumbling, rolling piece of equipment between himself and the gunners. When the earthmover exploded, Bolan shielded his face and turned a hard left, cutting overland, directly into the sights of any gunners still standing.

He heard the rattle of machine-gun fire. The earthmover's blast had been too distant to do much harm among the gunners from the main building, and several of them were still on their feet, tearing after him and triggering their weapons wildly. The battle had become a footrace. If Bolan won, he'd make it to the maintenance building before he was hit.

A round cracked into his back, slamming into the Kevlar jacket under his left shoulder blade. The bullet didn't penetrate his flesh, but the impact was like getting struck with a hammer, and the flesh of Bolan's back was already black with the bruises of his recent brush with automatic-weapons' fire at the Pentagon. He felt a burst of air rush out of his lungs, and twin rivers of pain flooded up and down from the impact site. He forced himself to concentrate on running, to stay on his feet. He knew that if he fell the squad of gunners would be on top of him before he had a chance to escape.

He saw the maintenance building ahead of him, feeling grave doubts. The dying man had been lying. The building was small and had a low ceiling, and it looked abandoned. He doubted he'd find Roger Kabat and his prisoner there. But it was the only option for cover he had at the moment, and he triggered the MP-5 K-PDW at the door latch. He didn't have time to determine if it was locked or not. The door sprung open a few inches, and Bolan dived into it as a fresh burst of fire rattled around him.

Instead of outdoor power equipment, Bolan found a concrete ramp that descended steeply into a second set of doors. He dropped a grenade at the top level and jogged down the ramp, flattening to the concrete and hiding his eyes as gunners pushed and shoved to get inside the entrance. Then there was the thump of an explosion and a sickening liquid sound. One mutilated corpse rolled down the ramp halfway to Bolan, leaving a bloody trail.

At the bottom of the ramp the door swung open and the soldier spun, landing on his back on the ramp and triggering a burst of rounds. The Asian guard staggered and flopped onto his face at Bolan's feet, dropping his assault rifle. Bolan plunged through the opening, finding another guard too dismayed by the attack to respond fast enough. By the time he thought to make use of his automatic weapon the Executioner was already cutting him down with the MP-5 K-PDW. He grabbed the ring of keys off the fallen guard and unlocked the prison-type, solid-steel sheet door at the end of the room.

Roger Kabat was inside.

The man was small of stature, scrawny and graying. He didn't look like a man in his fifties so much as a child actor who had been artificially aged with makeup. He stood behind an assault rifle that was too big for him, and he held it awkwardly, as if it were too heavy for his skinny arms.

"Stop!"

Bolan stopped.

He had found the laboratory where Andrei Sheknovi was being forced to manufacture the magnetic pulse emitters. The room was the size of a basketball court, with a low, dark ceiling hung with fluorescent light fixtures. The walls and ceiling were concrete. The fixtures were steel. The room was filled with tables and pallets, all covered with masses of electronic and mechanical components. The room contained one small bunk in the front corner. Next to it was a grimy toilet.

Kneeling in front of Kabat, his feet in chains, was Andrei Sheknovi, his skull inches from the wavering muzzle of the rifle.

"I'll shoot if you come any closer," Kabat warned. His voice was high-pitched, almost a whine. "Drop the gun."

Bolan lowered into a crouch, placing the MP-5 K-PDW on the floor.

"And the others."

The soldier's gaze pierced the relatively dim light in which Kabat stood. The man, he realized, was acting. The grip in which he held the Type 56, a Kalashnikov-style assault rifle, only appeared to be inexpert.

He wanted Bolan to think he was an amateur with an automatic weapon, when he was nothing of the kind.

Bolan wasn't impressed with the show, but he divested himself of the Desert Eagle, then the Beretta 93-R.

"Now we'll find out who you are, I think," Kabat said.

"I'm the man who was in Arlington, Virginia," Bolan replied, "when your men first struck Lipetsk Enterprises and gunned down Serge Gordetsky. I wiped them out."

Kabat's eyes became narrow and cold. "That was you." It wasn't a question so much as a hiss.

"When your men tried to kidnap Nicholae Dinitzin at the airport, I stole their Town Car and stopped the attack. And your boat in South America. I got on board and wiped out a bunch of your people and disabled the boat."

Kabat glared at him, then laughed. "You didn't

succeed, though. My man Leeke escaped you with my prisoner.''

"Nuala Leeke is dead now, though," Bolan said. "I left him hanging on the wall impaled through the liver on a wooden spike. Right after my helicopter pilot lifted off with Deolinda Sheknovi and the boy."

Andrei Sheknovi looked up suddenly. "They got away?"

"Yeah. They're being taken to safety right now."

"You're lying," Kabat stated calmly.

"I'm not."

Bolan wasn't looking at Kabat. He was looking at Sheknovi, and the Russian scientist saw in the soldier's eyes firm sincerity and conviction.

"He's telling the truth," Sheknovi said. "Your power over me is over."

Kabat smirked. "I can still kill you."

"Then kill me." Sheknovi turned on his knees and faced the man. The Type 56 was inches from his eyes. "Because I will not work for you any longer."

"Then I have no option," Kabat stated, and he moved the muzzle of the weapon slightly from Bolan to the Russian.

The Executioner snatched at the balanced Randall knife, leathered just over his shoulder, and sent the throwing knife spinning through the air like flying shrapnel. The blade slammed into Kabat's chest, slipping in below the collarbone, and the rifle fired a brief burst of rounds that bounced noisily off the ceiling. Kabat staggered and grunted. Bolan swooped to the floor, grabbed the Desert Eagle, then triggered the weapon. The round slammed into Kabat's hand and tore the rifle out of his grip, then the bullet continued into his stomach. The arms merchant hit the ground hard.

Bolan walked to him, kicked the gun away and searched him, coming up with a set of keys that he tossed to the Russian scientist. Sheknovi began to scramble to find the key that fit the padlock on his ankle shackles.

The soldier strode purposefully to a pair of low-profile wooden crates. Inside each, packed in wood shavings, was a magnetic pulse emitter.

"London and Moscow?" Bolan asked.

"Yes," Sheknovi said. He stood and crossed to Kabat. Without hesitation he closed one end of the shackles around the man's ankle, then he dragged him across the concrete floor to the steel bunk. The other end of the shackle went around the steel post. Kabat was moaning and whining, clutching his bloody stomach. Bolan didn't interfere nor did he assist.

The soldier marched to the entrance and slammed the steel door shut, locking it from the inside. Nobody was outside yet, and nobody was getting through without a key.

"Are we going to make it out of here alive, my friend?" Sheknovi asked. "I would like to see my wife and boy again."

"You will," Bolan said. "Soon. We'll go out that way."

The Executioner rearmed himself, then grabbed one of the emitters in both hands and hoisted it, moving to the rear door of the laboratory. Sheknovi was behind him, activating the other emitter, then raced beside Bolan and unlocked the door with Kabat's keys.

They marched up a ramp and closed the door behind them. The door was already heating up.

Kabat was already screaming.

AT THE TOP of the ramp they found themselves looking at the complex through a stand of trees. A large armed contingent was marching from the main building toward the laboratory's front entrance. The army paused when the smoke started. Soon, black clouds were billowing out of both entrances, and Bolan and Sheknovi used them as cover. They skirted north in the smoke until the west wing was between themselves and the army.

Bolan placed the emitter in a small flower garden. Sheknovi activated it with the flip of a switch.

"It will work for fifteen minutes," the Russian scientist said. "I hope that will be enough."

Bolan nodded, satisfied. "More than enough."

His radio was fried. They marched north, away from the compound, then west into the ring of mountains. Grimaldi had the Huey parked but running not far from the satellite uplink dish Bolan had staged. Deolinda Sheknovi was pacing. Grimaldi and the boy were playing checkers with rocks.

The game was forgotten when Bolan and Andrei Sheknovi marched out of the forest.

"I got worried, Sarge," Grimaldi said, "when I saw that."

The pilot pointed over the trees of the forest, where a column of solid black smoke spiraled into the sky.

Minutes later they were airborne. Grimaldi took them in a circle at two thousand feet, where they ~ould plainly see all that remained of the complex.

The low building that had been the laboratory was gone. The incredible heat generated by the steel reinforcement had caused the concrete to collapse. The two entrances were huge black stains, but the smoke that had created them was already gone. There had been little inside to burn once the emitter stopped operating.

The same couldn't be said for the massive, eight-armed building. It was made almost entirely of wood, with steel support framing. Even the state-of-the-art sprinkler system was mostly steel. The fire engulfed the great octopus in a conflagration that couldn't possibly be checked. It would burn until the last scrap was consumed.

Grimaldi pointed the Huey to the nearest airport, in the Malaysian port city of Miri, where they could transfer to the private jet that would return them to the U.S.

Where there would be other fires to command the Executioner's attention.

James Axler

OUTLANDERS™

SHADOW SCOURGE

The bayous of Louisiana, steeped in magic and voodoo, are the new epicenter of a dark, ancient evil. Kane, a renegade enforcer of the new order, is now a freedom fighter dedicated with fellow insurrectionists to free the future from the yoke of Archon power.

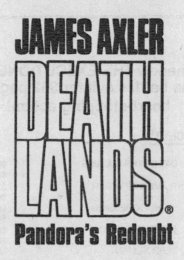

JAMES AXLER

DEATH LANDS®

Pandora's Redoubt

Ryan Cawdor and his fellow survivalists emerge in a redoubt in which they discover a sleek superarmored personnel carrier bristling with weapons from predark days. As the companions leave the redoubt, a sudden beeping makes them realize why the builders were constructing a supermachine in the first place.

Shadow THE EXECUTIONER®
as he battles evil for 352 pages of
heart-stopping action!

SuperBolan®

#61452	DAY OF THE VULTURE	$5.50 U.S. ☐
		$6.50 CAN. ☐
#61453	FLAMES OF WRATH	$5.50 U.S. ☐
		$6.50 CAN. ☐
#61454	HIGH AGGRESSION	$5.50 U.S. ☐
		$6.50 CAN. ☐
#61455	CODE OF BUSHIDO	$5.50 U.S. ☐
		$6.50 CAN. ☐
#61456	TERROR SPIN	$5.50 U.S. ☐
		$6.50 CAN. ☐

(limited quantities available on certain titles)

TOTAL AMOUNT	$ _____
POSTAGE & HANDLING	$ _____
($1.00 for one book, 50¢ for each additional)	
APPLICABLE TAXES*	$ _____
TOTAL PAYABLE	$ _____
(check or money order—please do not send cash)	

To order, complete this form and send it, along with a check or money order for
the total above, payable to Gold Eagle Books, to: **In the U.S.:** 3010 Walden Avenue,
P.O. Box 9077, Buffalo, NY 14269-9077; **In Canada:** P.O. Box 636, Fort Erie, Ontario,
L2A 5X3.

Name: _____

Address: _____ City: _____

State/Prov.: _____ Zip/Postal Code: _____

*New York residents remit applicable sales taxes.
 Canadian residents remit applicable GST and provincial taxes.

GSBBACK1